Eve Zaremba was born in Poland, lived in the UK in the forties and moved to Canada in 1952. A long-time feminist activist, she was one of the founders of *Broadside, A Feminist Review*. She has written three Helen Keremos mysteries and is working on a fourth. She works at Amanita Publications, and lives in Toronto.

Virago publishes *Work for a Million*, a Helen Keremos mystery, in 1990.

Sara Ann Raymond, the daughter of a right-wing US presidential candidate, has been missing for ten years. She has recently been spotted working on a road-gang in the interior of British Columbia. What seems at first like a simple chore in vacation-land for Helen Keremos turns out to be her most complicated and terrifying case involving a deadly game of multinational terrorism, murder and intrigue just forty miles from the Canadian-US border.

1

LIKE SO MUCH ELSE IN CANADA, this case began in the States. For me it started in California. I'd been visiting some old friends in San Francisco. At a late, loud and over long weekend party I bumped into a couple of people from Los Angeles. The three of us had left the crush of strangers inside for the coolness and peace of the fire escape. Over a quiet smoke we chatted and introduced ourselves. She was a TV writer, freelance. Her man was an academic, taught at UCLA. Both in their early forties, bright, articulate, affluent. In turn, I told them who I was and what I did.

"Helen Keremos. I detect," I said lightly. There are a number of standard reactions to my name and trade. I have learned to cope with surprise, disbelief, curiosity, competitiveness, pleasure, a variety of putdowns and aggressiveness. One guy once offered to hand wrestle me to prove he was 'a better man' than I. I told him that there could be no doubt about that. He hadn't understood. Then there are people who offer me jobs on the spot. That's the one reaction I hadn't expected this time.

"We know who you are. From Lynn." Lynn was one of the party hosts. "We came to San Francisco especially to meet you. Would you be free to take on a job in British Columbia for us? A very sensitive tricky job?"

We skipped down the fire escape and found a quiet bar. Their story started almost 20 years earlier. In the sixties they'd been revolutionaries. Looking at them now it was hard to believe. They were a little embarrassed about it. Embarrassed about what they had been and what they had become. It's not OK these days to have had hope. There are a lot of people like that around. Mostly they don't talk about the past. Children of the sixties making it in the eighties. Cool, cautious and comfortable.

Not quite all of them, it seemed. One of their group, Sara Ann Raymond (Ray) had been on the FBI 'most wanted' list since 1969. For bombing a branch of The Bank of America. She had disappeared then, nobody knew where. Nobody had seen or heard from her since. Nobody, that is, until my two potential clients had come across her on a road gang near Castlegar, British Columbia.

"It was pretty weird. Unbelievable, really. We were on our way back from vacation. On this road in the Kootenays. It was all dug up, getting fixed. So it was one-lane traffic. Long line of cars stopped, waiting for vehicles going the other way to get past. Signalmen with STOP signs and CBs at each end. Except the signalmen were women. In hard hats and orange vests. Well, they switched directions right in front of us. You know what I mean?" I nodded. She continued. "We sat there in the hot sun while a line of cars moved past us. Sat talking, not paying any attention. Then suddenly Bob said to me, 'Hey, that woman looks like Ray, doesn't she!' Meaning the signalwoman right in front of our car. She heard him, turned around — it was Ray. I'm sure it was her!" She stopped and lit a cigarette. Her hands trembled.

"Then what happened?" I prompted.

"Nothing, really," Pat continued. "The CB squawked; we hadn't noticed that the direction had changed, we were holding up traffic. Our line was supposed to move. So the CB said 'Hey, Carol, get on with it! Keep them moving!' She stepped back and waved us on. There were cars behind, impatient. We drove on; there was no place to pull off. And that's the last we saw of her."

"On the strength of this amazing coincidence you want me to find Ray. There is damn little to go on. But even assuming I could track her down, the question is why? She obviously doesn't want to be found."

"We don't know that." Bob stepped in firmly. "We figured she probably doesn't know how to get in touch with us without blowing her cover. She cannot know where we are at now. So it's up to us to give her a chance to contact us if she wants to. All we want you to do when you find her is tell her that. You could act as go-between if that suits her."

"If I find her. It's a long shot. It will take money and I might still come up empty."

"We know that." Bob was doing all the talking now. "We are prepared to give you $3,000 right now and take our chances. Will you do it?"

"Three grand and no strings? Three grand to a stranger, just like that? You're blessed with touching faith. How come?" I didn't like this one bit. It smelt of hidden agendas. A set-up. I only had their word for any of it. For who they were, for their past relationship with Sara Ann Raymond, for their motives. Meanwhile Bob turned to his companion.

"Pat, let's have the picture." Pat took an envelope out of her pocketbook and handed it to me. It held a graduation picture of an all-American girl. Long blond hair, straight teeth showing in a cheesy smile. Regular Anglo features, tall slim, athletic body. I turned it over. A faded red stamp — The Putnam Photographic Studio, Tucson, Arizona. *Memories are Made of This* and a hand-written date: June 23, 1967. If these two were to be believed, two years later the woman in this photograph was on a FBI wanted poster. I dropped the photo onto the stained table in front of me.

"Tell me more," I said. "Any family, other friends?"

They looked at each other quickly, signalling.

"Yes. Mother and father and two brothers. They live in Arizona."

Pat spoke, paused, realized that wouldn't do, went on quickly: "Her father is a U.S. senator, very rich, very powerful. Her mother ....,"

I interrupted. "Senator Raymond! Well, well. We've heard of him even way out in the Canadian boonies. 'Media magnate' the newspapers call him. Many times a millionaire, controls papers, TV and radio stations. All in the southwest. Reactionary Republican, right? Do tell!"

"Yes. Ray's the only daughter. Mrs. Raymond is very ill. Probably won't live long. You can check all that. It's public knowledge." Pat went on.

"Oh, I will! Fascinating. Would this $3,000 you are offering me come from Senator Raymond, by any chance?"

"No. Definitely not. He knows nothing about it. He disowned Ray long ago. And I don't think he even knows we exist. Ray never told her father anything. Knowing he would try to stop her. But her mother did get in touch with us hoping we could get a message to Ray."

I leaned back in the booth and looked them over carefully. They still looked like what they claimed to be. Which meant they could be working for Senator Raymond, the FBI or on some scam of their own. I didn't much like them or their story.

Bob spoke up, looking at me directly, attempting to dispel the impression these last revelations had created. The sincere touch.

"We know it sounds suspicious. But we really mean it. Take the money and try to find Ray. As soon as possible. Tell her what we told you. That's all. If she wants to get in touch with us or her mother — good. If not, we will have done our best. You've been well recommended. I don't think you'll rip us off. And you are the best chance we have to get through to Ray, wherever she is. Can you think of a better way?"

"And you don't expect me to tell you whether I've found her or not? Because if she doesn't want any part of you, it will be just as if I hadn't found her at all. Clear?"

"Clear. Of course. It's up to her."

They looked at me eagerly.

"OK. You've got it. Three grand in cash. No cheques. I never heard of you."

Bob relaxed, smiling. Pat again reached in her pocketbook. Another envelope. This time large, brown. $3,000. They had been all prepared. It didn't make me trust them any more. I checked the money quickly. Old bills, various denominations.

I put it away, and said, "Now. Exactly where did you see this woman Carol? When? I need the date and the name of the construction company she worked for."

They told me. And that's why a week later I left my crummy little office in Vancouver on my way to Castlegar, gateway to West Kootenays and Doukhobor country, British Columbia.

2

By noon the fat, self-satisfied lower mainland of British Columbia was miles behind me. I left the Fraser valley with no regrets. It wasn't often that my job took me into the interior of B.C. I enjoyed driving the lively little jeep through the green splendour of Manning Park. It was June and still too early for the annual invasion of tourists in lumbering RVs and overloaded station wagons. I was eager for the sagebrush desert of Similkameen and Okanagan valleys.

I couldn't resist stopping my borrowed trailer in Keremeos. Bought a bunch of the apples for which this area is famous and a post card. I crossed out the third 'e' in the name and sent the card on to Alex Edwards in Toronto. She never had believed the origin of my last name. My mother came from somewhere around Keremeos Creek and always claimed to have Kemano Indian ancestors.

With no real memories to feed on (I had been born in Vancouver and never lived in the interior) my moment of nostalgia was brief. I hurried on past the ghost mining towns and well irrigated fruit lands towards my destination in the Kootenays. There was a fascinating assignment in front of me. Whether I found Carol or not, this was going to be fun.

ARC (Arrow Road/Construction) was housed in a large white mobile structure on the outskirts of Castlegar, not far from the airport. That's where I found Peter Matakoff, general foreman. He was obliging and garrulous. No, they hadn't employed any Carol Edwards (I had to give a last name, so I used Alex's — she wouldn't mind) on road construction the previous summer. But there had been a Carol Latimer, with an address R.R.#1 Slocan. Probably using her maiden name, Matakoff instructed me sagely. Young women were doing that all the time now. Besides being unnatural it made more paperwork for proper hard-working men like him. I thanked him and escaped.

Castlegar nestles between mountains at the three-way

confluence of the Kootenay and Columbia rivers and Lower Arrow Lake. The Slocan River enters the Kootenay a few miles north.

The Kootenays have a reputation. What that reputation is depends on who you talk to. To some it's Shangrila, a place where good people lead good lives close to the land, where true community life flourishes, where alternative lifestyles have taken root in the beautiful mountain landscape. To others? It's where dope-polluted hippies push local inhabitants off their land, introducing unheard-of customs. A haven for atheistic strangers with no morals or decent work ethic, like those cowardly American draft dodgers of the seventies. Of course both sides are right. It's all true.

The back-to-the-earth movement combined with resistance to the Vietnam draft brought strange urban people and radical ideas to many a quiet valley in western Canada. The area of West Kootenays and especially the Slocan has been a magnet for such people since the sixties. Twenty years at least. Time and the realities of country living have changed the 'new people', as they are called. There is nary a wild-eyed revolutionary to be found among them now. But they also affected the country and the people among whom they settled. They had to have some ideological impact on the Doukhobors, a Russian fundamentalist religious sect; 19th century resisters against the modern world. Young middle-class Americans and semi-literate Russian peasants! Both groups anti-war, anti-state, anti-materialism. Yet how fiercely different! The 'new people' imbued with the spirit of the sixties — for life, love and peace; against race, sex and class discrimination, hierarchical structures and the dead hand of power. For them, the world was a place in which not enough had changed. The traditional, patriarchal, fundamentalist Doukhobors fought a rear-guard action in a society in which too much was changing. Both groups were refugees from the ugly power of state and money. As refugees they were held suspect by local mainstream Canadians — farmers, small town merchants, civil servants, functionaries of large mining companies, tourist operators, lumber and construction workers — who despised the Doukhobors and feared the 'new people'. Yet over time these three divergent groups had learned to live together, or if not together then at least beside each other. And inevitably learned each from each.

I mused over what I knew of this region as I entered Slocan Valley. Shiny new aluminum roofs and horses. Lots of horses. R.R.#1 Slocan is a mailing address and not much use as directions on the road. I stopped at the local Cooperative Store to ask for Carol Latimer. Russian language newspapers and records cheek by jowl with organically grown health foods, magazines on commune life and astrology. There were only two people shopping in the store; a surly man with beard and down-at-heel cowboy boots trailing a pale, sad young woman in a floor-length dress. She was pregnant. A toddler played with the car keys in a beat-up old pickup outside. If this was an example of the back-to-the-earth and family movement, it left me cold. I cornered one of the Coop workers. He didn't know any Carol Latimer. Short consultation with a co-worker. No. Name didn't ring a bell. Not a Coop member. I should try Vallican. At the Whole School. Whole School? Yes, alternative school built by locals for their kids. Centre of the community.

The bearded man and the pregnant woman watched me leave. Neither said a word.

I spent the rest of the day tracking down Carol Latimer. Not her in person, just anyone who'd admit to having heard of her. People lifted their heads from the innards of old autos, from mucking out the barn, from ovens full of bread, from farming catalogues, from the flickering images on TV screens, and shook them. Ask down the road, try Robert's Restaurant, or Jones's store in Winslow, or Silver Slocan Social Centre. At last a cheerful woman in a spotless apron over tattered jeans set me on the right track.

"Try Dean." She gave me directions "If she's good-looking and American he'll know her." She laughed.

Slocan Valley is long, narrow and very beautiful. The road follows the river all the way. Most places it has nowhere else to go. Where the valley broadens a bit there are sideroads. Dirt tracks. I went down one of them and found the farm of Dean

Greenwood. If that was really his name. I didn't ask. Always thought of him as L'il Abner. Except for the hair which was longer and blond, Dean was the spitting image of the old cartoon character. Tight bib-overalls over a large muscular body, enormous boots and a open, rather dumb-seeming face.

His place didn't amount to more than a two-room shack. There was an open-sided shed for a couple of horses and their feed, a chicken house, a few goats in a small pasture, some bee hives. A fancy four-wheel-drive pickup and an old VW sat out front in the evening sun. I found Dean at the back doing something important to a pump. He looked up and grinned cozily.

"Hi, be with you in a second. Have to tighten this nut or the damn thing will fall apart. These old pumps are well made but once they start to go .... hard to get parts. Had to make this myself ....," he went on muttering companionably. I stood back and waited. A very attractive man, no question about that. Charming. American draft resister? Probably. Been here a good while, feels at home with the country life but still very urban. I wondered how he made a living. Not from chickens, goats, or honey bees.

Soon we were inside, each with a beer, sitting at a beautiful handmade table in the kitchen-cum-livingroom. The place was spotless. No clutter, no normal signs of living. Furniture either handcrafted by artists or rustic treasures of the past. Herbs hung in decorative bundles from the rafters. Dry mushrooms on a string caught my eye. *Boletus Edulis*. Polished wood stove; kindling cut exactly to size. Whitewashed walls, posters, delicate prints in antique frames, brass candlesticks, an incense burner. Rows of canisters with varieties of beans, brown rice, whole wheat flour; tamari sauce in a large can, plates of nuts. Lots of spices, cookbooks neat on a shelf. Rough plank floor freshly scrubbed, hand-hooked rugs. Through the door to the bedroom, a large brass double bed covered with a glowing patchwork quilt. Perfect. You can take the boy out of *House Beautiful* but you can't take the *House Beautiful* out of the boy. It's one thing to be aesthetically pleasing but this was a bit much.

Dean centred his beer bottle precisely in the middle of the

middle plank of the shiny table, moved an ashtray an inch or two in my direction, lifted up his eyes, smiled and said,

"Carol Latimer. Sure I know Carol. Haven't seen her for, oh, months. But she's sure to be around. You won't have any trouble catching up with her. Unless she left for the city, looking for a job or something. Do you know her well? I don't remember her ever mentioning any Helen from Vancouver." Perfectly natural question. I ignored it and concentrated on what he seemed to be saying.

"Great! So you can tell me where she lives. Perhaps a phone number."

"Well, no. I don't know exactly where she is at right now. You see she used to live here with me," he continued bashfully. "Then she left."

"You split up?"

"Sort of. It's hard to talk about it. You can imagine what a bummer it is to lose a woman like her."

"Yes, very careless of you. To lose her, I mean. Where did she go?"

He laughed, unfazed. Still bashful, boyish, charming.

"She up and left me." Big blue eyes veiled in sentiment.

"Left you for another?" I intoned. "Anyone or anything in particular?"

He shook his head.

"No. I don't know. There's a commune near Kaslo, she kind of moved there originally. I don't know if she's still there. Doubt it. It's an all-women commune, 'Women's Acres'."

"She wouldn't stay at a women-only place, is that what you are saying?" I asked, perhaps a trifle sharply.

"No. I don't know." He was getting repetitious. "I wouldn't have thought so. Knowing her as I do. You are her friend, what d'you think?"

"Meaning she liked men. Sex with men."

"Well, yes." Embarrassment again.

"How do I get there? Have they a phone?" There was no point pursuing the subject of Carol's sexual proclivities.

"Not to my knowledge. And it's too late anyway. It's a rough

— *13* —

drive. Why not have a bite to eat with me, stay the night and start again in the morning. You can park your little trailer right there in the yard. No trouble."

He'd checked out my rig. And wanted to keep me around. Not due to any passion for my body. He couldn't have had any doubts that my interest in men was purely professional.

"No thanks. I'll carry on to Kaslo tonight. Make the commune tomorrow morning. How do I find it?"

"D'you know how to get to Kaslo? Yes? You have a good map. OK. Look, let me draw it in for you." Carefully he drew me a map, very specific directions. Very helpful. I thanked him.

"Y're welcome. If you find Carol remind her of old Dean, OK?"

He was smiling, relaxed and very unsorrowing. I said sure, climbed into my jeep, turned round slowly in the narrow lane and split.

3

THE ROAD FROM SLOCAN VALLEY to Kaslo leads over rough mountain country, virtually uninhabited. I left the river in New Denver and immediately started climbing. The road wound up, narrow, sometimes treacherous, broken pavement bouncing my egg-shaped fiberglass travel trailer. Through mountains, the dense woods of Slocan Provincial Forest, the road followed first Carpenter Creek and then Kaslo River. In the gathering darkness, the gaping structures of long-abandoned mine shafts poked out of broken hillsides. It was an eerie drive. In places, heaps of black gravel and ruined shacks marked sites of ghost mining towns dating back to the boom times of the 1890s. Almost no traffic except for an odd truck. Just once I saw the still figures of an Indian woman and half-grown child standing by the road. So people did live here. A few, perhaps.

It was good to hit a rise and roll down into Kaslo. My tired, ocean-bred eyes travelled gratefully to the expanse of lake water where no trees or rocks interrupted their focus.

Kaslo is a small, pretty town. Streets of wooden structures, couple of hotels, grocery and hardware, a government liquor store, book shop and art gallery in a converted bank building. Small houses with country-size yards. A municipal campground and beach. And in a sheltered cove a marina full of boats. A pleasant mixture of the run-down old and the trendy new.

I parked and checked out one of the hotels. Had a beer, rested, took stock. Next day I just might find Ray, alias Carol Latimer. Give her the message I was being well paid to deliver and be on my way back to Vancouver. End of case.

On the other hand, perhaps Carol Latimer wasn't Sara Ann Raymond. Or I couldn't find her anyway. Or there would be complications. I decided a good night's sleep would be in order. Didn't fancy a dingy hotel room, not when I had that nice trailer at my disposal. But a shower would be nice. I asked the bartender about a campground with facilities.

He shook his head dubiously. Couldn't say who would have showers.

"Most campers around here rough it. Try the Silver King Campground. They're new. Over near the marina."

Hour later I was comfortably settled on a sheltered site about 50 yards from a modern bathhouse, with hot water and showers. The campground was barely half-full. Some big RVs but mostly small trailers like mine, and tents. My only immediate neighbours were two men with a station wagon and a balky tourist tent they had some trouble pitching in the dark.

I decided not to bother with a campfire but to try out the shower and turn in. I undressed, collected my towel, soap and with a red jogging suit over my bare body, made for the bathhouse. Across the camp area bright flames of an enormous fire and the off-key voices of campfire vocalizers filled the night. I passed dark shadows of people walking their dogs or visiting from one site to another. A few said "good evening" or "good night." Most ignored me.

The shower was wonderful. It had been a long day. Tense shoulder muscles relaxed under prolonged pelting with hot water.

Out of the over-bright bathhouse, I walked blind. I hadn't brought a flashlight, trusting to the pale moon and the reflections of fires. My jeep poked its pork-like snout into my path. Behind it loomed the bulk of the Trillium. Suddenly a dark shadow moved into my field of vision, a figure sprang towards me.

"Hell! She's back!" it cried in a carrying whisper. Simultaneously the door of the trailer opened and another figure emerged, running. Both of them, straight at me.

I didn't have a chance but I fought back anyway. Just reflex action. Through the pain of blows I remember hitting out, connecting. One of them had me by the arm and was trying to wrench it from its socket. The other kicked. I couldn't have lasted if my attackers hadn't in turn been attacked. In seconds there were four men pummelling each other in the semi-darkness. I rolled under the jeep out of their way. My original attackers broke off the engagement and disappeared cursing and crashing through the bushes. They weren't up to fighting an even fight. My rescuers pulled me out from under the jeep little worse for wear. They insisted I lie down on the pre-prepared bed in my trailer. I looked at them. My neighbours of the balky tent. In these cramped quarters they still looked like regular tourists. Having seen them in action I knew better.

"You all right? Hurt anywhere? I am Harry Tower and that's Sid Bazerman." This one was short, dark, in his thirties. Chinos and a check sports shirt. Sid was taller, thinner and a little older. Leisure pants, a polo shirt, a windbreaker. They seemed more pleased with themselves than concerned about me.

I tried to sit up, decided against it.

"I'll live. But bruised. Thanks, you guys. Really, thanks a lot. They were about to stomp me into the ground. And my arm!" I fingered my left shoulder. "Ouch!"

"Did they steal anything?" Sid looked around the trailer. There wasn't much to see but what there was was scattered all around us. The duffel with my clothes had been up-ended. All cupboards gaped open. Books, maps strewn about.

"Want us to call the cops?" Harry said with no conviction. They were both busily picking up my scattered bits and pieces.

"The Mounties? No. These guys are long gone. What I need is rest, not making a break-and-enter report. Thanks anyway." I wanted them gone too. So I could think. Harry and Sid however were intent on 'tidying'.

"Hey, don't bother, really. I'll do that in the morning. I don't think anything valuable's missing. Not that I have anything valuable. It's OK." It was no use. The Good Samaritans wouldn't go away.

"No trouble, no trouble at all. Sorry we couldn't hold them. Wonder what they were after? Seems unusual to burglarize a little trailer like this. Perhaps they thought you had a map to a lost silver mine? This area's full of tales of lost lodes."

"Yes, have you heard of the Roderick gold treasure trove?" Sid chimed in.

"Oh, is that what you two are here looking for? Treasure?" This really was adding insult to injury.

Harry answered with a straight face, "Yes, just for a gag. Sort of. To give our vacation a purpose, you know. Sid is recuperating after a bout in hospital so we thought we would come out here, get lots of fresh air, exercise and poke around a bit."

"Well, you've had your exercise for tonight, that's for sure. Thanks again. Goodnight."

They weren't very good at taking a hint.

"Are you sure you're all right?"

I nodded vigorously, which didn't help the pain in my head.

"Yes, yes. A good night's sleep. Be fine tomorrow."

"OK then. We'll go now. But we'll be back in the morning. Check to see if you're OK."

"Yes, have breakfast with us." This was Sid. "Harry makes mean pancakes." Mean pancakes — just what I wanted right then!

"Great!" I pretended enthusiasm. "Love to have breakfast with you. Goodnight." Anything to get rid of them.

"Good night. Better lock up behind us." They walked clumsily out of the narrow door and waited outside. I staggered up and clicked the door shut. A child could open it with a nail file. Presumably a child wouldn't try. Apparently satisfied, Harry and Sid went back towards their tent next door.

Peace at last.

I got myself a drink of water and a couple of codeine pills. Tried to sleep with little success. Sore arm or bruises didn't keep me from it, it was my busy mind. Unfocused, it meandered over events. My trailer had now been searched by both the unidentified attackers and by dear Harry and Sid. Why? What could a woman have in a camp trailer that could so interest two separate parties? It's nice to be popular. Sid and Harry had acted very cool indeed. Not at all the way regular tourists would go about rescuing a female in distress. Had that lump under Sid's windbreaker been a gun? Did they really intend that bizarre treasure trove story to be believed? Did the original searchers mistake my campsite for Harry and Sid's? No, that didn't scan. "Hell, she's back!" one of them had said. They knew whose trailer they were turning over. Back to Harry and Sid. A map? If not of the preposterous lost treasure, then of what? Map, map — Dean had marked my government survey map of the area with directions to the all-women commune. I was going there tomorrow to find Ray, or news of her. I sat up suddenly. Were all those assorted dudes also looking for Sara Ann Raymond, alias Carol Latimer? It seemed safest to assume so. But why would they need to pulverize my trailer? The map wasn't hidden. And it couldn't be the only source of information. Perhaps they were also curious about me. Who I was, what I was doing. That made some sense. Only clues, aside from the map, were in my wallet. My private investigator licence and the snapshot of Ray. It had gone with me to the bathhouse. I concentrated on recalling whether Harry and Sid had a chance to go over it. Yes, sure. One of them had collected my belongings from under the jeep and brought them into the trailer. I picked up my wallet. Contents were intact. Again, the safest assumption was that my rescuers now knew who I was. And possibly, just possibly, knew of my interest in Ray. And the attackers? Probably didn't have any more than when they started. Except they might assume that Harry and Sid were my backup. That we were in it together, whatever 'it' was.

How did they, any of them, know where to find me? If they knew my jeep and trailer, it was easy. I had parked on Kaslo's main street, in front of a hotel. Harry and Sid had to have checked into the campground right behind me. And the others? Either they too were campers, or more likely they followed me here, parked outside, wandered around the site making like campers, spotted me on my way to the bathhouse and took the opportunity to ransack my rig. All well and good. But where had I been picked up originally? At ARC, talking to Matakoff? The Coop? Along the river road where I'd talked to a half-dozen random people? Dean. He was the most likely contact. He'd wanted me to stay the night. He could be in with either my helpful neighbours or my faceless attackers. In which case ....

Midnight musings by a groggy mind in a bruised body tend to lead round in circles. No way of telling whether I was right about any of it. Guesses. Just guesses. Finally the codeine took hold and adrenalin left my blood stream. I felt one thing for sure. The case wasn't going to be over tomorrow. I would get to earn that $3,000.

4

HARRY'S PANCAKES WERE AS ADVERTISED — 'mean'! Heavy blobs of thick dough. Inedible. I sat at the camp table in the site next to mine and picked at them. No bacon and only ersatz syrup. Instant coffee. No milk. Blah! Their station wagon had Alberta plates. Calgary dealer sticker. And unmistakably a rented look about it. So did the clumsy tent and much of their camping equipment. Propane stove and lamp. Brand new sleeping bags. 'CampeRentAll, Calgary'. So they hadn't come from Vancouver, as I had. Must have picked up on me here, in the West Kootenays.

"Hey, you aren't eating!" Sid stood over me, very solicitous. "Guess you wouldn't have an appetite after last night." I didn't tell him it was the cooking, not my appetite. But I ceased pretending and pushed away my plate.

"I guess not. Just coffee, thanks." I hate, loathe, and detest bad coffee. This was bad but I needed time to psyche out these two dudes. So I sacrificed my palate.

In spite of a sore arm and a large bruise on my leg, I felt good. Things were happening. I guess it's for times like these that I stay in this line of work. It's fine dealing with so many unknowns, sorting out the pieces and seeing where they fall. I meant to get a bead on what these two were up to. It was clear that this intention was mutual.

Sid poured more horrible coffee all round. Harry helped himself to the last pancake, drowned it in syrup and went at it. He ate in the European fashion, using fork in the left and knife in the right hand, simultaneously. Sid offered me a cigarette and lit one himself. We were in for a sparring session, each side intending to give little and gain as much information as possible. Whether by accident or design they were giving me lots of time, letting me set the tone. I took them up on it.

"What're you guys really doing here?" I asked. "Who are you?"

"We were about to ask you the same thing," Harry answered with his mouth full of pancake. Sid said nothing.

"You know who I am. You checked my wallet last night. What's it to you?"

"Yes. Helen Keremos. Vancouver-based private investigator. That much we know. But what brings you here, Helen?"

"Couldn't I be just a tourist, like you claim to be?" I grinned at him. "Even detectives take vacations." Harry shook his head.

"You aren't here on vacation, else why would these two hoods bounce you?"

"Coincidence?" I suggested.

"You aren't on vacation!" Sid spoke up decisively. "And neither are we." There was a pause to evaluate where this piece of frankness would get us.

"Ah. Good. So we are agreed that none of us are holidaying. Or hunting for maps to lost silver mines."

"I didn't say that. We're hunting for a mine. An old mine shaft, anyway. What are you here for? If it's the same thing, why don't we pool our resources?" Sid was speeding along leaving me with more questions than before his answers.

"An old mine shaft. Possibly. The question is, are we after the same treasure?"

"Yes, that's the question." Sid leaned back and seemed to lose interest. Harry finished his meal and began to clear the table. Ball was in my court.

"You've the advantage of me. You at least know who I am and where I come from. We aren't going to get anywhere until you reciprocate. That'll make us even and we could go on from there."

"What's to know? Harry Tower and Sid Bazerman. From points east." Harry tried to be funny. Sid looked at him sharply, then away again.

"What's to know? Well, certain things aren't hard to guess. I don't think either of you is Canadian. Harry's urban European, mid-Atlantic accent and all. My guess is that Sid is American. You two flew to Calgary, probably directly from the States, acquired very touristy outfits, rented a wagon and equipment and drove here. Where you are a little out of your depth. It's not your turf. West Kootenays is a strange place in many ways. Rural, remote, primitive and at the same time California-up-to-date trendy. You are looking for something and you got onto me, somehow. You're hoping I can help. But that's as far as it goes. You don't know if I am after the same thing. Well?"

"Not bad. Pretty obvious, though. Anything else?"

"You're agents of some kind. Government agents ...."

Sid lifted up his hand, palm towards me. I stopped.

"OK, OK. You're good. We checked you out last night by phone. Vancouver gave you an AOK rating. So I'll take a chance and tell you. We're government agents. Looking for a cache of stolen arms."

They looked at me expectantly.

"Nuts. What government? What agency? What stolen arms? Who in Vancouver gave me an AOK rating? Do better than that."

"We're Interpol. That's all I can tell you ...."

I got up.

"I'm tired of games. You aren't Interpol. It doesn't operate that way. If there are stolen arms here it's the Mounties' job to find them. You sure as hell aren't Mounties. My money says CIA. Good day, gentlemen."

I acted like they had leprosy.

"Hey, wait! Wait a minute! Not CIA! No way! Sit down. Please," Sid said urgently. I moved back and sat down on the edge of the bench.

"Tell me something I can believe," I said.

Their eyes conferred. Harry spoke softly.

"Have you heard of the Mossad?"

I couldn't repress surprise.

"Israeli Secret Service! What's it doing in the Kootenays?"

"Have you heard of Unit 101 — the Wrath of God?" Harry continued.

"Yes. But it's disbanded. Counter-terrorism unit."

"Disbanded as a unit. But counter-terrorism is an Israeli priority, Mossad's job."

Harry reached behind him and pulled out a deadly high-velocity .22 from under his windbreaker. Killer gun, used by Unit 101. Also favourite of the Mob and as a personal gun of the FBI boys. Some company I was keeping.

"So what are two Mossad agents doing in the interior of British

Columbia?" I repeated.

"Yeah. Wild goose chase most probably. But it had to be checked out. Anyway let's tell her. OK?" Harry turned to Sid, who sighed and nodded.

"Go ahead," he said. "You've blown everything as it is, already."

"You worry too much. We weren't getting anywhere so what's to blow?"

Harry turned to me and concentrated on his story. Sid sat and smoked.

"I guess it does start with arms. Not necessarily stolen. Know anything about the world arms trade?" He continued without pause. "So you know you can buy anything, any weapon, any amount for a price. High price. Not just rifles, machineguns, grenades and small stuff like that but everything right up to nukes. Well, Mossad likes to know who's buying what. Just so we know what's likely to turn up against us. Weapons are pretty specialized. Some are tailor-made for terrorist activities. So we keep our ears open. When these specialized weapons turn up or disappear, are sold or stolen, we try to track them down. Some time ago your police uncovered an arsenal of illegal weapons. A mixed bag. But interesting. Follow so far?"

"I follow and remember. Main find was in Ontario, thousands of kilometers from here. And it was reported as a mail order business to the States. Private enterprise: non-political. Maybe Mafia, but international terrorism .... seems unlikely."

Harry nodded vigorously as I spoke.

"Yeah. But don't believe all you read in the papers. Anyway, remember anything else about these weapons?" he asked.

"Yes. There were Israeli Uzis among them."

"Aha. That's the other thing. We don't like arms trade in our weapons."

"Hell, your government itself sells arms," I said. He shrugged.

"Governments will do anything for the sake of their balance of payments. Our job is to clean up the messes they make. Weapons we sell are supposed to stay with the original buyers, friendly governments, for defence. It doesn't work that way. Shipments appear and disappear all over the world. Our stuff is peanuts compared to what the big boys do. But it's ours and we like to know what happens to it."

"Very commendable. You mean to tell me that anytime any cops, anywhere bust anyone with an Uzi, Mossad sends along a couple of jolly agents like you? Must keep you busy."

"No, no. Of course not. That's just background. We noted these Uzis turning up in Canada, just for future reference. That's how intelligence services work, you know. Then lately we've been getting indications of clandestine activities of known international terrorists or their agents on this continent."

"Gobbledy-gook. 'Clandestine Activities of Known International Terrorists' — here? In the Kootenays? Sounds like some desk-bound bureaucrat's make-work project. Perhaps you guys really are on vacation."

"Just hold on a moment. I know it sounds far-fetched. Let me tell you the rest," Harry said. Sid moved uncomfortably. "Judge for yourself. You've been in security work. You know how it goes."

So they really had checked me out in Vancouver. I'd have to find out about that. Meanwhile I listened closely.

"For months it was nothing. Bits and pieces. Terrorist sympathizers moving about, travelling, visiting their old aunt Mabel in Portland. That kind of thing. All in this direction. Northwest. Then money moving around. That's always a dead giveaway. Now you must know that certain key people are of special interest to us. We like to know where they are at all times. One such man headed a terrorist cell in Europe. Name of Misurali. Has important connections in the oil business, too. He disappeared. We put a special trace on him." He paused for breath, then went on.

"We picked up his trail in Chicago. He bought a ticket to Calgary, Canada. Your oil capital. Travelling as an oil executive."

"Go on. How many millions was he carrying?"

"How did you guess? He deposited $100,000 in gold certificates issued by New York CityBank at a Calgary branch of the Canadian Bank of Commerce. He saw a few people in Calgary and then took a plane to Castlegar."

"$100,000 won't buy much, not oil or arms."

"Maybe not. Maybe it's just petty cash. But he came here.

And vanished."

"Impressive. Is that all you've got?" I asked.

"No. Not at all. Do you know how far Castlegar is from the U.S. border with Washington State?"

"At a guess about 40 miles to the border, 120 to Spokane. So maybe he went back to the States that way. Maybe he likes mountain scenery. Or just wanted to give you guys a run for your money."

"No. That's the point. While in Chicago our man called a hotel room in Seattle. The couple in it were registered as Mr. and Mrs. Albert Shoreman. No forwarding address. They left next day. But we were lucky. She'd left a new blouse. With a Nelson, B.C. boutique label in it."

"Oh. Now we're getting to it."

"Wait, that's not all!" Harry was loving this.

"We were curious so we checked their prints. In our files, you understand. It took some time. Our people in Seattle lifted them off the room. Nothing on the woman. But the man we knew. Knew well. He's an expert on weapons. Care, preservation, repair, handling and storage. How do you like that!?"

"You said it took some time. When did all this happen?"

"About a month ago. We've been here five days. It takes time to organize ...."

"So you checked out Nelson. Find your Shoreman couple?"

"No. We looked in all the obvious places. Directories, voters' lists, hotel registers. Nothing."

"How about the boutique? They probably know their customers."

"People there wouldn't give us the time of day."

Sid woke up suddenly. "Perhaps you could do better."

"I'll think about it. Does this Mrs. Albert Shoreman have a first name of her own?"

"Again we were lucky. The maid who found the blouse also remembered that Shoreman called the woman 'Carol'."

I kept my face impassive. Didn't want to distract them at this point. Time enough when it came my turn to explain what my job was. As it would and soon.

— 25 —

"So what have you been doing with this information? You've been here five days. How have you put it together?"

"Shoreman would be in charge of the weapons. He must be located in the vicinity. Misurali's trip was probably inspection."

"Inspection of what? Perhaps a crisis of some kind. A top brigadier would be sent to sort it out. Misurali notified Shoreman in Seattle to get back on the job and meet him here somewhere."

"Right. That's the way it looks to us right now."

It took another half hour to get all the details of the case. They had it figured for an arms dump in an old mine shaft in this area. So after they struck out in Nelson they decided to circulate. Looking for any sign of Shoreman and the 'Misurali connection'. Castlegar airport wasn't much help. It had been a busy day. Mining and construction people being picked up in company cars. Nobody noticed a passenger from Calgary. So prior to my sudden arrival on the scene they had been driving around Kaslo hoping something would turn up. Unsurprisingly, Mossad had no contacts in these hills. And they weren't used to operating without any local support.

"Your terrorists need local support even more than you do," I said.

"Precisely. There must be an established local connection. If they've been transporting and storing arms there must be a local cover."

"Hum. Did you get any reading on these two guys you scared off last night?" I asked.

"Not much. Young, out of condition. Definitely not local talent."

"So what does all this get us?"

"That depends what you are here for. Well?"

I opened my wallet casually and took out Ray's photograph.

"Missing person case. Name of Carol Latimer."

They liked that. Very much.

"Carol! No coincidence, that's for sure," Sid said. Harry examined the photo carefully.

"This picture's twenty years old. She wouldn't look like that anymore. Could be fat, with short hair, glasses. Never spot her from that! Who wants her found?"

I replaced Ray's photo.

"Oh, friends. Her mother's sick, wants to see her."

"So what's your game plan?" Harry was pressing.

"I've a lead. It's months old but all I've got. Plan to check it out this morning. After that, who knows? What about you?"

We were talking like colleagues. But none of us had any illusions. Sid produced a map. Scale 1:250,000. Same as that one of mine annotated by Dean. Sid pointed to the central mountain range between Slocan and Kootenay lakes.

"See this? Kokanee Glacier Provincial Park. Smack in the middle of this area. We're going there next. We'll play tourist and explore, ask questions. It's all that's left."

I had my doubts whether in five days they could have exhausted all other possibilities, but I let it pass. It suited me. And they weren't telling me everything. But then neither was I.

"OK. If my lead peters out I'll go to Nelson. Check that boutique for you. And flash Carol's photo. Then I'll join you up at the park."

Harry shook his head.

"I've a better idea. We'll meet you in Nelson tomorrow. At the Jam Factory. That's where everything happens in Nelson. Say, late afternoon?"

They had something up their sleeve. Something at the park. You don't 'explore' miles of snow-capped mountains in a day. They didn't want me around there.

"Jam Factory?" I asked innocently. I did recall a poster I'd seen at Dean's. A factory converted into a restaurant, gallery, bookstore, Women's Centre. Influence of the 'new people' entrepreneurs. "Sounds OK. Let's check with each other via the bulletin board. Bound to be one there. Leave messages if necessary."

Sid was looking at me thoughtfully.

"Likewise. Don't try to vanish on us. We would take that as an unfriendly act."

"Why would I do a thing like that?"

I walked away towards my waiting rig, their eyes boring into my back.

5

"HELLO, ALICE? HOW'RE YOU DOING?" I grinned like an idiot into the mouthpiece of the public phone in Kaslo's second-best hotel. Alice had that effect on me.

"Not too badly, not too badly. And what the hell are you doing in Kaslo making collect calls to us in Vancouver? Need bail? I knew they would catch up with you sooner or later."

"A good lawyer will do, thanks, Alice. That's why I called this number. It's engraved on my memory. It's serious but not desperate. Is Jessica around?"

"Jessica, Jessica. Oh, yes, I remember. My esteemed employer. D'you know she's finally managed to beat me at backgammon? But don't worry, it's just an aberration. We'll be back to normal soon."

"Your game will deteriorate as soon as you finish law school too. So watch it."

"Don't worry. I quit. Law is for the intellectually downwardly mobile. Do you need first class legal advice or will a sanctified member of the bar do?"

"Both. I want to talk to Jessica."

"In which case you'd better talk to her. Here she is. Stay loose, now." There was a click and Jessica's sleepy voice came on the line.

"Helen Keremos. Taking your vacation early this year, are you?"

"Vacation, nothing. I'm on a case which could get very, very sticky."

"Rough stuff?"

"Well, I've been bounced around by a couple of overgrown Hardy boys but that's not what worries me."

"It would worry me."

"No, that's not it." In spite of myself I was getting serious. Jessica heard.

"What can I do?"

"Nothing really right now. But it would be nice to know you are holding a watching brief on my behalf in Vancouver. You

— 28 —

see, it could involve the Horsemen and assorted international heavies."

"You've got it. Anything more you'd care to tell me?"

"Listen, I called Frank. You remember Frank Hanusek. I met him in the Navy. Dig? Now he's in Fisheries Protection Branch."

"Ah, yes. Your friend the sea dog. I remember. What did you call him about? My, you are stingy with information!"

"I don't have any, that's why. Someone has been checking up on me in Vancouver. I want to know who it was and what they got. Frank has connections in the right quarters. He's to find out and let me know tonight. I'll call him this evening. Clear?"

"Relatively. So what's my part in all this?"

"Call Frank tonight." I gave her his home number. "He'll tell you what he's found out and whether I've called back. If I haven't been in touch, say by 10 p.m., then figure that it's bad trouble. For me. And act accordingly."

"That's rather open-ended. What action would be appropriate? Just a border skirmish or the Third World War?"

"If only I knew! Use your judgment. D'you know anyone in Nelson? Or Castlegar?"

"No. A classmate of mine has a practice in Trail. But I would not exactly recommend him if it's a heavy international schtick. Trail's a company town. He's a company man. So ...."

"Forget that. If you don't hear from me you and Frank should put your heads together and follow whatever Frank's been able to turn up. It could be a clue."

"A clue." A deep sigh. "OK. Just do an old friend a favour and don't disremember to call."

"No chance. Thanks. Hey, what's this about Alice dropping out of law school?"

"Yeah. She says it interfered with her social life. Period. Perhaps it's just as well. British Columbia bar isn't ready for her."

"Was it ready for you? I seem to remember ...."

"Too late now. I'm in. And you can keep your highly selective recollections to yourself. 'Bye. I've a client waiting. Good luck."

Jessica rang off. I stood there for a second with the receiver in my hand remembering Jessica Tsukada. As I met her as a first-year law student. Eight, ten years ago. And Alice Caplan. Three years ago she was an actress. Currently working with Jessica as a legal secretary. And next year, who knows? Anything was possible with Alice. She and Jessica made a great combo. It would be a pity if it broke up. Meanwhile, it was good to have women like that in my corner. It's the only insurance I carry.

6

I TOOK HIGHWAY 31 FROM KASLO, north along Kootenay Lake. Dean's map and directions seemed clear enough, yet I managed to get myself lost once I left the highway. At least I could be sure no one was following me. Finally I managed to navigate the trailer over a narrow, rutted road towards a low sprawling house surrounded by new, half-finished outbuildings. A fence made of wire and lumberyard tail ends ran along one side of the access drive and around the vegetable patch. This looked like the only cleared area. The rest was badly overgrown: not a tree, bush or weed seemed to have been touched. A large woodpile proved this wasn't entirely so. A number of dogs of assorted ancestry loudly greeted my arrival. No one seemed to notice. I parked and walked around, looking. The area in front of the house, along and between the outbuildings, gave the appearance of a well-organized construction and junkyard. There was lumber in stacks, two-by-fours, boards, fence posts and scrap. Pile of builder's gravel. Rolls of wire fencing. Then there was a rough corral full of bottles — large and small, white, green and amber. Next plastic articles — pails, jugs, containers in various sizes. A heap of tin cans. Inside the fence at the edge of the vegetable garden a large covered compost pit. Recycling was a way of life here. Whether on principle or out of sheer economic necessity, this wasn't a place of waste. Except for tools. Sadly I spotted a steel rule, then a can of rusty nails and a hammer. Other good tools. Couple of hundred dollars worth of them deteriorating, uncared for. I poked around an old pickup, two wrecks of small Japanese cars and a newish, beautifully kept Honda 400 bike. By now I was at one corner of the house. Two large propane tanks marked this the kitchen side. Navigating a full rain barrel, under a rain spout dangerously at head level, I glanced at the window. The still face of a woman showed white inside. I waved to acknowledge contact, stepped into the porch and opened the door. It led directly into a large, dark farm kitchen. It was full. A long homemade table to seat at least ten ran along the window wall. Benches and old wooden chairs crowded around it. A functionally beautiful black and white wood-burning kitchen stove sent heat out in waves. Rough shelves holding an assortment of dry food covered the walls. Odd bits and pieces of furniture, kitchen cabinets and two enormous shabby armchairs took up the rest of available space. There were stacks of waste paper, two garbage pails — one for compost, one for burnable waste, a wooden box almost full of rinsed cans and bottles awaiting disposal outside. Firewood in a waist-high box. A refrigerator and, on a small metal kitchen table, a propane camp stove, shining copper pipes connecting them to the tanks outside. The unlit lamps were all kerosene. The place had no electricity.

I picked my way around a grouping of cat food dishes, disturbing a fat all-white beast which looked up at me with runny red eyes. Silhouette of a woman was dark against the window. I wondered how long she had been watching me outside. I tried to see myself with her eyes. Jeans, boots, a lumber jacket. Tall, dark, and probably older than any of the women in the commune. The jeep was fine; the trailer might be suspect, too fancy. But all in all I figured I would get by.

Neither of us had spoken yet. I moved closer, to where the pale light of day fell on her face. Her dark outline dissolved into a slim figure about 5'4" clad in layers of well worn clothes. Delicate features and dark eyes looking at me calmly from under home-cut hair.

"Hello," I said tentatively.

"Hello," she answered. We stared at each other, then grinned simultaneously.

"Like some coffee?" she said, moving towards the stove. Relieved, I sat down on one of the chairs by the table.

"Yeah, thanks," I said.

"Travelling?" she asked, pouring two mugs full of steaming black liquid from an enamelled tin pot which must have held half a gallon.

"Kind of. My name's Helen. I'm from Vancouver."

"I'm Nancy. I live here."

"I figured that." She brought the mugs to the table, placed one in front of me, then took hers to the other end and perched on a bench. Light from the window flooded the long table between us. We could see each other clearly now.

"How did you hear about us?" She paused and when I didn't answer continued. "In summer we get lots of sisters passing through. You're the first this year. Welcome." It was obviously quite a long speech for her.

"Thanks. I was in the area and thought I'd stop by and visit with Carol. Haven't seen or heard of her in ages. So I drove over to Dean's and he told me she might be here. Is she around?"

The second I mentioned Carol, Nancy became stiller than ever, if that was possible. Her eyes never left my face. I felt my lies crawling all over it. I was committed now.

"Carol?" She didn't bother looking puzzled. "So many women drop in on us, stay a while and move on. Carol? Maybe she was using a new name." That took me back momentarily but then I understood.

"You mean like Sky or Thorn or Lilith," I said. She smiled slowly.

"Sure, what else?"

"No, that doesn't sound like Carol. Her last name's Latimer."

"I never bother with last names," Nancy said. We weren't getting anywhere.

I took a chance. "Some old friends of hers from California used to call her Ray, I recall now. Does that help?" If it meant anything to her, she wasn't letting on. Her face held no expression. I would hate playing poker with this young woman.

"No." It was a very definite monosyllable. "Well, anyway. Sorry your friend's not here. But you are welcome to stay for a meal with us."

Sound of a motorbike invaded the quiet kitchen. Both Nancy and I looked out to see a slight anonymous figure encased in black leather jacket, jeans and high buckled boots circle the yard on an enormous blue Yamaha. Head and features totally hidden under a blue-and-silver helmet and goggles.

"Aha," said Nancy. A minute later the biker burst into the house.

Actually she just opened the door and walked in but it felt as if 130 pounds of positive energy had entered. She stood still for a split second accustoming her eyes to the dimness inside, took off her helmet, freeing a shock of bright hair which fell to her shoulders.

"Any coffee?" she asked, walking briskly towards the stove. Without waiting for an answer she poured out a mug, moved to the table and gave me a glance full of warmth and curiosity.

"You belong to that rig?" she asked. I nodded.

"Nice." She sat down and sipped her coffee. "Once I get biking out of my system I'm getting a jeep." Dismissing me and the attraction of jeeps she turned to Nancy.

"Hey, Nance. How come no one except me around here ever puts away any tools? I go away for a couple of days and the yard's full of them! Damn it! At our last house meeting we agreed to look after them with some respect. Even Artemis promised. She's the worst ...."

"Cool it for a minute, Laura," Nancy interrupted the outburst. "Helen, this dyke-on-a-bike is Laura. When she's not visiting her numerous lovers all over B.C. and Washington State, she hangs out here."

Laura laughed. She couldn't be more than twenty-two.

"Just as well. Or there wouldn't be a usable tool or a machine of any kind in operation left in this place. Hey, Nance. Someone else had better learn all that stuff. I'm moving back to Victoria."

"When?" Monosyllable again from Nancy.

"Soon. I guess Helen could have my space if she's planning to stay. You look like you'd be good with tools, Helen. They could use you." Laura went on a mile a minute. Nancy sighed.

"Laura. Take it easy. Helen's just looking for a friend. Called Carol or maybe Ray."

"Carol? Hey, wasn't that ...." Laura began.

"No. That was Carrie," Nancy interrupted her firmly.

"Yeah, I guess you're right." Laura sounded confused but she got the message, dismissed the subject and went on to the next thing on her mind. "Hey, Nance. Any news on that part-time job you were after? Bookkeeping for the lumberyard. Would be great! Get us real deals on scrap. Hey, where's the crew anyway? Isn't this a building day or is my schedule all off?"

"They're moving the privy and filling up the old hole, remember?" Now the danger was over Nancy spoke indulgently.

"Do I remember! Is it ever about time." Laura held her nose. "Guess I'll go give a hand. How are you at privy-moving, Helen?" Before Nancy could head me off I was up on my feet and following Laura out of the house like a tail on a comet.

"How many of you live here, Laura?" I asked as we crossed the yard, picking up tools as we went.

"Right now? Only four. Me and Nance, Rita, and Artemis. We stayed the winter together. I guess Chris will move in over the summer. She visits Rita a lot anyway. Probably here now, helping. The place is tight for more than five or maybe six."

I followed Laura with an armload of tools into a shed. It was fitted out with a workbench, pegboard for tools, jars and cans of nails, screws and an assortment of the odds and ends that accumulate in the country. Laura wiped, then examined every tool before putting it away.

"Look at this chisel. A chip out of it. That Artemis! Funny, she's good with wood. But anything made of metal disturbs her karma. She says." It was obviously a favourite complaint.

"How do you live? Make a living, I mean. Pay mortgage, gas, buy groceries?"

"Summer work, mostly. Last year we all worked on road construction. As flag women. I guess if ARC is hiring again this season that's what the rest of them will be doing. It's good money, better than any women's work we could get. Now me, I'm going back to Victoria."

"How come?" I prodded.

"D'you know Victoria? Geritol City. And the lesbian community is all couples, nesting. Not my scene at all! Wouldn't go back there except I've got this chance to get into a training program. I want to learn a trade. Mechanic. It's real hard to get in. And then once you're in the men give you a real hard time. So many women quit. And that gives them an excuse not to accept any more. It's a vicious circle. But I don't care, I'll stick it out."

— 35 —

"Yeah, I bet you will. Good luck," I said, and then as if suddenly struck with a random thought I continued "Did Carol work on the road with you last summer? When did she leave?"

"Carol? I thought it was Carrie." Laura wasn't really interested in either Carol or me. "Whoever, we all worked for ARC. Buddy boy Dean is always good for a couple of weeks or months of work for us every summer. D'you know Dean?"

"I've met him. He and Carol were lovers, weren't they? But I didn't know he worked for ARC."

"Sure. Project supervisor or something. Just seasonal work but he makes plenty. He's got a neat truck. Souped-up four-by-four, goes like stink." She'd ignored my implied question on Carol's relationship to Dean. Her mind was on his souped-up truck. Dean didn't hold her attention.

We made our way past the house to where from behind a dense jungle of growth, the sounds of young women's voices reached us. A well-worn path led past the unmistakable previous location of the outhouse. The hole remained unfilled but the contents had been liberally covered with lime.

"Have to fill that in next," said Laura indifferently. "Before someone falls in." She chuckled.

We reached the new site. Hole was ready, the dirt piled carefully to one side. A heavy two-holer had been rolled on logs and now lay on its side ready to be erected again. Three women in work clothes and muddy boots were grouped around it. Next stage in the operation was under cheerful discussion.

"We need more bodies. Two of us alone can't lift it and we need the third to back-stop." Woman who spoke was about thirty-five with a serious Semitic face and a New York accent.

"Relax, Rita. I see two extra bodies. Just in time, Laura, wouldn't want you to miss this." This came from a small, stout woman with close-cropped hair sitting on the roof of the privy kicking her legs. She looked like a mischievous cherub. The third woman, tall and very thin, said nothing, but she smiled at us and was first to kiss and hug Laura. The other two followed.

"This here is Helen. She's just dropped in looking for someone," Laura said once the customary feminist greetings were over. "She'll give us a hand."

"Hi, Helen." There were cursory introductions. The roof-sitter turned out to be Chris, the silent one Artemis, the New Yorker Rita. No one evinced any curiosity about me. I was there ready to work. That was enough.

An hour later we were through. The privy was up over the new hole, solidly anchored with two-by-fours. The old hole was filled and pounded down. There was toilet paper and a new stack of reading matter in the new location. Nancy came out to congratulate us. A joint made the rounds as we waited our turns to test the new facilities.

"Now that we've celebrated the occasion appropriately," Chris said, "let's go eat."

It takes a while for six very independent people to straggle in from outside and sit down to a meal. I cleaned up superficially and sat surrounded by pleasant chaos as five women went about their business of feeding cats, cleaning up, opening mail, cutting bread, arguing about lost objects, rolling a joint, stirring soup, finding the right number of clean spoons, discussing salad ingredients ....Finally we all sat down at the long kitchen table and ate. The conversation was sporadic and desultory. I felt Nancy's eyes on me a couple of times but nothing was said about my reason for being there until the vegetable soup, cheese, bread, and salad were finished and we munched on homemade carrot cake and drank tea out of pottery mugs.

Nancy spoke. "Listen, everyone. Helen's asking after Carol or Ray. Carol's a friend of Helen's from Vancouver. We don't know anyone like that, do we?" It wasn't a question. No one bothered to pretend it was. There was a silence while they all looked at me. It was up to me.

"OK. I lied. I've never met Carol. But you lied too. You know her and probably know where she is. It's important that I get in touch with her. I have a message for her. And her mother is sick." It was the best I could do.

"This Carol. What if she doesn't want to be found?" Rita said. "Why should we help you find her? We know nothing about you."

"Fair enough. And how much do you know about Ray, I

mean Carol?"

"Enough to know why she doesn't want to be found."

"So you know about Ray. Long ago and far away."

"Yes." Nancy chimed in with a monosyllable again.

"Look. I'm not here to blow the whistle on her. Do I look like a police stoolie? I just want to give her a message."

"She knows about her mother," Artemis said under her breath. Nancy looked at her sternly.

"Good. Listen. I did come here because of what happened all those years ago. I admit that. But now I want to talk to her about what's happening here and now. In this valley. Please help me find her. I believe she's in danger." It sounded weak even to me.

"Sure she's in danger. From you. And if she's involved in something here and now — that's her business. Not yours or ours," Rita replied.

"So you know about it! Have you any idea ...."

"Don't patronize us. Yes, we have an idea. It doesn't matter. She's a sister. She came here for help, for sanctuary, for a place to stay until she got her shit together. We knew she was into something heavy. Heavy political. Male politics don't concern us. That's her choice. But she asked us to preserve her privacy. And that's what we intend to do. You won't find her through us."

"I am sorry if I sounded patronizing. But you cannot just write it off as 'male politics' and therefore of no concern!"

"Why not?" Nancy interrupted. It sounded like she genuinely wanted to know.

"Because it does concern you! If for no other reason than because people may die and this sanctuary will be gone."

"Maybe. But that's a chance we'll have to take. It's not easy living the way we do. If we don't stick to our principles, what's the point?" Rita said. It was clear she merely expressed the consensus among them. Perhaps only Laura wasn't quite sure. She had already made her decision to leave. This too was accepted by the others.

"More tea, anyone?" asked Nancy.

I held out my mug.

"All right," I said. "I respect your politics even if we don't agree on this point. But is there any way you could get a message to her? About my being here and wanting to get in touch? Let her decide."

"No. We don't know where she is."

"But you know how to go about finding her. You have some idea. You must. OK, don't tell me. Let me tell you. I do have another lead. Nothing to do with you. I am going to Nelson. I'll be checking the bulletin board at the Jam Factory. If she wants to, she can leave a message of some kind there. OK?"

I received no answer.

7

It was still full daylight when I reached Kaslo again. I debated whether to call Frank from there or wait until I got to Nelson. Curiosity won. I got on the blower.

"Helen?" Frank Hanusek's voice sounded far off. "What the hell are you up to out there?"

"What did you find out? Come on Frank, tell me!"

"Well, we opened a can of worms for sure. I called a couple of my contacts. Places that would be likely to get asked about you. Nothing from the locals. The other contact called back within an hour. Told me there had been an informal inquiry about you late last night from a very prominent citizen. A lawyer called Beach. I checked him out. Morris Beach, big-time corporation lawyer. Director of a dozen companies plus the Art Gallery, Bonds for Israel, Cancer Society. You know the type."

"I get the picture. Very interesting. What did they tell him about me?"

"About what you'd expect. Said you checked out OK. Reliable, smart, honest. Regular girl scout."

"Thanks. What about the security angle, did he ask about that? Did they tell him anything about my past connections?"

"Ah. The security angle. That's where it gets really interesting. Yes, he asked and they told him. He's got lots of pull. No reason not to tell him."

"So? What's the angle?"

"So that was only the beginning! Couple of hours later, mid-afternoon I guess, I had a visitor. Very polite, very firm, very hush-hush. Wanting to know why I wanted to know about who wanted to know about you. If you follow."

"I follow all right. And?"

"I told him. Had no choice, really. Anyway couldn't see why I shouldn't. I told him you called from Kaslo, that you were on a case and obviously someone there had connections in Vancouver and had gotten information that you don't get from a telephone book. That's all."

"That's all!"

"That's all I told him because that's all I know. He did a fine job interrogating me about the job you are on. That's what they wanted to know. Pressed like hell. But not knowing, couldn't say. Helen, just what are you doing in the beautiful Kootenays to have stirred up this amount of interest among the security boys?"

"I wish I knew. Flying blind mostly. But this is a very interesting development. Did your visitor have a name?"

"Ronald Walters. D'you know him?"

"Ron! But ...." I stopped. Ron Walters was another memory from the past. Curiouser and curiouser. Were they keeping tabs on me or on Morris Beach? Whichever way the connection was originally made it was the combination of Keremos and Beach that stirred Ronald Walters' interest. Except that when last heard of Ronald Walters was in West Germany. So what was he doing inquiring about an insignificant private eye with a case in the interior of British Columbia? Which suggested that the lead had to be Beach. I just wasn't important enough to keep an eye on.

"Confusing, isn't it?" said Frank, right on cue. He knew about Ronald Walters, too.

"Did Walters leave any number or address where I could get in touch with him? Didn't he want to talk to me, personally?"

"As a matter of fact, no. But he did leave me a number 'in case I remembered anything else'. That's what he said. I checked it. It's not official. An apartment on the West side."

"You checked it! Frank you are a jewel! OK. I'll take it from here. Just keep your ears and eyes open. Do nothing. And listen. Jessica Tsukada will call tonight. Tell her everything you told me. I will keep in touch. And thanks."

"For what? It's been a pleasure. Like old times. Beats patrolling the 200-mile limit. Be careful. 'Bye."

I stopped for a while at the hotel window and cased the street. Cars, passers-by, my rig parked only a couple of stores down. Nothing. I shrugged and left. There wasn't any point worrying.

It's a beautiful drive down to Nelson along the lake. Traffic on the road was light. I had leisure to observe boats skimming over the water, small amphibian planes, tourist operators paint-ing up for the summer rush, kids fishing. Nice and peaceful.

Nearing Nelson I passed a road leading up to Kokanee Glacier Provincial Park. It looked rough but a four-wheeler would make it easy. I wondered about my two Israelis in their rented station wagon. If they didn't mind breaking a few springs and maybe having to rock themselves out of a hole, they could make it all right.

I like Nelson. Mountains all around except where the long narrow aperture of the lake stretches north. It's much bigger than Kaslo. Docks, lumber mills, wooden houses scattered on the hill sides and a small but busily urban downtown. I found the Jam Factory and drove past it. Backed into an out-of-the-way parking spot couple of streets over, uncoupled the trailer and went back in the jeep. No telling when the trailer would be a nuisance.

It was too late to check the boutique where a woman calling herself Carol Shoreman had bought a blouse. I went into the Jam Factory restaurant, passed the message board and had a meal. Good vegetarian food in very pleasant surroundings. I took my coffee out on the little patio. It was cool but I could see a small part of the street from there. Behind me were the rail yards and the harbour. On an impulse I turned to a woman cleaning up the table next to mine.

"Do you know a Carol Latimer, by any chance?" A stab in the dark. "About forty, blond?"

"Carol? Why sure! I haven't seen her for ages! Is she around? I was worried about her." Pay dirt!

"Worried? Why?"

"Oh. Men, you know. She got involved with this guy in town. He's got a pretty bad rep. Travels around, lots of money and treats women like dirt. I was surprised when I heard about them. Carol's always been pretty together. What would she want with a creep like that?"

"It happens. What's his name? Not Shoreman by any chance?"

"Yes, that's right. Al Shoreman. Engineer. Something like that. Mining or construction, I'm not sure. So you know him too, eh?"

"I've heard of him. Where does he hang out? Not here I bet."

She laughed. "Not a chance. We don't sell hard liquor and people here aren't his kind. I think the Admiral Tavern. It's where the rest of them booze up. But like I said, he's away a lot. Last I heard Carol went with him. Haven't seen her since. Perhaps they aren't back yet. Well, I must go." She picked up my empty plates and coffee cup and went on to the next table.

I went to find a phone. Admiral Hotel and Tavern. If he was registered there the Israelis would have found him. So I asked for the bar.

"Bar," a gruff voice announced itself over the sound of glasses and music. Moving my voice into its lowest register I demanded to speak to Al Shoreman. The voice at the other end sounded surprised.

"Not here. Haven't seen him. Didn't he get transferred?" I took a chance. "Hell, I thought he got fired. Figured he'd be drowning his sorrows."

"Well if he is, it's not here." Curiosity. "How come he got fired? A big shot like that!"

"That boss of his from back east. Bastards." Always safe to bad-mouth 'back east' bosses.

"Oh, yeah? Wouldn't you know! I'd figured ARC for a western company. But it's owned back east! Wouldn't you know it!"

"So I hear. Boss came, didn't like the operation or picked up some dirt on Al and out he went. Just like that."

"Well, there're no flies on Al. He'll make out OK. Sorry I can't help you, buddy. Gotta go."

"Thanks." I hung up. The barman probably knew where Shoreman lived. But it wouldn't do to arouse suspicion by asking a direct question like that. I could go to the Admiral, mix with the boomers there and probably pick up a lot more. But I had gotten enough. Shoreman was employed by Arrow Road Construction. I love coincidences. Gave me a strange feeling at the back of my neck.

That feeling was with me as I checked the bulletin board. No messages. That was strange. The Mossad boys seemed very keen on us picking up on each other that night. I went over our conversation in my mind. We definitely were to leave messages for each other. I got out a pen and wrote:

Wrath of God, where are you!? K.

Kind of cute I thought. Well, they couldn't say I hadn't left a message. I pinned it to the board, went out and sat in my jeep. It was dark and getting chilly. I tried to think of what more I could do that night. Nothing until daylight. Except possibly visit the Women's Centre. There would be people there who knew Carol. Suddenly I was tired. Especially of lying to women. My arms started to hurt again. My body was telling me to stop. I decided to heed it and get some sleep.

I drove back to the trailer, drew all the curtains and lay down hoping the local cops weren't big on checking travel trailers parked on city streets. It seemed a reasonable risk to take before full tourist season.

I slept.

When I woke I was looking into the barrel of a gun. A gun held by a young man with a black eye. There's a line in one of Holly Near's songs: "His smile was from Tucson." This was him. I groaned and rolled over.

"None of that," he said "Get up and let's go."

"Go where? I need my breakfast." I answered.

"Don't get smart." He was trying hard to act tough. It didn't quite jell. "We're taking a ride. Get dressed. And don't try anything."

"OK, OK." I said and got out of bed. I was wearing a T-shirt. "Like to search this place again or did you get all you wanted last night?"

"Don't get smart," he repeated. His script writer had quit on him. "Hurry up." I hurried. Jeans, shirt and high-top sneakers.

"Where do you keep your gun?" he said.

"Gun? What gun? There's a .30-30 rifle in the jeep. But no handgun."

"You're a private investigator, aren't you? You must have a handgun."

"Hey man! You've got the wrong job in the wrong country. We don't take handguns on vacation with us."

"Bull! Never mind. Let's go."

We left the trailer together and walked towards a flashy top-of-the-line four-door Buick with Washington State licence plates. The other man sat behind the wheel. He opened the far door for us.

"Get in," said my captor, slammed the door behind me and climbed into the back. He leaned forward with his hands on the back of the seat next to my head. The car moved away from the curb.

"I hope you guys will pay my fine if I get towed away," I said, just for conversation.

"Shut up," said the driver. He was almost a twin of my boy with the gun. No black eye and a trifle older. Thirty, maybe. I recalled referring to them as the Hardy boys. It was proving very apt.

Two bright lads from stateside. I tried to place them. Expensive high-quality sports clothes. Well groomed all over. Definitely not cops or run-of-the-mill hoods.

We drove out of town. Not the way I had come in, but up the mountain behind Nelson. I tried to engage them in light chit-chat but they wouldn't play. After about ten minutes the driver grunted with satisfaction and turned into a narrow side road. Almost immediately he pulled off into a small clearing among trees and stopped.

"This is it. Out," he said. The guy behind me leaned over and opened my door. A very foolish thing to do, proving this wasn't their kind of trip. I let him get away with it. They would make other mistakes, meanwhile I wanted to find out what their part was in all this. I got out stiffly, giving them plenty of time. Black-eye waved his gun. We moved down a slope through muck and undergrowth, finally stopping at a small stream rushing down the mountain. The driver swore, took out a fine linen handkerchief and wiped his Gucci loafers.

"Christ, what a country," he said.

"Let's get on with it," said the other. He sounded more nervous than ever. I had a moment of panic. Could I have miscalculated? Were these amateurs sent here to kill me? It didn't seem likely but stranger things have happened.

"Sit down," said the driver with clean shoes. "Over there." He pointed at an outcrop of rock. I went over and leaned against it facing them.

"OK. Now, where is she?" he said sternly. I calmed down. There were things they wanted to know.

"Who? Who is where?" I answered, sounding puzzled.

"Christ! Sara Ann Raymond, of course. Don't let's play games. We know all about you."

"Really. Then what makes you think I know any Sara Ann Raymond? And why bring me here? We could've had a nice chat in my trailer. Over breakfast coffee. Yeah, coffee would be nice."

"Oh, yeah? So those two goons you have protecting you could jump us again! Not a chance. Look, just be a nice lady and tell us where to find Sara Ann. Then you can go have all the coffee you want."

One, they didn't know anything about my Mossad pals. Two, it looked like they'd been sent to follow me and get Sara Ann. It would be nice to have them confirm that I'd been set up.

"Let's go back to square one. You've been sent to get this Sara Ann Raymond, whoever she is. You think I know where she is. Why? And if I did, why would I tell you? Under the circumstances. I've seen guns before. Even had them pointed at me. Am I supposed to roll over just because you ask me?"

"Shit!" The younger guy wasn't liking this, "I told you it wouldn't be so easy."

His partner ignored him and answered me, "Yes, we're here to get Sara Ann and take her home. Her mother is sick. That's all. Why not be a good girl and tell us what you've found out so far? Perhaps you don't know exactly where she is right now. But you have a pretty good idea how to find her. Just tell us that and we'll take it from there. What's it to you, anyway? You've been paid. You could be on your way home in an hour. A fast buck. If you don't, well, we don't want to hurt you but we will if we have to. Think about it."

"This is silly. Where do you get your information? I don't know from any Sara Ann. So how will it help if you hurt me?

Only trouble for you. You're a long way from home, boys. Why not go back and report that you've struck out?"

"Don't kid us. We know for a fact who you are and what you're doing here. How long do we have to bandy words before you'll understand that we're serious? Would you prefer we got nasty? And I mean nasty."

I laughed. Not that I wasn't scared but then so were they. And out of their depth.

"Oh, stop it. Why don't we go sit down somewhere over coffee and discuss this situation like civilized people? This cheap drama isn't getting us anywhere. You don't like it either, do you? Well, do you?"

I had the attention of the younger guy but the other one wasn't through.

"Tell us where to find Sara Ann. Right now!"

I just stood there. The two men looked at each other. Black-eye waved his gun and said to his tough pal, "You go. I'll cover you."

In that moment of their indecision I sprinted right for them. They stood quite close together about 20 feet from me with their backs to the stream. I split right between them, straight-arming the one with the gun. He didn't have time to fire. I kept going into the shallow, fast stream jumping from rock to rock, stepping into shallows, going like hell downhill with the current. I didn't look back.

It took them only a second to follow, one in the stream like I was, the other along the edge. I had lots of momentum and footing in my sneakers. They were younger and strong but taken by surprise and in city shoes. The driver lost one of his loafers in the water almost immediately. He cursed. I heard the other crashing and falling in the dense spring growth behind me. I knew that unless I fell and hurt myself they didn't have a hope in hell of getting me. Their guns were useless. It was impossible to aim. The terrain was with me. Then the stream narrowed between two outcrops of rock. I plunged into the deeper, faster water, lost my footing, was swept down and pushed under an overhanging bank, undercut by the force of the stream. At the point where it widened a tangle of logs and branches had been deposited there before me. I grabbed one large log and clung to it. As far as I could judge I couldn't be seen from either bank. Unless one of them made the journey I had, they wouldn't find me. The cold water pounded in my ears mixing with the pounding of my heart. I couldn't hear anything else but through the tangle above me I could just see the top of the rock on the other side. Black Eye appeared on it first. He still had his shoes on. The wet rock was slippery under his feet. He scrambled up awkwardly and looked down on the stream. His friend joined him within a minute, walking carefully in his bare feet, carrying one shoe. Now they both looked down. They talked, pointing here and there at rocks and trees, including my hiding place. Then the barefoot boy waved his arm in disgust, turned and scrambled back into the water the way we had come upstream. The other stood a minute longer, then followed him along the opposite bank. I dragged myself further under the overhang where a tree with naked roots hung precariously over the stream, creating a break in the bank. I crouched in the hollow for another minute shivering. From there I got occasional glimpses of the two men making their way slowly up-hill along the stream. I followed carefully, crossed the stream at a shallow point just above where I had lost my footing, cut sharply left up the ridge towards where I judged the car was on the side road. I didn't stop until I reached it. It wasn't locked. Even the keys had been left in the ignition.

Hour later I was back in Nelson in dry clothes, inhaling a big, big breakfast with lots of coffee. I had dumped their car across a laneway entrance just round the corner from the cop shop. Their luggage was all there in the trunk, along with a spare automatic they must have carried for emergencies. This was going to be an emergency all right. I left the trunk and doors unlocked, threw away the keys, and reported anonymously by phone the car illegally parked. That would take a while to sort out, one way or another. Our cops don't like tourists with hand guns, any guns. They would make more trouble about that than any other three things you can think of.

8

THERE WAS STILL NO MESSAGE for me at the Jam Factory. I got my rig back on the road to Castlegar. Best to let the Nelson scene simmer down without me. On the way, I decided to get rid of the trailer. It made me too conspicuous and slow. On an impulse I parked it at the Castlegar Airport. Then I went into town, got a motel room and prepared to make phone calls. It was time to check up on ARC's very special employee Albert Shoreman.

That white mobile construction trailer I had visited only two days previously turned out to be only a field office. Headquarters was in town. A woman with a nice voice answered. I did my baritone imitation again.

"Mr. Albert Shoreman, please," I said.

"I am sorry, sir, Mr. Shoreman isn't here right now. May I take a message?"

"Oh, that's too bad. This is urgent. When do you expect him? Or perhaps you might know where else I could reach him."

"I am sorry, sir," she had to say again. What a job! "I don't know where you could find him. He might be in the field on a job."

"Let me have his number in Nelson, then. Perhaps I can catch him at home."

"I doubt it, sir. But you can try." And like a lamb gave me a Nelson number. I thanked her and hung up. I called the number she gave me. A man answered.

"Mr. Shoreman, please," I said.

"He's not here. Who wants him?"

"Never mind, thanks. I'll call again." That was that. Now all I had to do was find the address that went with that number. As I expected, local B.C. Telephone wouldn't tell me. I sighed and reached for the Nelson telephone book.

It didn't take long. Al Shoreman's phone number was listed under D. Greenwood. Our friend Dean had a pad in Nelson. But that hadn't been his voice. So, another party heard from.

I took off my clothes, climbed into bed, set my portable alarm and was asleep before I touched the pillow. When it rang four hours later I woke up rested and hungry. I showered, dressed, went out to eat. On my way out of town again, I picked up a bottle of brandy, bread, milk and a bucket of chicken. I had decided to get to Kokanee Glacier Provincial Park going lightweight, sans trailer. I could always curl up in a sleeping bag at the back of the jeep. Going through Nelson to get to the park, I checked the message board again. Nothing. No message or sign of the Israelis. It was very unlike guys like that not to be dependably where they said they would be. They might be onto some hot lead or in bad trouble. Either way, I wanted to find them.

The sign on the road into the park said "No trailers. 16 kilo-metres to Gibson Lake. Very rough road." Almost halfway there I came across a small government truck blocking the road. I was about to go around it when a man with a chainsaw waved me down.

"We've got some trees down. You won't get through. But if you'll give me a hand with your jeep we'll get them cleared right quick. It's that storm we had couple of nights ago. Just terrible it was! Don't remember wind like that since I moved here from the coast. How about it? Otherwise you'll have to go back and try another road. You going backpacking? Very pretty it is up there. Not many people there yet. Lots of snow still, roads all tore up, washed away in places. You'll be OK in a jeep once we get them trees off the road. Amazing how people don't know enough not to take city automobiles up roads like that. Real amazing. Tourists now, they don't know from nothing. Hike in tennis shoes, drive dinky little foreign cars where you wouldn't take a mule! Then wonder why they get stuck." He prattled on and on. The sound of a chainsaw from behind the parked truck interrupted him. Only for a second.

"That's Win. My partner. Works real hard. For an Indian. You don't mind using your jeep, do you? To pull logs off the road. You see, gov'nment don't give us proper equipment. Chainsaws, sure. When they work, we can cut up the fallen trees. But then what? That truck! Hell, it's not four-wheel drive, see? So we got to cut them up small enough to roll by hand. And that's a lot of extra work. Now with your jeep and this chain I got right here we can get the road clear double quick. See?" He stopped for breath. I cut in immediately.

"Sure, sure. Glad to help. Move your truck so I can get through. Go on, man." He moved towards the truck reluctantly, still talking.

"You in a hurry, eh. Now why would you be in a hurry like that? Nothing up there but scenery. Hardly any tourists yet. Nobody there right now. Boy, it sure blew" .... His voice faded as he got in the truck, gassed it and backed off to let me pass.

The back of the other man with a chainsaw came into view. He was working on a large tree lying across the road. It was already cut in a number of places but the pieces were certainly too big to move without horsepower. I turned the jeep around and reversed up to where he stood. He turned round as I got out of the jeep.

"Howdy," was all he said.

"Howdy," I answered. From the ridiculous to the sublime. "Your partner there. Does he always talk like he was afraid of silence?" His face lit up.

"Echo? For sure. That's what we call him — Echo. Yeah, I guess he's afraid of silence, at that. My name's Win. You going to let us use your vehicle there?"

"Mine's Helen. Why not? You two get the chain around the logs and I'll pull them off the road. OK?"

"Fine." Win turned back to his saw and was finishing cutting when Echo arrived dragging a heavy chain.

"Ain't it great, Win, eh? Ain't it great! With the help of this lady and her jeep we'll be finished early. Short-handed and all, we'll be finished early."

Hastily I got back in the jeep and watched the two of them manoeuvre the chain around a six foot log. Echo kept talking. He was an odd-looking guy. About fifty, thinning blond hair, shaggy goatee beard, long, thin red-knuckled hands.

"Boy, won't Ben be surprised when we get back so quick. Yeah, Ben sure won't expect us for hours. Be time for a couple of beers and a plate of that good stew his woman makes. Eh, Win?"

"When didn't we have time for a couple of beers?" Win said as he waved me to get started. I engaged the jeep's front wheels and put it in low gear. The log moved with a teeth-jarring jerk.

"Wow, wow! Take it easy, easy now. You get this thing rolling and she'll go downhill and take you with her." (A balky log is a 'she'.) The men moved the chain to the uphill end of the log. I turned the jeep's wheels sharply left and tugged it slowly off the roadway.

"Great, great!" Echo was ecstatic. "You wouldn't want a job on this project, would you now? You and that jeep."

"Pay's lousy," Win commented. He too was enjoying himself.

"Lousy or no, it's a job, eh? Buys you booze and beads for your squaw, don't it. What else do you Indians need?" Echo continued as Win turned away to get the chain off and onto another log. "Don't mind it, lady. He's all right, for an Indian. Just fun, you know. Nobody should mind a little fun, like. Hey, Win! You don't mind a little fun, do you?"

"I don't mind," said Win. "Except the lousy pay."

"Quit bitching, I told you, Win. What else could you do around here. What else? Answer me that, hey! Dukies get all the best jobs. And 'Mericans. Ain't that the truth, now? All that's left for the likes of you and me is gov'ment project jobs. Wasn't for that we'd be on welfare. Ain't that the truth, now?" Echo seemed anxious to get Win to agree.

"It's the truth. God bless the gov'ment." Win answered with a straight face. I listened, fascinated.

"Right. So no more bitching now. You're lucky I got you this job, eh, Win. Just a couple more like that now, lady. Just a couple more and we'll have this road cleared. Then we go get a beer with old Ben and you can go on up top. 'Less you'd like to join us for a couple, eh? Always a pleasure to drink with a lady." They had the second log chained up. This time I got it moving smoothly.

"Beautiful, just beautiful. Well, what d'you say? Have a beer with us, eh. Not too good to have a beer with us, are you now? Would you be in such a hurry to join those two foreign gentlemen in a station wagon?" Echo let that drop and continued without a pause. "No, can't be that, can't be that. They've gone back out this morning. Must have. Yeah, must have. So what's the hurry? Stop, rest, have a beer."

Something about Echo was getting through to me. This talk wasn't just random blather.

"What two men in a station wagon? What'd they look like?"

" 'Mericans, maybe. But not local 'Mericans. Alberta plates they had on that heap. Alberta, weren't they, Win?" Win nodded at me. Echo continued, "Barely made it in yesterday, road was so bad. We saw them, yeah, Win, Ben and me saw them yesterday. Then today they're gone. Not worth the ride I guess it was, for them." I couldn't restrain my curiosity.

"How d'you know they're gone? And how did they get up this way? If that tree's been here for days, like you said?"

"There was a way around until today, tight but passable. Then the bank gave. See?" He pointed to a large bite out of the road bed. Broken wheel tracks. He continued, "So you may as well stop by Ben's with us and have a beer and plate of stew, maybe, eh."

"I might as well, I guess." I said. Echo was proving a very interesting conversationalist after all. Win looked but said nothing.

After that it didn't take the three of us, plus my jeep, very long to get the road cleared. Once we finished and the two men were packing up their gear into the truck, I got out of my car and disappeared into the bushes on the side of the road where the tree had stood. Delicacy required that they look the other way. They were ready when I emerged. Echo said, "Just follow us. It's not far to Thrums, not far at all. Old Ben's a Douk, but it's the best stew you ever tasted."

"Let's go then," I said, and followed them back down the mountain. We had to go through Nelson again to get to Thrums, a Doukhobor settlement on the Castlegar road. I had passed it unknowing.

Ben looked to be in his late sixties. When we arrived he was sitting on a bench under an apple tree, drinking beer and chewing sunflower seeds. A collie-like dog lay, tongue lolling, at his feet. Picture of a bucolic 'oldest inhabitant in his natural habitat.' Pretty and probably misleading. Behind him was the farmhouse, shining aluminum roof and all. Through the open window we could get glimpses of a woman bustling about the kitchen. A baby crying. Warm smells wafting out.

"Nice setup old Ben has. Them Dukies got it made. But Ben's the smartest of them all. He don't hold with all that religious guff most of them go in for. Don't pay no tithes to nobody. And no taxes either, you bet. No, not old Ben. You got it all figured, eh Ben," Echo said as we came up to the old man. He seemed to be showing off Ben as a local curiosity.

"Who that you got with you, Echo? Don't know she. Howdy, mam." Ben didn't move except to spew out a good mouthful of sunflower seeds, all split and empty as if individually shucked. It's a skill I've admired and tried to learn in a certain Vancouver tavern frequented by Ukrainians. It can't take a lifetime to learn; kids can do it. I never could.

"Howdy, Ben," I said. "I am Helen. Been helping the boys on the road. Nice place you've got here."

"Pretty good, yes. Sit down, have a beer." A twelve pack sat in the shade of the bench. We each got one out and made ourselves comfortable.

Echo took a pull at his bottle and started right in.

"Yes, Helen here's been real helpful. She kind of lost her party. Them two guys in an Alberta station wagon up at the park. Wonder what happened to them."

"It's a big place, that park. Could be anywhere." Win contributed. "Easy to get lost if you don't know your way."

"Her here for something special?" Ben said. It was obviously addressed to me. I decided to borrow the treasure story.

"Just visiting until I met Harry and Sid. That's the two guys in the station wagon. They got me interested in some lost silver mine they're trying to find. Thought we could join forces and explore a bit. Just for something to do. More fun that way. Seems like there's lots of old mine shafts in these parts." Both Win and Echo looked interested.

Ben spat out another mouthful of seeds and chuckled.

"Yas, lots and lots. All over. Strangers won't ever find nothing. For sure."

"Maybe you could help. You must know this area real good."

"Maybe," Ben said and fell silent.

Echo jumped in at once.

"Old Ben here knows them mountains like the back of his hand, eh Ben. Him and that dog of his been everywhere. Knows every shaft and old mine site there is, eh Ben."

"Yas. Lots and lots. Strange things all over. Such goings on!"

"Goings on? What do you mean?" I asked.

"Nothing, nothing. Youse won't never find nothing," he said.

There was a shout from the house. Echo was on his feet.

"Ah, stew! Best stew you ever ate, like I said." He and Win went into the house and moments later came out carrying four large tin plates of stew with two-inch slabs of black bread on the side. The woman didn't appear. The four of us sat and ate. Except for the slurping and occasional exclamation of enjoyment from Echo, there was silence. Finally Win wiped his plate with his last piece of bread and said, "Time we was getting back now, Echo. Pleased to have met you, Helen." Echo looked up, surprised.

"You reckon we got to go back to work? Hell, there ain't no more trees we know of to clear. How come, eh Win? How come you want to go back to work?"

Win shook his head.

"Back to the office. It's pay-day, remember?"

Echo struck his forehead with his hand.

"'Course, 'course. Should have known! Pay-day it is! Right folks, we're off. You be OK now, eh Helen. Just you find your treasure hunters before the bears get them." He laughed.

"They're OK, I'm sure. If you happen to see them somewhere just say I'll meet them in Nelson. OK? 'Bye, boys." We shook hands. Win collected the plates and carried them back to the house. Then they left. Ben and I were left alone.

After a moment he took out his pipe, already filled with tobacco and lit it carefully with large kitchen matches.

"Her smoke?" he asked.

"Some. Not right now, though," I answered.

"Good, good. Tobacco good friend. What people scared of?"

"Oh?" I didn't understand. He drew heartily on his pipe, sending pungent smoke into the clean country air.

"Lot new people against tobacco. Against much food too. Don't make sense."

"How come?" I still wasn't following.

"Yas. Drive big truck everywhere, smoke weed, drink funny stuff, take pills like crazy then come tell Ben tobacco no good. Don't make sense. Yesterday young woman come on motorbike said not to smoke tobacco. Raised dust, made smell and noise, scared chickens. No sense."

"Who was it? This woman on motorbike?"

"Nancy, up at Women's Acres. Smart girls. Look after themselves. Don't work for man, smart." He chuckled that surprising chuckle of his. I'd have liked to pursue his reasoning regarding 'smart girls' who didn't work for men. Instead I said, "What did she want?"

"Looking for Ursula. Granddaughter. Her work in Nelson. Brings dollars home. Good girl. Help my woman work farm. Good girl, not smart."

"What she want with Ursula, do you know?"

"Her had message for Carol. But Carol and man not here. Her man no good." He spat.

"What's her man's name? Al Shoreman?"

"No more Shoreman. Now, new man, Huber. Her call he 'Huber'. Came, went. Maybe looking for treasure like youse." He looked at me from under his eyebrows. His eyes twinkled. I had the feeling this old man had told me just what he'd wanted me to know. I'd been led on. We're conditioned to assume imperfect English equals lack of intelligence and knowledge. I knew better. At least I hoped I did. I got more beer for us.

"So you think women aren't smart to work for men. But your woman does most of the work around here, doesn't she?"

"Her good woman. Me smart to have woman like that."

"I see." And I did. He had it figured.

"Yes. Her smart too." He meant me. I was smart too. That was encouraging.

"And Carol? Is she smart?"

"Some. Her man no good." He spat again into the fine white dust. Whoever Huber was, hadn't made a great impression.

"Who's Huber? Ever seen him before?"

"Niet. No good."

"How about Al Shoreman. Do you know him?"

"No good." He didn't spit this time. Seemed to lose interest in conversation. His pipe was going well, his eyes almost shut.

I finished my beer and stood up.

"Well, gotta go. Thanks for the beer. And thank whoever made the stew. It was great."

"Nothing, nothing. Good day. God bless." He said.

I walked away, knowing his half-closed eyes were on me.

It's easy to be a total sceptic, in my business. Was this man for real? Funny how his English deteriorated as we went along. Did Nancy mention that a woman called Helen might be around asking questions? She had obviously jumped on that Honda immediately after I had left. Trying to get my message to Carol. Or a warning. Via Ursula, Ben's granddaughter. Now this Huber. Mossad boys hadn't been very informative about the Misurali guy. Could it be Huber? Then where was Shoreman? For that matter where were Carol and Huber? A lot of people seemed to have dropped out of sight suddenly. Including Harry and Sid. I couldn't be sure about them yet. Perhaps they were back in Nelson drinking coffee at the Jam Factory. Perhaps. But I wouldn't give odds on it.

Anyway it was a fair guess that these unanswered questions were tightly connected. I had a freaky fantasy of all five of the missing playing catch with hand grenades in some abandoned mine shaft. When you start to fantasize like that it's usually a good idea to stop, rest, think. Which is just what I didn't do. I knew I was suffering from 'stimulus overload' as Alice Caplan calls it.

As it was I got myself thoroughly tired, wasted half the night and came up empty. There was no sign of Harry, Sid or their vehicle. Kokanee is a large piece of mountain wilderness. Most people stay in one of the roadside campgrounds or leave their cars at a parking space to walk up to see the glacier, with its pinkish snow cover. Why would Harry and Sid have packed up so soon? They hadn't had time to 'explore' as planned. I could think of a couple of reasons. They could have been jumped and disposed of, or they'd seen or heard something which made them burst out of there bright and early.

I spent the rest of the night in the jeep drinking brandy and eating stale chicken. In the morning, stiff and cold, I made my way back to Nelson.

9

IT WAS EXASPERATING. After the frantic activity of the day before now everything was stuck dead centre. No message of any kind at the Jam Factory. D. Greenwood's address, where Shoreman presumably hung his hat, was a small house on the edge of town. There was no sign of life, no car in the driveway. I would've settled for a glimpse of the Buick with the stateside boys but no luck. Nothing.

Of course I had lots of options. I could tackle L'il Abner Dean again at his shack. He was up to his handsome neck in whatever was happening here. There was plenty to question him about, the ARC connection just for starters. Dean certainly knew more about Carol's activities than he had let on. But if he wasn't home or wouldn't talk I could be wasting a long trip. Then there were Nancy and the women at Women's Acres. As it stood, were they likely to tell me any more? Why would they? The situation hadn't changed.

Ben. That old man knew something about Carol, Shoreman and the mysterious Huber. I had gotten the distinct impression from our conversation, both before and after the departure of Echo and Win, that Ben was trying to communicate something to me. In his own inimitable way, which didn't allow for more than hints. No close questions, no specifics. Thinking of Ben brought me in turn to Echo. Just a loquacious redneck? His interest in me and the Israelis could be natural curiosity. But I didn't believe it. Both he and Win had lied about that tree. There had been no storm two nights before; the tree had been cut down to block the road. Were they making work for themselves? That could be. On the other hand .... There were so many possibilities. I'd been successfully distracted from looking for the two agents. Did that mean the Mossad boys were blown? Endless questions and no answers. I let it drop. Sat and worried. Back again. Where were Sid and Harry? And Carol and Shoreman and Huber .... Nuts, I decided. This wasn't getting me anywhere.

I found a telephone booth and called Vancouver. Jessica was glad to hear from me but had no information or suggestion to offer. I kidded with Alice for a minute, then called Frank. He was full of news.

"The plot thickens," he said. "Your old friend Ronald Walters was here again. He badly wants to contact you now. I don't know what's changed but something has. How can he get in touch with you? Immediately."

"I'll call him now. That number you gave me. That's the place to get him, right?"

"As far as I know. OK. Try that. Do you know what's going on? Why this flap all of a sudden?"

"I have an idea. If I can't reach him, I'll call you back and we can arrange something for later on. OK?"

"OK. Be careful."

"No sweat. 'Bye."

I gave the operator Walter's number and my name since I was calling collect. He was on the line almost immediately.

"Yes, yes, operator. I'll accept the call." His voice was distorted but still familiar after the span of years.

"How are you, Helen? Long time."

"Long time, indeed, Ron. Frank tells me you want to talk to me. Well?" I said.

"Still the same old Helen," he laughed. "Straight to the point. Very well. Regarding that inquiry about you. The same person has now been back to us. He's concerned. Lost touch with his 'clients' — let's call them clients — they are in your area and he was expecting to hear from them regularly. But he's had no word since the day before yesterday. Follow?"

"Sure. Beach has good reason to be concerned ...." I began.

"No names over an open line, please Helen. Let's observe the usual precautions." It's fascinating how nervous government agents are about taped phones. It should be a lesson to the rest of us.

"All right. His clients have disappeared. I assume you know who his clients are?"

"We have a pretty good idea. It's not good, not good at all.

I've been hoping we could keep out of this. What's your part in this matter? What have you been doing?"

"I've been looking for them. We made contact my first night here. In Kaslo. Arranged to meet or leave messages in Nelson. Then they went one way and I went another. Since then no sign of them. I've checked the place they intended to visit. They reached there but left very soon. Too soon."

"Oh." He was trying to read between the lines of my story. "What sort of a place was it?"

"Provincial park. Miles of mountain."

"Could they have gotten lost?"

"Sure. Someone could instigate a formal search. Two tenderfeet lost in the mountains. No need to suggest anything else. That man in Vancouver who is so anxious about them could report them missing. Search and Rescue could be called up. Well?"

Silence. He answered slowly,

"I'll talk to him. But I suspect it's not in his interest. I know it's not in ours. Look Helen, this is serious. Phones are no good. We need to get together and discuss. I can't go there yet; could you fly back to see me? Soon. As soon as possible, in fact. Please."

"I'll see what I can do. Be in touch." I hung up before he could press me any further. I wasn't all that keen to get embroiled with spooks. Contact with Walters, in whatever capacity he was operating, would tend to tie my hands. All the same, it was interesting that he knew of Mossad's presence in the Kootenays and wanted to keep out of it, at least officially. Politics, bah!

Strictly speaking I wasn't any further ahead, but somehow it gave me a kick to know that I knew more than Ron Walters.

10

I DROVE BACK ALONG ROUTE 3A towards the road up to Kokanee Glacier Provincial Park. A Mountie car with lights flashing passed me going like hell. On a hunch I stopped at the Sandspit Campsite and found a park ranger. Were there any cars up on the park road, I asked. He seemed agitated.

"No tourists. But we have a crew up there now trying to get down to a vehicle what went off the road into Kokanee Creek. Must be two hundred feet down. Mounties on their way there now. You missing anyone?"

"No. But you mean there might be people in that car? Bad accident, eh?"

"Don't know yet. Real hard getting down to it. All you can see is the back of a station wagon way down in the gorge. Place in the road with no big trees on the down side to stop it falling all the way. Only spotted the place it went off the road by accident. Must have skidded .... Yeah, if you know whose car that might be you should wait for the Mounties. They'll want to talk to you." He looked at me curiously.

I had no interest in getting interrogated by any local law. I shook my head as if reluctantly.

"No. I'll be no use to them. Just thought I might do a little exploring myself. But I guess the road will be blocked until they get that car up. Guess I'll pass it up for now."

"Yeah, we've closed this road. You might try the Kaslo entrance." He turned away satisfied. I got into my jeep and drove to Ben's place. There, the scene had changed. There was no sign of Ben or of his dog.

I went into the warm kitchen. A solid middle-aged woman with bright blue eyes said, "Ben, he's gone. Don't know nothing", without ceasing to knead a basin of dough. I asked for Ursula. She shrugged,

"Working." Nothing else.

I thanked her and left. On my way back to the park road I

passed a truck towing a familiar station wagon with Alberta plates. It was totalled. No one inside could have survived. I turned back and followed it into Nelson.

Back in town I had no trouble finding out that the car had been pulled out of Kokanee Creek empty. No one could figure out how it had gotten there. But the Mounties were organizing a search for the two men reported to have arrived in the area in that car. They had last been seen at the Silver King Campground near Kaslo. "Anyone having any information is asked to contact … etc." It wouldn't be long before the Mounties connected an inquisitive female in a jeep with the two missing strangers. It was decidedly time to disappear myself. But first I had to check out the spot where the car had left the road and especially the Gibson Lake parking lot where the Mossad boys had to have been just before the 'accident'. My jeep was too noticeable. There was nothing for it but to hike up.

Having some idea what I was in for I prepared as for a polar expedition. Hiking boots, down vest, ropes, small backpack with a propane stove, food, rain gear.

It was early June, too early. There was still snow in the gullies; now a multitude of small streams fed the rushing creek. Ground was wet, slippery, crumbly and unsafe. In addition it was cool and windy. At 6,000 feet it often is, even in summer. There are bears, both black and grizzly. Nice prospect.

Reluctantly I left the safety and warmth of my jeep, parked at an out-of-sight spot close to where the creek fell into the lake. Shouldering my pack I worked my way slowly and carefully up the banks, until I judged it safe to climb onto the fateful gravel mountain road. I figured I could hear any vehicle approaching and hide until it passed. But there were no vehicles. Not even Mounties or park personnel. Just the jagged mountains, cool breeze in the firs and the leafy brush, pale sun and red rocky earth underfoot. The road follows the creek, up and up the mountainside, splendid views at every turn. I passed no one and no one passed me. Two hours from the highway, I stopped, made a cup of hot soup on my pocket stove and rested. I figured I had made maybe six kilometres up the mountain.

The place where the car had left the road couldn't be that far ahead. Lying down on a hard but dry piece of rock I wondered what the hell I was doing there. Who was I hunting for, anyway? This was no way to find Sara Ann, was it? And even if it was, I was crazy to continue this search. Everyone in this puzzle was turning up missing. It could be my turn next. Idly I wondered what Jessica and Frank would do if they didn't hear from me by next day. And Ron. What steps would he take, if any? I was close to sleep, soothed by hot food and wind in the high firs, when an unexpected sound sat me up suddenly. An animal. Definitely the sound of mammalian panting in the surrounding bush. I was reluctant to think of bears but the possibility did present itself. With absolutely no enthusiasm I picked up my pack and turned towards the sound. Anything is better than not knowing. The sound was now a definite whine. A coyote? Before I could make up my mind whether to press on, a brown and white creature pushed its way through the young undergrowth. It was Ben's small collie. Soft brown eyes, a tongue like a piece of wet rag, she whined up at me, sat down, and licked a bloody paw. She was hurt.

"Hey, you poor beast," I said in the soothing tones. I searched my memory to recall her name, patted and examined her. One paw was badly cut; whether by stone or manmade object was impossible to tell. I judged the wound more than half a day old, maybe over 24 hours. Had the dog rested and slept since the wounding, then the natural process of healing would be well under way, but she had obviously been travelling over rough terrain methodically licking fresh blood as it appeared. That hadn't helped the wound to close and scab. I had to prevent the poor beast from doing any more damage to herself. She had to be carried. Not a chore I looked forward to. Even a small dog weighs 20 pounds or so. Fortunately this one was thin. I picked her up carefully, murmuring encouragingly and started back in my tracks, the smelly shaking burden passive in my arms. But the second my direction became clear the dog started to struggle and whine. I put her down. She turned her back on me and slowly dragged herself uphill in the direction from which we had come.

"Is Ben up there, is that what you're trying to tell me?" I said. "OK old girl, we'll go up together. We'll find him." I got the dog up on my shoulder again and together we pushed through the thick undergrowth. For about half a kilometre the way was relatively easy although the forest was thick with hemlock, larch and western red cedar. Then we hit a rock slide area and there was nothing for it but to go around it and back to the road. The collie bitch in my arms whined and struggled until we were off the road again and heading straight up the steep slopes. I knew we couldn't keep this up. Or rather I couldn't. I was thoroughly exhausted, bruised and pissed off. Apart from the physical impossibility of complying with the dog's demands for vertical ascent, the whole enterprise smacked too much of an episode in a Walt Disney movie. The faithful pooch, the lost master and the heroic rescuer. I put down my furry burden and contemplated the situation as coldly as I could. This was no time or place for foolish sentimentality. I couldn't look for Ben cross-country with a 20-pound dog on my shoulder. I had two options. Take the road down and rescue the dog or leave the dog and keep looking for Ben. But Ben could be hours away and I was good for perhaps one or two kilometres at most. And yet the idea of leaving that old man lost, obviously hurt or dead here on this wild mountain didn't sit well. Added to my natural distaste for retreat was the knowledge that I would have to report the incident to the Mounties and get involved in an official search. Reluctantly I picked up the dog again and despite her struggles made for the road which at this point curved sharply along the cliff with nothing between its south edge and the creek rushing violently below. Taking a rope from my pack I attempted to tie the poor wounded beast to a tree, so I could proceed on my mission alone. My cold and clumsy hands weren't up to controlling both dog and rope. With a heave the collie sprang out of my reach and disappeared limping into the trees. There was nothing for it but to follow.

I don't know how either of us survived the next period. The dog was better at picking our way over the mountainside than

I had been but still the path would have taxed a mountain goat. I was about to say the hell with it and quit, when the dog whined louder and just about threw herself down a gully. I reached the edge and looked down. There, like a sack of potatoes, lay the body of Ben with the dog sniffing around his head. I scrambled down. There was no doubt Ben was dead. His body was stiff. Been there since the previous night, at a guess. Dark congealed blood covered the chest and disfigured his face. Instinctively holding my breath with distaste I cut the shirt open. Below the breastbone a black hole as big as the palm of my hand gaped at me. I stood up hastily. The dog was still. So, for a second, seemed the surrounding forest. Death, sudden and bloody.

Then it was time to get myself together, search the area and decide on the next step. The gully was deep but not very large. A fissure really. I moved around it, carefully checking for disturbed soil and vegetation, dropped objects, blood splashes, any signs. I had no doubt Ben had been killed elsewhere. The body had been carried there and then thrown in from the north side. There were broken branches and a few small blood spots on leaves which must have brushed his blood-soaked body. I moved north and very soon reached the road. The damned dog had led me straight up the mountain to within 50 metres of the road! The road twists and turns; not the collie's idea of the shortest distance between two points.

I went back to the body. Someone had blown a hole smack in the middle of old Ben and then went to a lot of trouble to dump him here, just off the Kokanee Creek road. Why? And the Alberta station wagon down the creek. Coincidence? I had the feeling that whoever was responsible had been setting the scene for the Mounties. How were they expected to read it? I thought about that quite a bit as I made my way down the rough gravel road carrying the exhausted dog. June days are long. It was 9 p.m. and full daylight when I finally staggered to the waiting jeep. I hadn't met anyone on the way.

I dropped the dog off at a nearby vet's. Playing dumb, I described finding it on Route 3A at Kokanee Creek. That should give the Mounties the clue they needed to find Ben's body as soon as his disappearance became known. I was taking one hell of a chance in not going directly to them with the whole story, but right then couldn't face the consequences of being a good citizen.

Sleep almost overcame me on the drive to the Castlegar Airport, where my faithful trailer still stood undisturbed. I barely made it to bed.

11

Ronald walters was a tall, thin fragile-looking man in his late forties. His face was furrowed with vertical lines emphasizing its length. The perpetually worried look and the slow gray eyes were immediately familiar. But there was evidence of the passage of time since our last meeting years before. The top of his head was almost bare. Sideburns, with which he compensated for hair loss, were longer, bushier and grayer; tufts of grizzled hair poked out of his ears. Instead of the cords and tweed jacket which I remembered, the pants and vest of a sharp three-piece brown suit hung unbecomingly on his lanky body; matching jacket had been discarded. He had on a cream shirt and a fashionable tie. But the shirt was unbuttoned and the tie out of place. As he moved towards me, hand outstretched I noticed the bulge of a small gun tucked away under the vest. I wondered how much I had changed in his eyes.

"Ah, Helen," he said smiling. "You haven't changed."

"Much," I finished for him as we shook hands. He laughed an uncomfortable laugh and ran his hand over his bald head in a habitual gesture soon to become familiar.

"Just older and wiser, I hope, both of us," he answered, "Come in, sit down." Quickly he turned and led the way through the sunny livingroom to a desk at right angles to the open window and balcony. A fine view of English Bay spotted with giant tankers and tiny sailboats. He sat down behind the desk and immediately fished out a pencil from among a pile of papers. Safely settled in his usual place, with a pencil to play with, he relaxed somewhat. I looked around me. The apartment looked properly lived in but probably not by him. It was in a posh highrise, one or two bedrooms, kitchen and this well-furnished livingroom. It didn't have that rented-furnished-by-a-government-agency look about it. There was old-fashioned taste and a personal touch. A very unlikely place for Walters to stay, considering who and what he was. But perhaps that was the idea.

Whatever changes had overtaken him, his sharp mind was still there. He picked up my unspoken question immediately. "My mother's," he said shyly. "She's just retired and moved out of the city. So I took over her lease. Until the end of the month. These are her things." He waved an arm.

"OK. But why?" I asked.

"I'm here on detached duty."

'Detached duty' meant that he wasn't in Vancouver officially at all. So he couldn't use any facilities which might connect to his job. Not even 'undercover' facilities of the regular kind. Which meant that his job was so secret it was undercover from local undercover. Under undercover. That's spook business all over. Not merely that the right hand doesn't know what the left hand is doing but sometimes even the fingers of any given hand don't know what the thumb .... It was all sadly familiar. Didn't he ever wonder if there was someone under under undercover — even further than he? Of course. He knew and expected it. That's why he had the job he had. Whatever it was. Holing up in his mother's apartment was smart. Normally no agency would dream of setting up a base in the home of a family member of a well known agent. Therefore it was the perfect place. But, since the opposition followed the same thought processes, it might not be so perfect. On the other hand .... It was a shell game. Double, triple, multiple bluff. Like all shell games, it only worked at speed. Walters would be safe in his mother's apartment as long as nobody tried to figure out where he might be. Soon he would have to move. Again. And again. Then again, it might not be his mother's apartment at all. He might have lied. And so it went. The endless, silly game. I laughed, relieved I wasn't a part of it. Or was I?

At my laugh, Walters nodded. He had followed my thoughts as if I had spoken them aloud.

"Yes. Details don't matter. I am here. It's safe for the time being. You weren't followed."

"No. And now I am here."

"What are you doing in the Kootenays?" he asked. I didn't answer, just looked at him. He moved deeper into his chair, looked out at the gorgeous scene outside. "Come, come, Helen. You're a smart woman. Do you really want to get sucked any deeper into what can't be your business? Because if it is, if you are involved in this ...." He smiled sadly. "It would be too bad."

"What business? You tell me."

"Arms. Arms smuggling. Are you?" he asked. This was silly. He couldn't seriously expect me to answer that.

"Aren't you going to offer me a drink? Coffee or something? The way you are handling this, we could be here all day," I said. Again that familiar sad look on his face.

"There is coffee in the kitchen. And beer in the refrigerator. Help yourself," he said finally.

I got up and fetched myself a cup of coffee. He sat staring out of the window. After I sat down and made myself comfortable again, he swung back in his swivel chair as if having made some decision.

"An important citizen, one Morris Beach, inquired about you. Then the two men for whom he was acting disappeared without trace. In the Kootenays." He spoke the name as if it was some exotic spot across the globe. "You were there. You are connected to these men. Explain."

"Right. I was in Kaslo on a case. Met two men, obvious agents, at a campground. We agreed to meet next day in Nelson. They never showed. No messages. I don't know where they are."

He shook his head as at a recalcitrant child.

"Helen. We've been over that." He shuffled the papers in front of him as if looking for some item of information. "You know and I know these were Mossad agents. Right?" He went on without looking at me or waiting for an affirmative answer. "You talked to them. You aren't dumb. So you picked up on what they were up to. Beach told us a couple of men, strangers, were after you and the Mossad boys helped you out. So you and they compared notes. It's clear from what they told Beach that the case you are on connects to their job. Helen, what are you doing in the Kootenays?"

"No. The question is what are Mossad agents doing in the Kootenays? What are you doing cooperating with foreign agents like Beach? On what? Smuggled arms? Clearing up a smuggling ring? Balls! Information, yes, but foreign agents operating in Canada on a police matter? And what are you doing on a simple criminal case? You said I wasn't dumb. Act like you believed it."

"OK, OK." He waved his hand at me. "Well, we aren't happy about these agents on our territory either. There has been some cooperation with Beach in the past, yes. These are difficult times, internationally. Beach is important. He's the front-end contact. We watch him, we like to know what's happening. OK so far?"

"So far."

"Good. To cut a long story short, we don't know why these agents are here. We want to know, but until we do, until we know what complication it might cause, we are playing it cool. Nothing official. No word to the local law enforcement. But we want them found!"

I said nothing.

He took a long breath and went on "It probably does have to do with the arms trade. But nothing simple. Look." He opened a drawer, took out a map, and spread it open on the desk. "Look at this." He was standing now, tapping the map with his finger for emphasis. "This is a unique area. Geographically and topographically. The Columbia River crosses into the States. Look at these dams .... Do you know how much water is behind them? We dammed all these rivers so the Yanks can have flood control and reliable power downstream. Flooded millions of acres of our best valley bottoms for a song. Now look up here." He was excited now. His arms moved over the map like semaphores. "North-south valleys, only one highway east-west, few airports, lots of lakes, wild mountains and hundreds of old mines and abandoned shafts." He stopped, sat down and looked at me. Calmer now, he said, "What does it all suggest to you? Just fantasize."

"I understand the importance of the Columbia to the western U.S. What are you trying to say? Say it."

He seemed to be holding his breath. Then softly, "West Kootenays are the perfect base for terrorist sabotage of north-west

United States. Especially the Columbia system."

Having said it, Walters folded his map, put it away, sat down and went on in a more normal tone. "Perhaps that's overly dramatic. But it's a possibility. Something is happening in that area. You will grant that?"

"Sure. A possibility. Anything is possible these days. But how probable? Any real data, solid fact? Or just normal security service paranoia?"

Mention of paranoia was designed to taunt him into telling me what, if anything, he knew. I acted cool and skeptical but had no doubt that my concern and curiosity were obvious to his trained eye. But he appeared to take my comment at face value, answering carefully.

"Paranoia. Perhaps. That's the trouble, we know very little. A bit from the Israelis. Their single-minded concentration on terrorism is helpful. They take risks which are unacceptable to us. They take hair-curling chances to get information." Automatically he ran his hand over his scalp. "That's great if it works out but the consequences of a foul-up could be horrendous. A very, very delicate situation all around." Walters fell silent, playing with his pencil. Then continued. "Now you are there, right on the spot. Another possible source of information. And you won't talk. You see the spot I am in?"

"Is that a threat or a plea for sympathy?" All that grandstanding with maps and dark hints at sabotage! "Next you'll be threatening me with licence cancellation or asking for my cooperation in stopping World War III! Make up your mind, Ron. I got up early to catch my flight to Vancouver and haven't got the patience for all this to-and-froing."

Ron Walters laughed good-humouredly. "I haven't lied to you. I want your cooperation, that's all. Starting with the nature of your job. Once I know that, I can evaluate the situation, possibly let you continue. Without it, well, no threats need be involved but I guess I could make it hard for you. On this case and any future jobs you undertake. We both know that."

"That's a risk I'll take. Occupational hazard. Look, I've been here an hour and nothing real has been said by either of us. Don't you ever get tired of these games?''

Walters changed gears, ignored my comment and said, "Did the Mossad agents kill that old man?" He watched my reaction.

"You know the answer to that. Nuts."

"The police think so."

"They were meant to."

"Maybe. But that means that there is a terrorist unit of some kind operating in the area. And I think you have a lead on it. Look, Helen. Chances are the Israelis are already dead. Their bodies may or may not show up. Regardless, they will get the blame for the old man's murder. Case closed. Are we agreed, so far?"

"That's the way the scenario seems to have been set up. But it doesn't have to be that way. A word from you and the area will be crawling with cops looking under every bush, into every shaft. Ultimately they will find whatever there is to find."

"No. You know I can't do that. How about you? You could tell them your story. With the same result. Well?"

Now we were getting to cases.

"That would blow my job and probably take me out of circulation. No deal."

"Oh, I wasn't asking you to do it! Just presenting the possibility. But if I won't and you won't, the scenario stays in place. Murderers go free. Only alternative is for you and I to put our heads together, cooperate on this one. Nice quiet undercover operation. No cops, no publicity."

"And if I don't? Takes two to cooperate. And I only 'cooperate' with people I trust. How trustworthy are you, eh, Ron?"

He pretended to consider the question seriously.

"As long as our interests coincide ... trust needn't be involved."

"Our interests coincide only to the extent that we have each other over a barrel. You can't afford to have me tell my story and blow that scenario. Any hint at terrorist activities so close to the U.S. border will bring the Americans in, in spades. Publicity, hundreds of FBI, CIA and other assorted security agents making mincemeat of Canadian sovereignty, falling all over each other, taking the play away from you. No, you want to keep it hush-hush, figure it all out and scotch it your way. Nice quiet operation. That's the Canadian way. And for that you need me. I am there, on the spot, with possible leads."

He didn't like it but didn't deny it.

"Your cooperation would be useful, I admit. However, if you are just in the way, well, you could be rendered, shall we say, inoperative."

"Sure. That's why I said we have each other over a barrel. Stalemate. You make a move I don't like and I'll sing; I don't cooperate and you have me taken care of, one way or another."

"One way or another, yes." Walters leaned back carefully.

I smiled.

"Sure. But not before you know what I know, and not unless you can be sure there won't be any comeback. And there would be, believe it."

He sighed.

"I believe it. OK. Stalemate. For the time being. But surely not for long. Situations have a way of not standing still. Sure you wouldn't rather have me on your side in this? Surely you don't approve of terrorism? We could work together."

"Terrorism is where you find it." I looked around the sunny livingroom. "Don't get up. I'll let myself out."

I got out of there fast. On the way down I had trouble holding onto my last meal. Perhaps it was only the elevator.

12

I WAS SCARED. In the circumstances, anyone who wasn't didn't understand the situation. But I was also angry. After shaking off any possible tail I made my way to Jessica's to pour out my story. Soon Jessica, Alice and I were sitting around their boardroom table with a cassette tape recorder turning slowly in the background.

First a modified precis of the Sara Ann Raymond case. Just the highlights. Then finding Ben's body. Jessica was concerned. She turned off the machine and said, "And you didn't report it. Bad. Not sure I understand why not. Perhaps I am old fashioned, but a murder … !"

"What good would it have done? And the Horsemen would have zapped me for sure. Material witness or some such."

"Hmm. Not necessarily. Would've had to let you go eventually. But yes, police would've wanted to know what you were doing there. Awkward. Go on."

Alice turned on the tape again. I continued with that morning's confrontation with Ronald Walters. Alice enjoyed the early sparring. Even Jessica smiled. But as I got to the crunch they both sobered.

"Wow!" was Alice's reaction. "He really threatened your life! Wow!"

"Not in so many words. But the intent was clear," I said.

"You realize all this isn't evidence?" said Jessica lawyer-like. "Just your say-so. Unsupported word."

"Oh, sure. That's not the point. This is for the record as protection. Apart from the episode with Walters, which would never come out in public, any good detective or journalist could pick up this story at any point and start unravelling. There is enough there to blow every cover three times over. Can you imagine what would happen if this tape got in the hands of the police or the press? Publicity. Lots of it. Last thing Walters wants."

"I can see it all now. Squads of agents, road blocks, headlines!"

Alice mused easily. "Hell, it would make the Kootenays a tourist attraction! Great stuff! OK. So Walters wouldn't like it. But neither would the terrorists. Seems to me you are playing into their hands too by keeping it quiet." Both Jessica and Alice looked at me.

"You are suggesting a moral dilemma. I don't see it that way. If there are indeed wicked international terrorists in them thar hills, and we don't know that for sure, could be just a bunch of crackpots ...."

"Crackpots who murder. What's the difference?" Jessica interrupted.

"Let me finish!" I pressed on, clarifying my thoughts as I went. "Let me start again. I have some knowledge which as far as we know no one else has. That means responsibility. My responsibility. OK so far?"

Alice looked at me as if seeing me for the first time. This was hard for all of us. Jessica nodded. "Yes. And you take this responsibility as yours alone?" she asked.

"I have no choice. Tell me. Can I, can we, trust Walters? For that matter, can we trust 'the proper authorities' any more than we can trust terrorists or crackpots? Is there any reason to believe that many lives wouldn't be lost or destroyed in the process of 'cleaning up' this situation? That it wouldn't be used in ways we cannot even imagine? Think of it! Threat of sabotage would mean guards on every dam, every road, every generating station. Searches, deportation of undesirables! Can you see it? And that's not all ...."

"That's enough. I understand your fear. You are describing public hysteria leading to a police-state type crackdown. But how real is that possibility? Can you be sure the outcome would be so awful?"

"No. I can't be sure. But that's one risk I cannot take. I have to stay loose and smart. I must try to defuse the situation, find the murderers, conclude my case with a minimum of danger and disruption to the people involved. And to the rest of us."

Alice stirred uneasily. "Helen, I appreciate what you are saying. But isn't that rather a tall order? Maybe you are overestimating yourself."

"Maybe I am. But like I said, I've no choice."

There was silence.

"What can Alice and I do to help?" Jessica said softly.

Breath I hadn't known I was holding escaped me in a rush.

13

I CAUGHT A FLIGHT back to Castlegar where my jeep and trailer waited patiently. On the cramped little plane I made myself some notes. Working backwards chronologically, I started with a roundup of what Walters had added to my knowledge both openly and by inference.

• Walters had been in the case since before the first call from Beach. Walters' last known assignment had been in Germany where he was deep in anti-terrorist work, learning from and cooperating with European and Israeli security forces. His transfer to Vancouver must have been prompted by some secret information. There had been no overt terrorist activities in this area recently to account for the presence of the top Canadian expert on international terrorism. Question: What brought him back here?

• Israelis were tops in this field. Walters would obviously monitor them at all levels. Beach's interest in me would be of special interest. The two men would cooperate with each other to a limited extent, both holding out on the other through habit, if nothing else. Questions: Did Walters know about Shoreman, Carol, Misurali? Harry and Sid had a lead they hadn't told me about, that was obvious. My guess was it had been Ben .... Did Walters know that?

• Walters had at least one undercover agent in place. Who?

• Walters had access to details of the official investigation into Ben's death, the junked station wagon and the two men missing from it. He could follow its process but wouldn't interfere in any way. It looked like the scenario was going to hold: two strange Americans murder an old Doukhobor and then disappear. That's what the papers were saying. No motive was apparent yet but there was speculation about a lost silver mine! No one with any sense could buy that. Question: Would Harry and Sid be allowed to surface, dead of course, perhaps as a result of an 'accident' in Ben's truck, which was also missing, or would they just disappear? Were the Mounties likely to pursue the matter and turn up anything else?

● Strongest impression I'd received from my encounter with Walters was that under no circumstances was any hint of terrorist activities, possible sabotage, or even arms smuggling to become public. Once that was out, there would be no possible way to prevent American interference, political meddling and general escalation which would take matters out of his hands. Question: How far would he go with a cover-up? For instance, would he engineer a cover-up with the Mounties if they got close? More dangerously for me, would he take the risk of putting me out of commission 'one way or another' in spite of the tape? This was a definite possibility. In Canada at least he could probably have the tape buried under 'National Security', 'Official Secrets Act' and the like. Wouldn't work in the States, though. The press and politicians there would jump at any hint of terrorism near their borders. So probably I was safe. But it was nerve-wracking to be protected ultimately by a weapon I couldn't use.

Next I turned to the tangle of people and events 'on location'.

● The ARC connection was no coincidence. Carol, Dean, the commune women, Shoreman, all worked for ARC. A construction company was perfect cover for building up a terrorist cell in these mountains. Arms, personnel, equipment could be transported, hidden, prepared. Questions: Was the company as a whole a front or was it just infiltrated and used? There had to be central control. What exactly was Dean's role? Did Huber equal the mysterious Misurali connection which had brought the Israelis to the Kootenays? And where did Carol fit?

There were too many questions to list. I went on.

● Old Ben Soteroff, the dead man, had intimate knowledge of the whole area. Abandoned mine shafts, etc. It was a good bet that he'd spotted some suspicious activity somewhere, dropped hints and had to be silenced. Also a good bet the Mossad boys were onto him, hoped for information, and walked into a situation they couldn't handle. Whoever arranged Ben's death was no dummy. Cool. Snatching Harry and Sid and leaving their car near Ben's body made them natural fall guys for the old man's murder. Plausible enough to fool the Mounties if they didn't look too hard. Strangers make good suspects. Questions: Where were they or their bodies? Where was Ben's truck? How did he get to the park where I'd found him? What was the role of Win and Echo in all this? And again — what about Carol, Dean, Shoreman, Huber?

I dropped it. Too many questions, not enough data for further speculation. I went on to the Hardy boys.

• They had undoubtedly been sent to get Carol. I'd been hired to bird-dog for them. Their boss must have assumed that a female detective would be a patsy; good at finding another woman but easy to scare. Questions: Was this a side issue or was it connected to the ARC action? Was the error of sending boys to do a grownup's job likely to be corrected?

Mulling it over I decided that the answer to the first questions was no, there was no connection, but that I must expect another attempt, this time by the real thing, heavies, not boys. That was my working hypothesis, as they say in academic circles.

So far, so good. My scribbling had clarified a few things. Gave me a sense of direction, where to go from there. Of immediate concern was my freedom of action. Would the Mounties be a problem? Even without any prompting from Walters, did they want me for questioning? I must have cropped up a number of times in their investigation. At the campsite next to the missing suspects, on the park road looking for them, at Ben's house with Win and Echo. If they managed to unsnarl all my comings and goings, all my contacts of the last few days, they just might get onto the real story. That would be disastrous. My instinctive distrust of cops didn't lead me to underestimate their capabilities once on the track of something this big. Perhaps Walters would head them off, after all. But there was bound to be a time lag between events in the Kootenays and Walters' possible reaction to any threat of exposure. His two-way pipeline wasn't instantaneous. The Mounties could still grab and hold me. That had to be avoided. By the time I got to Castlegar my mind was made up. I had to leave the highly visible trailer and use the jeep only when and if absolutely necessary. I needed a hideout and another set of wheels. Women's Acres and their speedy little motorbikes were the obvious solution. But first I had to check out Nelson again.

Castlegar airport is small and generally quiet. There is always a uniformed Mountie or two on duty. But that turned out not to be a problem. They weren't checking deplaning passengers. Since they weren't going to any great lengths to get me I concluded it was reasonably safe to take the jeep. Just to make matters harder for the police, assuming they were on the lookout for it, I decided to get the jeep off the main highway as soon as I could and take the Beasley road to Nelson.

Driving carefully towards the unmarked road entrance at Bonnington Falls, crossing the river and later along the steep dirt road on the other side, I observed the dams and holding pools with special interest. The river and all its adjacent lakes and tributaries were totally under man's control. All part of the Columbia control system. Walters' paranoic speculations took on a certain plausibility. Nothing is too farfetched any more. It wasn't hard to visualize armed guards on every dam, machine gun emplacements on road approaches and the whole beautiful area in the grip of martial law. It was only a little more difficult to imagine the havoc both here and downstream if these dams were destroyed. I shook my head clear. There was no shred of evidence for the latter danger. It would be a massive enterprise to carry out sabotage on a scale large enough to be effective. On the other hand, even a hint of such a possibility could bring on disproportionate counter measures and probably vicious retaliation against anyone, no matter how innocent, who fell under suspicion of complicity. I'd no doubt which represented the greater danger. Ronald Walters was right, regardless of his motives. In a peculiar sort of way we were on the same side.

I stopped in a lumberyard on the edge of Nelson and waited for darkness. There was no point making it easy for anyone who might be out to get me. So it was almost ten before I ventured out on foot, carrying a knapsack and looking as much as I could like a hiking tourist. In a motorized society a pedestrian may be more vulnerable but is also more likely to be overlooked.

I debated with myself whether to make first for the Jam Factory or for the house where Shoreman was supposed to live. Mentally I tossed a coin and it came up tails. So it was Shoreman's house. That chance decision turned out to have significant consequences.

14

THE HOUSE WAS DARK when I arrived. Except for a car parked in the driveway I would have taken it for as empty as it had been on my earlier visit. The car, an inconspicuous old VW, was unlocked and at a pinch could be used to get me around. I walked quietly up to the back door, opened it with little trouble and slipped inside. Dark and no sound. The house was of the open plan variety. My pocket flashlight flickered over the sparsely furnished interior. Standard rental junk. The phone might be in Dean's name but sure as hell nobody that fastidious spent any time here. Circle of light moved to a closed door. A bedroom or possibly the bathroom. I put my ear to the door. Someone was breathing fairly regularly inside. Asleep? At 10 p.m. of a summer's night? I turned the handle as softly as I could. The door wouldn't budge. Now that was strange. Why would anyone have a lock on a bedroom door in their own house? I looked again. There was no lock but a new heavy slide bolt had been installed on the outside of the bedroom. Whoever was inside was locked in! I didn't stop to figure it out, slid the bolt over, opened the door and walked in.

A woman lay in the middle of a large unmade bed. She was fully dressed in neat pants, blouse, sweater, and covered with a small tattered rug. Her head was squarely in the middle of a pillow, her hands at her sides. An unnatural position. She had been 'laid out' by some not uncaring hand. Looking at her I had no doubt I had found Sara Ann Raymond, alias Carol Latimer. Her eyes were shut. She wore no makeup, her hair was darker, and there were definite lines around her mouth, but in repose this 40-year old face bore more resemblance to that old photograph than it would when animated.

Gently I lifted an eyelid, picked up an arm and let it fall. Like the position, her sleep was unnatural. Ray had been drugged, left on the bed and locked in. Why and by whom? She wasn't meant to come to any harm, that seemed clear. I'd at least one good guess at who might've been a party to keeping her on ice like this, but the full import of the situation was still beyond me. A decision had to be made, fast. Putting an arm around her shoulders I lifted her to a sitting position. There was a small sound, a dribble of saliva fell from her mouth, but she didn't wake. I pulled her feet off the bed hoping she could stand up. No way. Her body was as flaccid as a string puppet. She had to be carried. I put my left shoulder to her middle and with a groan got her up in a firefighter's carry. She felt like the newly dead, totally relaxed, her head hitting the small of my back.

It wasn't far to the car outside but I did have trouble getting her into it. I finally got her stowed in the back seat and covered with the rug from the bedroom. Back in the house I hunted for a bag or purse until I found it under the bed. Among the usual junk I found a fair amount of money, an ID in the name of Carol Latimer, and even a set of VW keys. They worked, saving me the trouble of hot-wiring the ignition.

My passenger was out so thoroughly and the car so inconspicuous I took a chance and stopped for a look at the Jam Factory bulletin board. There I got another surprise. A message. It said, in full: "Dear Troy. Got your message. Love to see you. Meet me at the Kaslo Municipal Campground tonight (Thursday) after 10 p.m. Ray."

It was almost 10 now. Obviously Ray wasn't going to meet me there or anywhere. But more than likely someone else was. Had I gotten that message first I wouldn't have known that for sure. Lucky I went to the Dean/Shoreman house first. Pure chance. Fate has a way of hanging on such random decisions. Not a comforting thought. No matter how 'smart and loose' you are, circumstances, chance, bad luck or whatever-you-call-it had better be on your side. This time it was. Next time, who knows?

So I'd a date with someone in Kaslo. But first there was the matter of my helpless passenger. She needed care, a 'safe house.' Women's Acres came automatically to mind. Not that it was really 'safe' but somehow I'd faith in the women there. They'd cope. We were off on the long drive north, past the Kokanee Park road, through Kaslo. This time I'd little trouble finding the right dirt track, even in the dark.

Soft kerosene light shone through the windows when we arrived at the house. Dogs greeted us noisily. Rita and Nancy were at the door before I'd time to set the brake.

"Hello, what are you doing in Dean's old bug?" Rita asked. Tiredly, I lifted myself out of the seat, flipped over the back and pointed. Ray's bundled body hadn't stirred since Nelson.

"Christ!" said Nancy as she pushed past me into the back of the car.

"Relax. She's alive. Drugged, that's all," I said. Nancy ignored me. She said, "Rita, give a hand." Together the two women lifted Ray — or Carol, as I decided to think of her from now on — and carried her into the house. I followed slowly, wondering what reception my second appearance here would produce. Artemis sat at the large kitchen table, by a lamp, laying tarot. She looked up incuriously at Rita and Nancy's burden, then went back to her cards. Neither Laura nor Chris were in evidence. I poured myself a cup of coffee from the ever-ready pot, sat down, and tried to pull myself together. For ten minutes or so no one spoke to me; Artemis ignored me, the other two were busy with Carol in the back room. Finally Rita returned, closing the door softly behind her.

"Well?" she said, sitting down across the table from me.

"How is she?" I asked. "Can you tell what they gave her?"

"Not for sure. But her pulse and breathing are strong. Nancy is trying to walk her. You know? Keep her moving. We might have to do that all night. Well?" she repeated.

Artemis got up, put away her cards. "I'll go help Nancy," she said and walked out without a glance at me.

"I found her like that. In Nelson," I said, trying to explain myself. These women intimidated me somehow. I felt inadequate and vaguely guilty. Not feelings I am much familiar with. "Snap out of it," I told myself and took a big gulp of coffee. Rita let me flounder. I continued.

"The door was bolted on the outside. There wasn't anything in the room to show what the drug was or that she'd taken it herself. Someone had drugged her to keep her out of action.

I think I know why."

"Do you?" Rita said skeptically, then relented and went on. "There is a puncture mark in her right arm. She's right-handed, so she didn't do it herself. Otherwise she seems to be OK."

"Well, that's a blessing anyway. But she's in danger. Ultimately."

"We all are, 'ultimately'. Especially with you around. Well?" That was all the leeway she was about to give me.

"OK, OK. You've made your point. I realize my coming here increased everyone's danger. That can't be helped. Look, I found a message at the Jam Factory to meet her in Kaslo. From Ray. Ostensibly from Ray, I mean Carol. Just like we'd arranged when I was here last. So you passed on my message. But someone intercepted it and set me up using Carol's name." I wasn't being very clear. "The trap didn't work only because I found her first. But I have to make that rendezvous regardless. So I'll be off. Thanks for looking after her." That was the wrong thing to say, I realized as I said it. Rita's look despised me.

"We look after each other," she explained calmly as if to an imbecile. "Go then. Preferably a long ways from here."

Neither of us had noticed Nancy's return. She'd heard the last part of our conversation and uncharacteristically broke in.

"Take it easy, Rita. Don't take it out on Helen. We're all under strain. Helen, you should know that we never got your message to Carol. So it wasn't through us."

"Who then? How?" I said, knowing what the answer had to be. I'd arranged with the Mossad boys to check the Jam Factory bulletin board. Anyone who knew that and also that I was trying to reach Carol could've baited a trap with that phony message. There wasn't any point thinking any more about it. The trap had to be sprung. Without further explanation I put down my cup and left. It was a relief to leave that house and go into action, no matter how dangerous. Action is my forte, not dealing with emotional tension.

It was well past midnight when I got to Kaslo. I was tired and impatient. Rather than doing the right thing, leaving the car and reconnoitering on foot, I took one of the back streets which led directly to the rendezvous site. Kaslo Municipal Campground is not much more than an unpaved parking lot near the beach. I approached slowly. Campfires were forbidden but the moon was bright enough to see a number of tents and scruffy pickup campers lining the edge. Suddenly, the dark figure of a man emerged from the shadows on the right and grabbed for the car's doorhandle.

"Damn it, Dean! What the hell are you doing here?" Seconds later a short dark man was in the car beside me. Almost instantly he realized his mistake but by then I had stepped on the gas. Gravel flew from under the wheels of the little VW as we careened over the campground wrestling for the steering wheel. His hands were large and strong. They were all I saw as I tried to keep control. With my foot firmly on the gas pedal I leaned over and bit the thumb of his right hand which was about to break my index finger. He let go, swore and flung himself abruptly out of the car just as the little machine left the beach area and plunged into the lake. As I struggled with the pressure of water against my door I heard him sloshing away.

Our excursion into the lake wasn't all that dangerous. Dean's car was firmly stuck dead — in two feet of water on Kaslo's shallow beach. I got myself out of it and looked around. Whole episode was over so swiftly it hadn't attracted any attention. The waterfront was quiet until the sudden snarl of a marine engine. As I stood stomping my wet feet, a good-sized power-boat with a flying bridge detached itself from the shadows and took off down the lake, leaving a white phosphorescent trail on the black water. I had no doubt that my large-handed enemy was on board. So, presumably, was the rest of the welcoming committee I had come to find. My stupidity in arriving as I did had left me wet, wheel-less and not much further ahead. Still, it could've been worse.

I grinned to myself as I squished my way up the empty street to the nearest hotel. To hell with it all, I needed a good night's sleep. Tomorrow would come soon enough.

15

Tomorrow arrived immediately. I hadn't walked half a block from the VW beached on the shore like a dead turtle when I became aware of being followed. A familiar brown-and-white dog limped towards me, tail wagging. She wasn't alone. A silent figure walked up to me from the moon shadows. As I braced myself for another attack, I recognized the tall, slim shape of Win.

"Hello," he said, teeth flashing. "How's the water?"

"Water's fine," I replied, relief flooding over me. "What are you doing here?"

"Long story. My truck's over there. Use a lift?" he asked, grinning.

"You bet."

Without another word, Win scooped up Ben's collie, turned and led the way back towards the campground. A small Toyota pickup was parked inconspicuously among the sleeping tents. He got in behind the wheel and we drove slowly and relatively silently away with the dog between us.

"You two know each other," Win stated, indicating me and the dog.

"Yes. What's her name?" I answered, making conversation.

"Dotchka. Where did you find her?" he asked.

"Find her?" I acted stupid.d

Win shrugged. "Don't tell me if you don't want to. You took her to the vet. Bet you found her on the mountain. Did you find Ben's body too?"

"Yes."

"And you didn't report it?"

"No."

"Ah." We drove a few minutes in silence.

"Where are we going?" I asked idly.

"Where d'you want to go?"

"My jeep's in Nelson."

"I wondered what happened to it and where you got that

old Beetle."

"I stole it. Jeep's too conspicuous."
Win looked at me curiously, nodded and turned his eyes back to the road.

"You didn't answer my question," I said. "What were you and Dotchka doing in Kaslo in the middle of the night?"

"I could ask you the same thing. But since you asked first you might as well know. We were looking for Ben's killer."

"In Kaslo?"

"Why not in Kaslo? Can you think of a better place?"

"And you found me instead. D'you think I killed him?"

"No. Sure you didn't."

"Because of Dotchka?" It was pretty clear, really.

"Yes."

I patted the dog. She licked my hand. "She would recognized the murderer," I pressed with the obvious.

"Sure. She must've been there at the time. Ben and Dotchka never parted."

"Maybe."

"No maybe. She knows."

We drove down the moon-lit lake road in silence. Outwaiting each other. We were both good at it. It could get to be a stalemate. I gave up first.

"Did you see the boat?" I asked, wondering if he'd answer. He did.

"Big Chris Craft. 32, 36 feet. Too far, too dark to see details."

"Seen it before?"

"Maybe."

"Recognize it again?"

"Maybe. Cannot be sure." He was being very, very careful.

"We could check all the marinas on the lake. Tomorrow."

"We could. What are you suggesting?"

"Working together. How about it?" I asked.

"It's an idea," Win said. And fell silent again. But this time not for long.

"I am looking to find Ben's murderers. What are you looking to find?" It was a fair question. I took a chance.

"I am looking for the two guys who belong to that Alberta station wagon."

"Same thing," he said.

I wasn't sure whether it was a question or a statement. I took another chance. "No," I answered, hoping Win wasn't an RCMP stoolie.

Again that curious look at me. Then Win sighed and said, "You would say that. They are friends of yours. What were you doing in Kaslo if not meeting them?"

I considered the matter from his point of view. I had arrived surreptitiously, expected by a man who got in my car. There must have been another man in the boat. It might look like a meeting of three conspirators. Except for the struggle in the car and their hurried exit in the Chris Craft.

"I came because I'd a message. But it wasn't from the men the police are after. It was a trap by the real killers to get me out of the way. Just like your suspects were gotten out of the way. It didn't work for a whole lot of reasons. One, I knew it was a trap. Two, I was late. Three, they mistook the car. Four, A VW going berserk in the middle of the campground was bound to attract attention sooner or later. They cut their losses and split."

Win listened carefully, biting his lip. We both knew I'd left a lot unexplained. "OK, so these were some other guys. Still doesn't make your friends innocent of Ben's murder."

"No. But it makes the matter less simple. Lot more than two strangers in a station wagon are involved."

"Oh, I knew that all along," he said and stopped as if he'd said too much. It was my first opening.

"My friends, as you call them, only arrived a week ago. So when did you notice something weird was going on around here? Did Ben put you onto something?"

Win nodded. And proceeded to make what for him was a long speech.

"Yes. A while back Ben started acting real strange. He was a strange old man, anyhow. Didn't have much to do, his old lady and Ursula look after him like he was god. He wanders around on foot and in that old truck of his. With Dotchka. They know these mountains like no one else. No one takes no notice of old Ben, you know? Real secretive, never a straight answer out of him. Enjoyed bamboozling people. Making them think he was dumb, like. But he wasn't. Oh, not old Ben, you bet. He liked to know things. About other people. So I don't rightly know when I figured out something was going on. Over and above the usual shit he was always into. A hint here, a wink there. But then I spotted he was real excited about something. Something he'd found. Come across in traipsing around. More than just a liquor still or somebody's crop of dope. More than some guy balling someone else's old lady or two women making out in the grass. Bit of a Peeping Tom old Ben was, for sure. But it wasn't anything like that. It was real big. Something he couldn't get a real grip on. Couldn't figure out. So I asked him, once. 'Bout a month ago. I guess. He wouldn't tell me. Liked his secrets. But he was real pleased I'd asked. Just chuckled, pulled at that pipe of his and didn't let on. So when he got killed I reckoned he'd really been onto something. Real big."

Win fell silent. We were almost into Nelson.

"Real big. Yes, you could say that," I commented wisely. "Any idea where or who? Ever follow him?"

Win laughed. "Like following a fox. No luck! And me an Indian!"

We both laughed. Win continued. "He was interested in the new people. Always was, so that wasn't nothing new. 'Californians' he called them all, regardless. Tried to figure them out, how they lived, what they thought, stuff they did. He was a real strange old man. A good friend, too."

"Any 'Californian' in particular he was interested in?" I pressed.

"I'd thought about that. Tried to remember. But no, cannot say as there was. He knew most everybody in the valley and in around Nelson, Castlegar, Salmo, up in Argentia. No."

We were driving through sleeping Nelson. An RCMP car passed us slowly. Win took no notice.

"So where's that jeep of yours?" he asked. I told him.

"OK. Assuming it's still there, what will you do now?"

"Get a good night's sleep. I hope."

"And tomorrow?" Now he was insistent.

I answered with a question. "Where would somebody keep a big Chris Craft on this lake if they didn't want it spotted?"

He looked surprised. "Forgot about that, almost. Not in any regular marina, that's for sure. Hum. Up the lake, away from the road, I reckon."

"That's what I think too. But it would have to be accessible from land too, you know. Else they would be immobilized."

"Old logging road, maybe. Or to an old mine. They shipped stuff by water at one time. Yes, could be."

"Yes. So how about you and me, and Dotchka of course, renting us a boat tomorrow. Go for a nice ride? See what we can see."

"Great. Sure. I'd better tell Echo I won't be working ...."

"You tell Echo nothing!" I said firmly. "Just don't show."

Win laughed out loud. "You're right. Might as well act like what he would expect from an Indian."

"Yeah. Pity to disappoint him." We grinned at each other. "Where's the best place to hire a boat?" I asked.

"Oh, I'll get us a boat, don't worry. One of our rich brothers owes me a favour. Where and when?"

"How about Kaslo? At two or so?" I answered.

"Kaslo again, eh? OK. Good night." He spun his steering wheel and took the Toyota out of sight, little Dotchka still sitting beside him.

My jeep was as I left it. I climbed into it wearily and in minutes was back on the lake road between Nelson and Kaslo for the third time that night. Weary or not, I had to make it back to Women's Acres and Carol Latimer.

It was daybreak but still dark. Mountains on the eastern side of the lake cut off most of the dawn light. My eyes kept closing, unfocused. Couple of times I barely avoided an early morning truck. After each of these near misses my back straightened, my hands clutching the wheel, my heart pounding. Keeping my eyes firmly on right side of the road and counting mailboxes, I again passed the turnoff for the Kokanee Glacier. The road wove along the steep lakeshore, in places lined with houses on both sides, in others crowding the edge of the lake. There were no real side roads, only a few driveways and short dirt tracks to nowhere. Just the road I was on and the lake. Keeping myself awake, I speculated how Ben's truck and the Mossad agents had been spirited away. Together or separately? The phrase 'one by land and two by sea' came unbidden into my mind. I couldn't concentrate; the idea had to be filed away for consideration later.

The sun was over the mountain's horizon when I reached Women's Acres. The house was dark and still. It was barely 5 a.m.

Inevitably the motley crew of dogs greeted me, milling about the jeep, barking hysterically, tails wagging. I took my sleeping bag out of the jeep, made my way into the barn, lay down and was out like a light. If anyone came out to check on the noise, I didn't know about it.

I woke up slowly to full daylight. After a moment of panic at the possibility that I'd overslept, I relaxed. My watch said 10 a.m. Plenty of time. Time to talk to Carol, assuming she would talk; time to parry Rita's hostility; time to meet Win at 2 p.m. And time for a good breakfast. I was starved. With the rolled-up sleeping bag under my arm I crossed the yard. No one was about, only two dogs were visible and they kept quiet. After depositing the sleeping bag in the jeep and finding some clean underwear in my pack, I entered the kitchen. Still no one. Panicked again, I searched for Carol. She was there, sleeping normally in a back room. Back in the kitchen I poured myself coffee and foraged for breakfast. I was just breaking a second egg into the cast iron frying pan when the door leading from the bedroom opened and Carol stood there peering uncertainly at me. She was wearing a long flannel nightgown, obviously belonging to one of the regular inhabitants of Women's Acres. Her feet were bare, she held onto the door jamb and said, "Hello, I am Carol. How did I get here?" Pause. "I don't know you."

"Hi, Carol. I am Helen. I brought you here. Last night."

We stared at each other.

"Helen ...." uncertainly. She was trying to remember.

"Yes. Want some coffee?" I waved the pot. The familiar, welcome sight distracted her.

"Oh yes, please! I feel real wobbly. What happened to me?"

She moved to the long table and sat down. I put a cup in front of her, moved milk and honey in her direction. She ignored them, grabbed the coffee in both hands and, elbows on the table, took a long swig. Another addict.

"Ah!" she said.

I was on the horns of a dilemma. On the one hand here was a perfect opportunity to get things out of Carol Latimer/Sara Ann Raymond, an opportunity which might not come again. On the other hand, if I took advantage of her vulnerable condition, of the absence of the other women, on their return they would be on me like a ton of bricks. I would lose any credibility I'd gained here. And that wasn't much.

As it happened, decision was taken out of my hands. Carol finished her cup, got up, poured herself another, sat down again.

"OK, Helen. Now tell me what happened." Her eyes were clear, her voice firm. Poor vulnerable victim was interrogating big, bad Helen. I had to smile. Should've known. This woman had lived on the run for years, mixed up in all sorts of dangerous and difficult situations. She hadn't survived by being dumb and helpless. Weakened by some unknown drug or not, the likelihood that I could zap her into telling me anything she didn't want me to know was nil. I relaxed gratefully. It was better this way. Bullying the weak is not my favourite occupation, although I have been known to do it. I gave her the address of the house in Nelson. She frowned.

"You found me there, unconscious from some drug. And brought me here," she repeated. I nodded. Let her draw me out. It was a nice switch. "Why here? And what were you doing in that house?"

"I was looking for Albert Shoreman. That's his address, according to his employers. As for bringing you here, it seemed the best place. I couldn't just leave you, could I?"

"I don't see why not. But never mind. What did you want with Albert? And surely the house was locked, and looked empty. How did you get in, and why?"

"I wanted to find out what he knew about a murder. Since he wasn't there to ask, I checked the house."

"You are a detective?" Carol asked.

"Yes. Helen Keremos of Vancouver. And you are Sara Ann Raymond, late of the U.S. of A. I came here to find you and give you a message. Now I can do that."

Her eyes flickered momentarily but otherwise she gave no sign my words had shocked her in any way.

"Never mind about that. My part is immaterial. Tell me about the murder. Whose murder?"

"Immaterial! Carol, don't be dumb. I can help, whatever you are into, I can help. I brought you here because it's sort of neutral but friendly ground. A sanctuary, Nancy called it. Think about yourself, think about what you are doing, think whether you want to go on with it. Revolutionary activities of the sort you were involved in in the past are one thing but this!" I admit I was flying blind. I'd no ideas how she would react.

"What makes you think I haven't? Thought about it, I mean? What makes you think I don't realize what I'm doing?"

"Because you were knocked out and locked up in that house. Held against your will. Whatever you say now, that's the truth of it. And do you know why?"

"They must have had a good reason. It's sometimes necessary ...."

"Nuts. Sure they had a good reason. So they could dispose of me without you even knowing I was around. Before we had an opportunity to meet and talk with each other. Well, we're doing it now." I grinned at her. She managed to smile in reply. Perhaps we were getting somewhere.

"How do you know that?" she asked.

"They set a trap for me using your name. They used you as bait while you were lying there unconscious. Tell me, can you ever trust your comrades again? And now that we have met, are they ever likely to trust you? Well?"

She didn't answer for a while, just looked at me. "You made sure of that by bringing me here, didn't you? That I couldn't go back. But I believe in what they're doing! It was my choice to make and you took it away from me. Damn you!"

"I had to do what I did. Tell me, what would you've done

— 95 —

in my place?" I asked.

She shrugged."Where does that leave me?"

"You could start by telling me all you know. Then together we can figure out what to do."

"Tell me how you found me."

I told her more than that. I told her about the assignment I was given in San Francisco, $3,000 cash to find her and tell her how to get in touch with her 'old friends Pat and Bob'. Then I went on to Matakoff giving me the name 'Carol Latimer' and my long day's search until I found Dean.

"I didn't trust your erstwhile friends Pat and Bob worth a damn. With good reason, it turns out. But I took the money, wherever it came from, and yes, conscientiously tried to find you. And that endangered you, which could make me an enemy. But remember how easy finding you turned out to be. Once you'd been spotted your cover was blown anyway. Seemed best I find you and fill you in rather than leaving it to someone else. As I expected it turned out to be a set-up. There were a couple of dudes around here a few days ago following me and asking about you. Someone wants you back in the States. Your Daddy perhaps?"

"From the states? Who's ...? Did they know ...?"

"Not when I met them. And they weren't real heavies. Just errand boys. Which proves, to me at least, their employer had no idea what's going on here. But that won't last. Next lot will be different calibre. They may be here now. Then we got trouble."

I described the wake-up call I'd gotten from the Stateside boys, our trip out of Nelson, episode at the creek and leaving them stranded. I told her what I'd done with their car. I omitted any mention of our previous encounter in the campsite. That would involve the Mossad agents. Best to keep a little in hand.

"Nice, very nice. You know your way around."

"A girl has to know how to look after herself," I said modestly. We laughed together.

"You're right. There'll be others. May not be so easy. What will you do?"

"First they'll have to find me. I am being more careful these days. Since Ben's murder."

"Ben's murder! Is that what you came to talk to Al about?"

"More or less. Just wanted to find him. And you. For a while there everyone had dropped out of sight. But you knew about Ben's death, eh. Your comrades killed him."

She considered. "No, I didn't know. But it doesn't surprise me, I guess. He was such a curious old man. We made jokes about him sneaking around, eavesdropping. But they were worried about him, finally. Whether he'd really found anything and figured it out. Then more recently things got very tense. Something was up but I wasn't told. Maybe they figured he'd gotten too close. I am sorry. He was a nice old man, really. And for Ursula." She fell silent, probably not satisfied with what she'd said.

"You're sorry. That's nice. He got in the way. So, bingo! Let's off him. Too bad."

"For God's sake, Helen! We cannot be sentimental about such things. We are involved in world revolutions. There have to be sacrifices."

"Sacrifices! Whose? They killed a harmless old man."

"He was a danger. We have to work that way. Don't you?"

"I try not to."

"That's what it will take to build a new society. Like it or not."

"What's so new about killing?"

"Aha. You're one of those. So why don't you just leave it to the authorities?!"

"For the same reason that I'm not blowing up dams. Because the cure is too much like the disease. So a plague on both your houses."

Carol looked into her empty cup with a small smile on her face.

"Blow up dams. Is that what you think this is all about?"

"It's a possibility. One of them."

She stood up and stretched. "I am ready for breakfast."

That was to be the end of my first solo conversation with Carol. As if on cue, Nancy, Rita and Artemis appeared in the yard from the woods. Grubby with sweat and dirt but cheerful. Coming in for a break from work. It was about noon.

I'd two hours before I was due to meet Win in Kaslo. Keeping well out of the way I watched the emotional greetings between Carol and the three women. There were hugs, exclamations of joy and concern. But the only question asked was the conventional, "How're you feeling now?" Nothing about how it happened, who did it, what will you do now. Strange, and quite in line with the atmosphere at Women's Acres.

"I'm fine, just fine. Thanks to you. And Helen, of course," repeated Carol after it was over. Everyone looked at me.

"Helen. Yes, she was right to bring you here, wasn't she?" This surprising bit of approbation from Rita. Especially surprising because of its implied criticism of Carol's personal and political choices.

"Yes. Now that I am here, could I stay?" Carol's tone was subdued, almost pleading. I looked at her sharply. She went on: "Just for a while, until I get myself together. I can work, contribute."

"Oh, for sure! Stay as long as you like. Laura's left, there is lots of room." Rita was enthusiastic. The other two women added their agreement, but I thought I detected a note of hesitation on Nancy's part.

"Great. Thanks a lot. I guess I'll go get some clothes on." Carol left the kitchen without a glance at me. I turned to Nancy who was busy breaking endless eggs into a pan. Scrambled eggs and homemade bread, goat cheese.

"You're for a heap of trouble. She won't be hard for them to find. For sure Dean will figure out where she'd hide."

Nancy didn't answer. Rita did, with exasperation.

"I thought I explained to you. This is what this place is for."

"Don't you think she owes you an explanation? At least. So you can evaluate the danger she's putting you in? Shouldn't trust work two ways?"

"Yes," Nancy said suddenly. "I think Helen is right. I don't like us being manipulated like this. Rita, it's no good. We've got to deal with this."

Rita gave in gracefully. "OK. Let's have a house meeting tonight. Discuss it between ourselves," she said.

"No! That's not good enough. I want to hear what Helen has to say."

"What about Carol?" Artemis asked. It was the first time she'd opened her mouth.

"She must be here too. I'm sure we can come to some agreement."

"Nancy, don't be naive. You know Carol's politics. We can never agree," Rita answered. "By all means let's sit down with Helen and Carol tonight. But don't count on any resolution."

"I won't," said Nancy, ladling out the scrambled eggs. Carol was back in the kitchen, looking good as new in her tailored slacks and elegant boots. They sat down and ate. I drank more coffee.

"I wonder what happened to my car," Carol said idly. "Be nice to have it back."

"Your car? I didn't know you had one currently," Rita said.

"Dean lent me his old VW. For keeps, I guess."

Rita looked at me. "Ask Helen. She brought you in it and left in it last night. Now she's back in her jeep."

"It's in Kaslo," I said. The situation struck me as absurd. "I'll take you there to collect it, if you like. I am due in Kaslo at 2 p.m."

"At two sharp, I suppose. Nobody makes appointments like that here. 'Sometime in the afternoon' is what we would say. Better leave your city ways behind if you want to make any headway here, Helen," said Artemis, much amused.

"Thanks," I said. "Well, Carol, want to go to Kaslo with me? If you are, then let's go."

"Sure." Carol pushed her plate away. "I'll do the dishes tonight." Together we left the kitchen, leaving the three women still sitting over their half finished meal. They had a lot to talk about.

16

"It's all very interesting," said Carol. "How did my car end up in Kaslo? Someone must have given you a lift to pick up your jeep. Is that who you are meeting this afternoon?"

"Yes. We are going for a boat ride. Like to come?"

That shook her. "A boat ride! What for?"

"Looking for a big Chris Craft with a flying bridge. Know where we'll find it?"

"OK, I'll come with you," Carol said after a moment. "Who are we going with?"

"Win. And Dotchka."

"Win! Why the dog?"

"She'd met the murderers."

"And you think she'll point them out to you!"

"Cut it out, Carol. You can't get under my skin. You heard that discussion between Rita and Nancy while you were getting dressed. You wanted to know where you stood with them. You know the danger you're getting them into. Is it worth it?"

"You tried to get me kicked out. Turn them against me." She laughed. "We will struggle for their hearts and minds between us, eh, Helen. Their stupid bourgeois hearts and minds! What a gas!"

"Why is it so important to you then? Since you despise them as you do." I tried to keep my anger in check, knowing she wanted me to lose it.

"Don't be stupid! I've nowhere else to go. Thanks to you," she burst out.

"So you are trying to 'take over' Womens Acres, infiltrate this outpost of the women's movement, so to speak."

"I'll give it a try. They're so easy to manipulate, to guilt, blind with baffle-gab. You do it very well too, you know. 'Trust should work both ways.' Neat. You and I should be working together."

"We aren't."

"No."

We drove in silence.

"Why did you tell me about Win and offer to take me on your boat ride?" she said finally. "I could sabotage the whole enterprise."

"To confuse you. We'll find the boat sooner or later. Just knowing it's around is enough."

"Oh?" She thought about that for a moment. "And will you also tell me what you know about Ben's death? Just to confuse me further?"

"Sure. You can buy a paper," I said.

I told her where Ben's body was found, about the station wagon with Alberta plates, and about the RCMP hunt for the two strangers missing from it. She listened closely, following all the implications with no trouble at all.

"These aren't our two guys from the states, I take it," she said.

"No way."

"Well, it looks like an open and shut case. Nice work."

"Yes, your ex-friends are very thorough. I wonder how they plan to dispose of you."

"Oh, don't try to scare me. I know the score. I am not a dumb tourist from Alberta."

"Neither were they."

"You know who they are!"

"Yes. And I intend to find them. Dead or alive."

"And avenge them and Ben, I suppose. Very commendable."

"If I can."

"With me as bait."

"Possibly."

"Beautiful, just beautiful! So you don't want me at Womens Acre's when the shit hits the fan. You have a soft spot for your sisters."

"Something like that."

"How do you justify setting me up for the sacrifice? Thought it was against your principles."

"You're in the game. I'm not sacrificing you. You are doing that all by yourself."

We pulled into Kaslo with time to spare. The VW was still

stuck on the beach. I let Carol off to find a tow truck before the Mounties did it for her. I stayed around to watch for Win and discourage underage vandals who showed a lot of interest in the abandoned vehicle. She was back in 10 minutes.

"Charlie said he'll get it out and fix it. He knows it belongs to Dean so that's all right. Why don't we go get a beer?"

We had a beer. Then another. Win didn't join us until almost three. Artemis was right. Nobody keeps time in the West Kootenays. Win was natty in brand new jeans and a freshly laundered check shirt. He and Carol seemed to know each other well without being close friends. I explained to Win.

"Carol knows where we might find that boat. She's been on it, haven't you Carol?" I sprung it on her.

"Oh?" said Win.

"It's probably the ARC company boat. Al Shoreman got to use it sometimes. So I've been on it. Its just an executive perk. Tax write-off, you know."

"No, I don't know. What was it doing here in the middle of last night?"

"Perhaps some bigwigs went for a moonlight ride."

"So we're no further ahead, is that it, Helen?" Win turned to me.

"I wouldn't say that. That boat explains a good deal given the geography of this area. There's only one north-south road on this side of these mountains. Easy to block, to monitor. Takes time to get from one end of the valley to the other. It figures they would use water for the really tricky stuff. Like bodies, dead or alive. In my opinion neither Ben nor his truck were anywhere near Kokanee Glacier Provincial Park when he got killed. He was brought there to make us think he was and to point to the two strangers. They were kidnapped and spirited away across the lake by boat. Nobody saw any other vehicle but theirs."

"You sure it was ARC?" asked Win. "Al Shoreman killed Ben?"

"Perhaps we should ask Carol," I said. "She and Shoreman are good friends. At least they registered as Mr. and Mrs. in a Seattle hotel not too long ago."

For a moment too dumbfounded to speak, Carol managed to collect herself in record time. "What's that got to do with Ben's death? I know, I know, Al did a bit of smuggling on company time and with company equipment but so what? Everyone does that at one time or another. Anyway he got fired last week or so. I don't see how either he or ARC are involved in Ben's murder."

"Good try, Carol," I said. I turned to Win. "Rather than a nice boat ride, I suggest we check up on ARC directly. Where do they keep that boat officially? What other unlikely equipment do they own or rent? Like a pontoon plane. What contracts do they hold and where? Are all their crews where they are supposed to be? Know anyone who might give us a lead on all this, Win?"

"Yeah, sure," Win replied but he was looking at Carol. "Leave it to me. Yeah, sure. But I wish I knew what you're up to, Helen. If you're right about Shoreman and ARC it doesn't make sense to bring Carol here and plan in front of her. Won't she tip him off?"

"Carol didn't murder old Ben, Win. Why would she help those who did?"

We all knew that was more for her benefit than his. But Win nodded, apparently satisfied.

"Ok. Same time, same place tomorrow?" he asked. "It's Saturday."

"Right. Good luck," I said.

Rather reluctantly, I thought, Win finished his beer and drifted off.

Carol sat over her second beer, silent. Her face was drawn, her body slumped, her eyes almost closed. She put her head down on her folded arms and sighed. "I'm tired," she said.

"No wonder. Reaction. Better get some rest. Wonder if your VW is ready."

She lifted her head. "You're not going back to the farm?"

"Not yet. But I'll be there tonight. Count on it."

"Aren't you worried about leaving me alone with Rita and the rest? I could influence them," Carol prodded with a flash of her old spirit.

"Worried? Not a bit. You are in no shape to influence anybody.

Anyway, I've faith in them. Let's go get the VW."

She heaved herself onto her feet and followed me out of the hotel bar. I stopped at the front door and looked around.

"What's the betting that your Charlie at the garage called Dean about his car? And told him you were around? Dean could be waiting for you."

"God, I never thought of that. My mind's not working. Yes, of course. But, ... it doesn't matter ... I mean, Dean wouldn't ..."

"Oh, wouldn't he! Now who's being sentimental! Call him. Call Charlie's."

Back in the hotel lobby, I gave Carol a quarter, watched her find the number and dial.

"Charlie, it's Carol. Is that VW ready?" She listened. "Oh good. I'll be right there to pick it up. Thanks." Carol hung up and turned to me. "It's ready. But I bet he called Dean and expects him there momentarily."

"How did you figure that out?" I was curious.

"By the way he spoke. Sort of cutsey. Like he expected a lovers' meeting. He wasn't like that before."

"OK. Here, take the jeep keys. Get in it and drive back like hell. Stop for nothing. I've been wanting a talk with Wonder Boy."

She took the keys and looked at me wonderingly. "Boy, you take some chances," she said. I didn't know whether she meant giving her my jeep or going to meet Dean. Probably both.

"It's all designed to confuse you, remember," I answered.

"Well, it's working." She smiled tiredly and walked away. I followed at a distance. The jeep was parked on the street, not on the hotel lot. From a shaded doorway I watched her get in, and pull away.

I went back, had another beer and a hot dog. In spite of my flippancy I knew I was running a grave risk in trusting Carol. Yet she was surely the key. If she would only cooperate ... She couldn't be brow-beaten, tricked or argued into it. It had to be voluntary.

On the face of it, it was ridiculous to expect an instant miraculous conversion, against the grain of years of political commitment reinforced by personal loyalties. Yet that was exactly what I was looking for from Carol. Admittedly, circumstances were on my side. The stress of dangerous and quickly moving events works like a microwave oven. Fast. Ideas which normally take months to absorb now have only days; crucial decisions must be taken in minutes rather than weeks or hours. Carol knew she would be destroyed unless she made some changes. She knew it was the doing of her terrorist comrades, none of mine. If they hadn't exposed so clearly how little they trusted her, how little her loyalty counted, nothing I did or said could make any difference. It could prove a fatal error on their part.

I finished my beer and found the back door. Out into the parking lot and back alley. First I wanted to find Dean's wheels. Probably that souped-up truck I saw at his place that Laura had a hankering for. Kaslo is a small place, he wouldn't have left it very far.

It was mid-afternoon and hot. Not many pedestrians on the streets. I walked from alley to alley, keeping in the shade and crossing streets only after a thorough check in all directions. Of course Carol could've been wrong. Charlie mightn't have called Dean, the whole thing could be a figment of her imagination. But my bet was on Carol's ability to psych out any sexual implications in a man's voice, even over the phone. She'd had lots of practice.

Charlie's Garage wasn't one of the slick ones catering to tourists but rather a two pump, one-man-and-a-boy operation where the locals had their old cars fixed. Charlie was a mechanic, not a gas jockey. Low overhead in a rundown building on a side street and all the business he could handle. I figured old customers used the alley entrance to the shop rather than the tacky front drive with its outmoded pumps. That's where Carol would be expected to appear. Through the back. So I tried the front. The little street with its assortment of cheap bungalows and one-and-a-half storey wooden houses was almost empty of people. Just cars and a few trucks parked here and there along its length.

I scanned them carefully. Dean's truck wasn't among them. I tried the closest cross-street and there it was! Dean must be very sure of himself to have left his rather distinctive opulent vehicle just around the corner from the garage. A half-assed attempt at concealment by an arrogant man who wasn't really expecting to be challenged.

I walked up to the truck boldly. It was open, keys in the ignition. Well, that wasn't unusual in this area. I pocketed the keys and went on to find Dean.

17

As it happened, Dean found me first. I'd just crossed the street and entered the alley behind the garage when he appeared, striding purposefully towards me. He was obviously on his way back to his truck. Recognition was mutual. We both stopped, took a few moments to evaluate the situation. Dean made his move first, coming at me like an express train, his outsize boots digging into the white dirt. I just had time to get out of the empty alley and step into the street. He slowed down once he realized I wasn't running any further, so that we met in the middle of the street more like friends than like pursuer and pursued.

"Well, Helen. Fancy meeting you here! Where's Carol?" He was trying to be casual for the benefit of any watching eyes or ears but I sure didn't like the smile on his face. Dean was scared and in a hurry.

"She decided to leave. I was on my way to tell you not to expect her."

"Oh, yeah? Where did she go?"

"She didn't say. I think she left for the sake of her health. It's not been so good lately."

"That's too bad." Dean was right beside me, his large hands hovering over my right arm. He grabbed it and in a movement which could pass for friendly tucked it under his left arm. His hand closed like a vise over my knuckles. "Why don't we go and find her. Perhaps I can help."

I dug my heels in and said sharply, "Cut it out, Dean. I know you are stronger than me but I'll give you lots of trouble, believe me. D'you want an audience while you beat up on a woman? Everyone knows you. Be bad for your rep."

Reluctantly he let go. I stepped back a pace.

"Won't work, Helen. I know where I can find Carol. Only one place for her to go. I'll take that dyke haven apart with my bare hands."

"Bare hands, eh. Go ahead. Try it. But I suggest you bring

your army. If they aren't too busy elsewhere." For a moment I thought he would hit me. I had struck a nerve. He didn't have any help in the vicinity. It occurred to me that he'd casually offered to find Carol and bring her back to the fold alone. It would be like him. With his charm and strength he hadn't had many setbacks in his life. Believing himself to be virtually invincible, he'd taken on a task he now wasn't sure he could carry out. What surprised me was that Huber and Shoreman, who should know better, had apparently bought this plan. Perhaps they really believed he was Tarzan. More likely they just couldn't spare any more men at the moment and decided to risk it. If so, something pretty important must be keeping them from pulling out all the stops to find and silence Carol. It wasn't a comforting thought. I'd absolutely no idea what they were doing, where or why. Dean would know, of course. I looked at him speculatively. Perhaps I could turn the tables and grab him?

Suddenly his attitude changed. He dropped his threatening stance and backed off.

"Oh, never mind. It's not important. Carol'll come to her senses soon enough. Tell her to join us when she's ready. Everything is going along as planned. And she is part of it all. She should be proud." It was hard to see whose benefit this nonsense was for, since Carol wasn't there to hear it. But it gave me an idea.

"Why don't you tell her yourself? We could arrange a meeting. Neutral place. Of course, I'll have to ask her. She may not want to see you."

He was taken aback. The situation seemed to have reversed. But he saw the possibilities. It might still be possible to trap Carol somehow, meanwhile lulling me into thinking he'd given up. Or something equally unlikely.

"I guess that would be OK. When do you suggest?" So he had time problems.

"Tomorrow. Give her time to ... recuperate," I said. He considered the implications. Giving Carol time to 'recuperate' also meant giving her time to blow their whole plan. On the other hand, time was obviously what they needed to complete whatever it was that was keeping their 'army' so busy at the moment. Dean was in a spot.

"No, you don't. I want to see her now," he said grimly.

I shrugged. "Suit yourself." As I said it I turned and sprinted towards his truck. In seconds I was burning rubber. As I turned the corner I saw Dean disappear back up the alley. Presumably to get the VW and give chase. Only question was, would he try to stop me on the road or concentrate on getting to Women's Acres before me? For there was little doubt it had to be one or the other. If the first, then I could lead him away, take a road in another direction; if the latter, any diversion I tried would merely give him more time to get to Carol first. It was safest to assume he would ignore any attempts to lead him on a wild goose chase. Carol was his goal. Zipping along in the powerful truck I didn't think he had a chance. I had too good a start, even if he managed to get his hands on a fast car, never mind that VW with its old sewing machine for an engine. Automatically I glanced at the dashboard. I was doing 60 k/h on Kaslo's main street and the gas gauge was showing empty! A gas guzzler like this would run dry in minutes. I wondered whether he knew how low on gas he'd left it and was counting on it. There wasn't any choice. I pulled into a self-serve station, jumped out and then watched helplessly as the familiar little car with Dean behind the wheel buzzed past going flat out .... I pumped five bucks worth, hoping it would be enough, threw the money at the curious attendant and got out of there as fast as I could. My lead was gone but I still had the more powerful car. In any case I was on his tail and barring accidents wouldn't be far behind him all the way. Perhaps I could even get ahead of him, going cross-country. I looked around the cab for a survey map. Mine was in the jeep, with Carol. There was a map stuck behind the visor. It was hard to read, driving the narrow, curving road. There were no bush roads marked across the Goat Range. Route 31 ran between it and the lake. It was the only way. Perhaps once we got onto the dirt track leading to Women's Acres I could cut him off. I tucked the map into my pocket and concentrated on driving. For the moment the fast, powerful vehicle gave me no advantage over the lighter, more manoevrable little VW. I saw it ahead, taking the bends at a speed I couldn't match without a grave risk of going off the road and into the drink. There wasn't any point in stupid heroics. On an open stretch I might catch up. But there were no straightaways. Road curved like a dizzy snake. Still, I was getting close. We arrived at the side road to the farm with only 100 metres between us. Both cars hit the uneven gravel at high speeds, throwing up showers of dirt and rocks. Dean could drive, had to give him that. We tore through the trees like dirt-bikers, the VW only a few lengths ahead of me now. Suddenly its brake lights blossomed and continued to glow. Panic stop. I slammed on my brakes and swerved to the right. Crippling the car ahead of me on this narrow road would only hold me up. As the truck finally came to a halt I saw what had led to the VW's sudden stop. Sitting across our path was my jeep, abandoned. It was empty, both doors hanging open, key in the ignition. Carol was nowhere to be seen.

For a minute Dean and I stood silently looking at the empty vehicle together.

"Well, well," I said. "I guess your friends didn't trust you to grab Carol and silence her all alone. They sent reinforcements."

"No, it couldn't be them," Dean said, then fell silent considering. "Had to be someone else. The cops, perhaps?"

"Would they leave the jeep like this? No way. Had to be Shoreman or Huber," I answered, knowing very well that it had to be the US contingent. The only question was, was it the original Hardy boys or someone more dangerous. But Dean needn't know any of that. While I in turn had no hint what was keeping Shoreman and Huber so busy that 'it couldn't be them.'

"I tell you it cannot be them," Dean repeated with exasperation. "What they are doing is important ..."

"What's more important than taking Carol out of circulation? She's a danger to you all."

"No. I persuaded them she isn't. I can deal with her. No. It's either the cops or someone else."

"Well, we aren't doing any good here. Get in the VW and let's ride to Women's Acres. Or would you prefer a lift in the truck?"

Dean turned and glared at me. "You've got your nerve. Why should I go there now? I've got to find Carol."

"Because I am inviting you. And I have your gun. And Carol is safer without you after her," I said. In my hand was a high-power automatic I had found under the truck seats. It pointed at him. "Let's go. We'll take my jeep. Get in and drive.

Unbelieving but unresisting Dean manoevred the jeep up the road. He wasn't quite sure what lay ahead. Neither was I.

As soon as we arrived in the yard I jumped out, waved the gun at him and led him to the barn. Nancy and Rita arrived to see what was going on.

"What are you doing with him?" Rita demanded.

"Carol's been snatched. I have to go find her. Buddy boy is in the way. Can you hold him here for me until I get back?" I was out of breath, my voice urgent.

"Snatched!" Rita would've argued but Nancy cut her off.

"OK. We can lock him up in one of the small bedrooms. There're shutters on the windows. He'll be safe till you get back."

"Hey, come on, Nancy. It's me, Dean. What's the idea?" Dean couldn't believe what was happening. "Let me go, for Christ's sake! I'm just as keen as you are to find Carol. What's this about locking me up?"

I ignored him. Turning to the two women I said, "Lock him up by all means. But don't trust him. It was him drugged Carol. Now he has orders to dispose of her. I've got to go."

I hit the jeep running and was out of there before they could ask any more question.

18

"PLEASE FOLLOW ME," said the cherubic Mountie politely. Then he turned and got into the car with the RCMP/GRC logo on its doors. Sighing, I complied. This wasn't my day. To be stopped at this time! To be identified and scooped up for interrogation. Damn! I fumed, preparing to tell my pack of lies and get myself out of there as soon as possible. It took me a minute to realize that we weren't going to the Kaslo cop shop. Instead the Mountie car turned into one of the many long driveways off the highway, passed the house and stopped at a large barn. Curious, I followed. By the time I stopped the Mountie was waiting for me.

"Please follow me," he said, polite as ever. We entered the cool, dim interior of the barn. A man with all the old familiar signs of a government agent dropped his newspaper, got up from a chair, and said, "Thank you, constable, I'll take over."

"Right, Sir," said the young Mountie, impressed. He almost saluted, restrained himself, then turned smartly on his heel and left.

"Let's have the gun." The agent sounded bored. Without a word I turned over Dean's gun. He looked at it with professional interest.

"Nice," he said. "Nice."

"Yes. Let's get on with it," I said. "Where is he?"

"In there." We walked through an inner door into what must have, not long ago, been a series of horse stalls. The smell of horse-shit and hay was not unpleasant. Then out the back to a trailer with a long antenna and all the accoutrements of a field office. Tables, chairs, file cabinet, radio transmitter, battery of telephones. Maps on the walls. And the indispensable teletype, copying machine, and shredder. Even a coffee maker. My escort motioned me to a chair and picked up the phone, pressed one button.

"She's here, Ron," he said. I went and poured myself some coffee. It was good. Just as well. Bad enough having Walters descend upon the scene like this without a good brew to sustain me.

"So, Helen, here we are again." Ronald Walters walked in rubbing his hands. He looked the image of a skinny, balding cat which had just dined on one bird and was about to have another for dessert. I didn't feel like dessert.

"Yeah, let's stop meeting like this. People will talk," I said insanely and unnecessarily.

Walters laughed. "People will talk, indeed. That's good. Yes, I trust people will talk. Would you like to start?"

"I don't have anything new to say."

"Too bad. And unlikely. Considering all the things that have been happening around here."

"What things? What brings you down here, Ron? Yesterday — was it yesterday? — you were in Vancouver. Now a command post in the boonies. Very fast work. But why?"

Walters was so pleased with himself he almost popped a vest button.

"Just moving with events, Helen. Remember what I said yesterday? 'Situations have a way of not standing still,' eh? I said that. Right. They didn't. And here we are again."

"So what makes you so happy?" Needless to say I wasn't happy. Despite all this bullshit Ron Walters was no fool.

"A bit of luck, I admit, luck. But well deserved, if you know what I mean. If I hadn't made the decision to move up here personally then I wouldn't have been in a position to get lucky. Follow?"

"No."

Walters turned back to the door through which he had entered and pointed. "Come and see."

We went out and back into the barn. One of the stalls was fitted out into a rough facsimile of what the English call a bedsitter. Right down to a hot plate. It held only one occupant. It was Carol. She sat in a folding rope chair, her feet planted firmly and defiantly in front of her.

"Oh, it's you," she said woodenly on seeing me. "Welcome to this charming old country retreat. All the comforts of home, including bullshit.''

"Horseshit,'' I corrected. "We wondered what happened to you. Dean and I were most concerned.''

"Dean.'' Her face froze again. "Ask your friend.''

I turned to Walters who had watched this by-play carefully. "OK. So you've taken to snatching people right off the road. How come?'' I asked.

"No, no.'' Walters was delighted at my error. "It was all purely fortuitous. Like I said, luck. Miss Carol Latimer, whose prints we are currently checking, and who will undoubtedly turn out to have names other than Carol Latimer, was picked up in the company of three Americans in a routine speed trap. It turned out that some of the American tourists haven't adjusted to our metric system. They were travelling at over 80 miles per hour, where only 80 kilometres per hour are permitted. Naturally our efficient police force pulled them over and tried to show them the error of their ways. Those American 'tourists' first tried to intimidate, then bribe members of the RCMP. Well, you can imagine what happened,'' Walters went on, enjoying himself. I looked at Carol. She was looking down at the tops of her boots.

"Who were they, Carol?'' I asked her.

She shrugged. "Like you guessed.''

"Where are they?'' I asked Walters.

"Being held in town. They will be properly charged, be out on bail tomorrow. That's not what matters. What matters is that this young lady is Mrs. Albert Shoreman, isn't she?''

"Where did you get that? Your friend Beach?''

"Of course. Come, let's leave Miss Latimer to consider her position. I am sure she will agree to talk sooner or later. Meanwhile you and I must have a chat.'' He led the way out of the barn and back to the trailer with the coffee machine.

"OK. You've had your fun. Now, what brought you to the Kootenays?'' I asked, testing the rich, hot liquid gratefully.

"Developments. Beach is really worried about his lost clients. So he came to me and this time told me the whole story. Or at least enough of it to give me leads which are worth following up. Like Shoreman.''

"What about Shoreman?"

"As it happens I know a great deal about Shoreman. He's a weapons expert. Every terrorist organization needs a man like that. He is highly prized. Reputed to be an arrogant, self-willed bastard. But indispensable."

"So?"

"So he disappeared from his regular haunts over a year ago. The West Germans have a big question mark on his file. Will they be surprised to hear he has been sitting in these mountains all this time!"

"Come on, Ron! Shoreman is a mechanic! A technician. Not a leader, planner or organizer. So Shoreman is here. So what? Where does that get you?"

"He's the end of the string. You know that once we have a good lead like that we can crack this. Shoreman's been here a year. He lives somewhere, has a job, connections. It's just a matter of time. And having that Carol Shoreman fall into our hands! That's just gravy. She's in it, whatever it is, and she will talk."

"I wouldn't count on it."

"No?"

"No."

"We'll see."

Ronald Walters sat down carefully behind the table and picked up a pencil. "We'll see," he repeated. "I have leverage. Lots of it. She'll talk."

"What leverage?"

"Her past. Her prints are on file somewhere, I'll bet my pension. Those three gorillas she was with. There's something there and I'll find it. But you know all about that, don't you, Helen? Carol was your little secret. Don't need you any more, Helen. A little pressure, and we work out a little deal with this Latimer-Shoreman-whatever-her-name-is broad and I'll have the whole story. Just a matter of time." He leaned back and grinned at me.

"You don't have time, Ron," I said. He looked so smug. I wasn't sure I could shake his confidence enough. I thought of Dean at Women's Acres, my arrangement to meet Win tomorrow. I had to get out of there and take Carol with me.

"Oh, a day or two isn't very long. Anyway it may not take that long. Nice, middle-class Americans like Carol break like matchsticks. Even men."

"You've got it wrong, Ron. In the first place, things are moving fast and you don't have one or two days. In the second place Carol Latimer is no nice misguided middle-class American innocent. She's been a full-time revolutionary for almost twenty years. You won't intimidate her by breathing hard and showing your biceps." I was taking a chance but what were my choices? I had to shake his faith so he would listen to my proposition. I leaned over the table and said urgently, "Did Beach not tell you how the Mossad got onto Shoreman? Anything about a man called Misurali, a.k.a. Huber? His arrival in this area?"

Walters looked uncertain. "No."

"His Calgary connections?"

"Calgary? No." He looked away, back at me again. Then he sighed. "OK. I knew it was all too good to be true. That bastard Beach! OK, talk to me, Helen."

"Forget about holding Carol and wanting to crack her. She's not that important anyway. We have to find Huber."

"Who's Huber?"

"Shoreman's boss. Man from headquarters. Huber flew to Castlegar from Calgary only a few days ago. He had business in Calgary and Chicago and New York. He called Shoreman, probably, arranged to meet him here. Israelis intercepted the call, that's how they found Shoreman. So it's not simple at all. There had to be a good reason why Huber would drop by unexpected, like .... Something important, big and urgent. You don't have time to sit around pulling wings off flies, much less waiting for Carol to tell you a pack of lies. If she tells you anything." I sat down and took a gulp of my luke-warm coffee. Ronald Walters watched me speculatively.

"You know where this Huber is?" he asked.

"No, but I know how to find him," I answered, hoping it was good enough, hoping it was true.

"You have a plan?" he continued.

"I have a proposition. Give me Carol and 24 hours. That's all. Stay out of the way that long. Call off these cops. Let me do it my way. 24 hours."

Walters played with his pencil, his eyes closed now.

"Helen. You do appreciate the fact that if you are conning me even a little, you are through. I promise. Through." Suddenly his eyes were open, looking at me.

"I know, Ron. It's my neck on the line."

"OK. Take Carol." He looked at his watch. It was 7 p.m. "24 hours. I'll be here."

"I want my gun back," I said.

He nodded. We didn't shake hands.

19

At FIRST SHE WAS SILENT in the jeep on the way back to Women's Acres.

"How'd you do it?" Carol asked finally.

"I persuaded him that you wouldn't tell him enough that was useful, soon enough. I told him I had a way of speeding things up. That's all," I replied.

"How?"

"You and Dean."

"What about me and Dean?"

"I want to find Huber. With your help."

"Is that all?"

"That's the beginning."

"God, Helen! Are you nuts, or what? You cannot have any idea what you're talking about! D'you really think Dean and I will just tell you where to find Huber, Huber will turn himself in, we'll pack up all our plans and quietly get back to growing rutabagas? Just because of you or that asshole Ronald Walters? Get real!"

"Whoever killed Ben isn't going to get to grow rutabagas, I promise. And you forgot to mention the two guys who've been set up for his murder. Where are they? Are they alive?"

"I don't know. Ask Dean. He might know. But he didn't do it. I know he didn't."

"You mean Dean didn't personally kill Ben. But I bet he arranged for the body to be moved and possibly for the kidnapping of Sid and Harry. That's his job, isn't it?"

"Yes. Dean's logistics: transportation, supply, communication. That's his job."

"Who's the boss?"

"Shoreman's our contact and cell leader."

"No, I mean the real, overall boss."

"I don't know."

"Does Dean know?"

"Maybe. There are at least two cells in this area. Maybe three. We get orders passed on to us. We carry them out. Our cell is the only above-ground part of the operations. Well, our cell is ARC. We deal with the outside world, and like I said Dean's job is logistics. He and Shoreman are responsible for transportation, materials, all of that. All through ARC facilities."

"Where do you fit in?"

"I provide cover, carry messages, generally help out."

"And recruit."

"Yes. Not much any more."

"Did you ever try to recruit Rita, Nancy and that lot?"

"Yes. It didn't take."

"I wouldn't have thought so. Go on, how about the other cell or cells?"

"I'm not sure exactly how it works. We aren't supposed to know any more than we need to."

"Yeah. 'Need to know'. But you have some idea."

"There's a security cell or group. But whether it's separate or part of the leadership cell, I don't know. I've met a few of the members, that's all."

"How many people, altogether, do you estimate?" I asked.

For the first time she paused. "About 20, but it may be more."

"How about Huber. What's his position?"

"I don't know. All I can tell you is that Shoreman's scared of him."

We drove a while in silence.

"What's it all about, Carol?" I asked.

After a moment she answered. "I am beginning to realize how little I really know. We aren't exactly encouraged to ask questions. Dean recruited me about a year ago. Our politics were always pretty close. So when he said that we were to set up safe houses for comrades to hide, rest and regroup, I went along. Mostly my job was to meet people, look after them and pass them on. Like being part of an underground railroad. Sometimes there were large shipments of goods in crates. Weapons, I guess. That's when Shoreman showed up. He took over."

"What about ARC? How does that work?"

"I think it belongs to the organization. Corporate HQ is in Calgary. But it's a legit company. Builds roads and things like that. All on the up-and-up. Shoreman has access to all their equipment, including the boat."

"It all figures. OK. Tell me more. How about Dean?"

"Dean works with Shoreman. He's the local above ground organizer. He does the actual work, like a foreman. Dean recruited some of the men locally, you know. Others arrived from outside. As far as I know all the ARC personnel are here legally, they're on the regular payroll, have social security numbers, all that. Above ground, like I said."

"How many men are involved on that level?"

"No more than ten or so on a regular basis. Last summer Dean hired a bunch of us as casuals. We did regular road work mostly. It's all very fluid. When something major needs doing, Dean organizes it. The rest of the time ARC operates like any other construction company. It's a very safe arrangement."

"What's it all about, Carol?" I replayed my original question. "What is being planned, what are Shoreman and Dean preparing?"

She seemed willing enough to answer. "Preparing is the right word. Up to this point we've been working on infra-structure. Hide-outs, weapon storage, supplies, training areas. We've never actually *done* anything here. Orders are to keep a low profile and not raise suspicions."

We were on the dirt road leading to Women's Acres. I braked gently as we approached the spot where Dean and I left his truck and VW. Then I had to stop. The two vehicles had been moved and were blocking further access quite thoroughly. Good thinking on someone's part. It took me three tries with all four wheels engaged to get past them and on the road again. Only a jeep could get past this obstruction. That needn't prevent a surprise attack but did cut down on potential visitors. Minutes later we circled the yard. Dogs barked as usual as Carol and I left the jeep and walked through the low doorway into the dim kitchen.

There were greetings, explanations, food and coffee served all round. Carol, Nancy, Rita and Artemis talked and laughed at once in excitement and relief. I took a piping hot mug of coffee into the back room occupied by Dean. I knew he would try to jump me so I was ready. Cursing he wiped the hot coffee off his face and glared at me.

"Carol is here. Now we can have our meeting," I said. "A bit delayed, but we have all night if necessary. So you will get your chance to talk to her, persuade her, whatever."

"Hah! Thanks a lot!" His face red from coffee and anger, he tried to keep himself in check. "And what do you want from me?"

"I don't know yet," I lied unconvincingly. "We'll see how it goes." I took out his gun from my belt and waved it at the door. "Go on, let's join the ladies." Excitement has a way of producing facetiousness. I promised myself to guard against it in future.

I followed Dean into the kitchen where four pairs of eyes immediately focused on us. I pointed to one of the two old overstuffed armchairs. Deep, they were hard to get out of in a hurry. Perfect. I sat down across the room in a hard chair.

"Sit. Now would you like a coffee? To drink this time?" Without a word Nancy passed Dean a fresh mug, carefully avoiding getting between him and me.

I looked at Carol, wondering how she would react to Dean's presence. I couldn't see her eyes but her mouth set in a hard line. Good, I thought, we might get somewhere after all.

And so began one of the tensest nights of my life.

It was clear early on that Dean had no idea what tack to take with Carol. Of course, being a prisoner, even a comfortable one, is not to everyone's taste. Having a gun pointed at you concentrates some people's minds wonderfully, while others tend to go to pieces. Dean did neither, but the stress of not being in charge — clearly his natural habitat — took its toll very quickly. He started out with the obvious ploy: he and Carol were on the same side, in a nest of enemies. It didn't work. Carol got to the point immediately. She interrupted.

"Why did you drug me and use me as bait for Helen?" That was putting it succinctly.

"Look, Carol. What's it matter now? Perhaps it was a mistake.

Seemed a good idea at the time, that's all."

"Which do you mean — drugging me or trapping Helen? If trapping Helen was a good idea I would have seen it too and cooperated. On what basis did you and Al decide it was necessary to get me out of the way?"

"We weren't sure you would go along, that's all. It just seemed simpler." He couldn't avoid saying all the wrong things, rubbing Carol's nose in the fact that she had been only a part-time comrade; just a convenience which could be dispensed with once it became an inconvenience.

Dean turned on Carol all his not inconsiderable charm, heavy with sexual vibes, trying to placate her. It had worked in the past; this encounter had some of the earmarks of a replay. But this time Carol wasn't buying. Her eyes examined Dean as if seeing him for the first time. Still, as long as the argument stayed within the realm of their personal relationship, as long as the issue remained on the plane of their undoubted feelings for each other, Carol was unable to disentangle herself. But then Dean made a mistake. He reminded Carol of her commitment to their cause. A true revolutionary should go along with anything without question. Carol's concern was an ego trip. He dismissed it as a sign of bourgeois individualism. She must learn that personal considerations had to give way before the political cause they served.

Carol laughed. Her face, which had been flushed, turned pale.

"Bullshit," she said. "You serve no cause but your own. What nerve, talking about ego trips. Bourgeois individualism, indeed!" She laughed again. Then she got up and got herself more coffee. Phase one of the encounter was over. The ground had been cleared.

I looked around the crowded kitchen. Pools of soft kerosene light surrounded by darkness. Nancy, Rita, and Artemis all sat at the long table with their backs to the window. Like a theatre audience, they faced the remaining three of us: me by the stove, Carol and Dean in armchairs in the middle of the room. To this point only those last two had spoken. Dean especially ignored the presence of anyone else in the room. Carol's trip to the coffee pot relieved tension all round. Like a seventh-inning stretch. Artemis sighed and proceeded to roll a joint. Nancy reached up to get a sketch book from a shelf. She dropped a pencil, said "Damn," and sat down again. Rita merely leaned back and watched the two protagonists in the foreground with a side glance at me from time to time.

I cleared my throat and said, "What happened to Harry and Sid, Dean?"

Dean turned at me as if stung. "Your precious friends Harry and Sid are Israeli agents."

"I know who they are. I asked what happened to them." All four women stared at me.

Dean couldn't hid his exasperation. "Look, Helen. You have no idea what you stumbled on here, much too big for you to understand or do anything about. So stop playing female Bond, give me my gun back, and get the hell out of here yourself."

I pretended to consider this suggestion seriously. "Thanks for your advice. But haven't you left out a few minor details?" My sarcasm was too obvious to be anything but an insult. "Ben's murder, Harry and Sid's disappearance, the recent arrival on the scene of the RCMP plus one Ronald Walters representing established authority. I couldn't just pack up and leave even if I wanted to. Walters or the Mounties would zap me. Even if I dealt myself out of this game altogether, they wouldn't. Your peaceful days are over. You have to admit, Dean, that your plans are in something of a disarray."

"Disarray," he mimicked, "So you admit that you, Walters, and the cops are all together on the same side." He glanced up triumphantly. "The side of international Zionism and im-perialism. Against the people."

"Quit making speeches. You know, Dean, you are an anach-ronism. Nobody buys those simple polarities any more." I raised my voice. "And on my right, ladies and gentlemen, in white hats the bad guys, and on my left, in black hats the good guys. Or vice versa. Take your pick." Someone by the window giggled. I continued. "What, apart from your out-of-date rhetoric makes you the good guys? How are you different from the bad guys?"

"Nevertheless, nevertheless, a choice has to be made. By all of us. What side are you going to be on when the time comes?"

"When what time comes? When you set out to destroy the Columbia system?"

"So you think we plan to do that? Well, it's certainly a possibility, isn't it?"

"Is it? A real possibility? I doubt it. Shoreman is an expert in weapons, not in demolition. You would need a lot of expertise, a lot of very accurate plans, a lot of people to carry it out. You haven't got any of that."

"So why mention the Columbia then? Where did you get the idea?"

"From Walters. Which is significant. He really knew nothing about the situation here. Yet he was all paranoic about dams. Why? Because he'd been fed some information by someone. I am convinced it was a plant. I think you were laying the groundwork for some gigantic con. The dams are hostages. You don't have to do anything. Just sit tight and bluff. It doesn't matter whether Walters believes you or not. He and his bosses cannot take a chance. The merest threat and their country would be invaded by hysterical Americans. Meanwhile you are after something else. Well?"

Dean listened, smiling politely. The strain was showing. There was a sag to his handsome, muscular body, a slight twitch in his left eye, and his thumbs repeatedly pressed into the side seams of his jeans.

I turned to Carol. "Well, Carol? Wouldn't your father want to send in the Marines or at least a pack of CIA if the Columbia system was threatened? He's a Presidential candidate, isn't he? I can see the headlines now." I waved my hand, palm out. "'Marines land in Castlegar to protect American interests.' 'Senator Raymond pledges that if elected President he will rid North America of terrorists at all costs.' 'Canadian government signs over security in B.C. interior to the U.S.' 'Just a temporary measure,' says the Prime Minister.' Nice eh?"

Carol didn't answer. Rita spoke. "That's all very interesting, Helen. But it doesn't add up, does it? Where does Ben's murder fit in? Surely that was a mistake. And drugging Carol and trying to trap you. It's … it's all so petty. Compared to what you are suggesting."

"Exactly. The rot sets in. Correct me if I am wrong, either of you." I motioned at Carol and Dean. "I am most interested in Huber's arrival. It hadn't been planned in advance. Shoreman had to be summoned back to his post from Seattle. Now why did Huber come here like that? My guess is that he had been sent to sort out some internal problems within the organization. Most likely dissension in the ranks. Factions. In any case, he was sent for by one of the sides, the more orthodox side obviously. So the trouble was already here when Huber arrived. But he brought more of it with him. The Israelis followed him here. Through him, they identified Shoreman and got a lead on Carol. They picked up on Ben's hints, made contact with me and generally managed to change the problem from one of internal discipline to an external threat to the whole project. How am I doing?"

No one spoke. I continued. "My guess is that the original problem was between the leadership cell on the one hand and Dean-Shoreman on the other. It's a common situation. Differences between the underground part of an operation and the above-ground people. But it must be more than a difference of opinion or tactics. Something more basic."

"God, this is a waste of time." Dean had finally found his voice. "What the hell does it all matter? Play guessing games all you like. Sure, we have problems. You think it's easy? Dealing with stubborn assholes who have no real grasp of the situation, no idea of potential, no imagination yet insist on giving orders. We have to follow instructions. There is a plan and we had to stick to it no matter what. Anything else is 'opportunistic' and 'inauthentic'. Can you believe it! We could have achieved so much!" He was almost shouting.

As if on cue a bullet hummed across the room. Then another and another found their marks in the kerosene lamps. In seconds the room was in pitch darkness and all of us were on the floor.

Phase two of the long night was definitely over. At that moment I wasn't sure whether any of us would survive phase three.

20

COUPLE OF HOURS (at a guess) later I found myself jammed along with two other bodies into a cold, damp space rather too small for all of us. We were underground.

The siege of Women's Acres hadn't lasted long. Possessing only one gun and no extra ammunition against the kind of force exemplified by the accurate snuffing-out of all the lamps in that kitchen, resistance would have been stupid. I gave them no trouble; turned over my gun to the first man through the door. He was medium height, with a five-o'clock shadow and a reassuringly competent way about him. After me he turned his attention to Dean, who was delighted to see him.

"At last, Paul! Hey, give me back my gun and let's go."

"Shut up," said Paul.

"What? What's going on?" Dean struggled against Paul and two other men who followed him in. One carried a big flashlight, the other simple handcuffs which he slipped on Dean as well as Carol and me. As they marched the three of us out I saw Paul turn his flashlight on Rita, Nancy, and Artemis.

"Just stay put. You know nothing. Understand? For your own good."

Paul was a man of few menacing words spoken with a French accent. Their effect on the Acre's women must have been satisfactory because Paul joined us almost immediately. We were helped up into a big gravel truck. The two other men came with us. Paul climbed in with the driver, who had remained outside during this short successful raid. They had pushed the cars off the road with the truck. The dogs had been quietly silenced. Everything had gone like clockwork, with a minimum of talk or expenditure of energy. Professionally. It seemed clear that the security cell was taking over. Presumably under Huber's orders. And Dean was now *persona non grata*.

Our trip was too excruciatingly uncomfortable to permit mellow reflection. Riding in a gravel truck over rough roads with your hands shackled is not recommended. Finally we were off-loaded into the same boat that Win and I got a glimpse of, was it just the previous night? I would've passed out from sheer exhaustion if it wasn't for dear old Dean. He was still trying to catch Paul's attention and persuade him of his commitment and loyalty. Paul remained unmoved. It did give me an insight into — not Dean, I already had his measure — the dynamics of the organization he and Paul were part of.

All through this jaunt Carol said nothing either to us or to our captors. In turn, they ignored her. I wondered how Huber, obviously the heavy, would deal with her. All that, to avoid thinking about my position and how Huber intended to deal with me. Maybe, given a chance, maybe I could convince him that I could be useful to them. Prognosis wasn't good, however. I couldn't think of any really good reasons why they should keep me alive and many good reasons why they shouldn't. Good from their point of view, that is.

Cold hands handed me out of the boat and into another truck. Somewhere in that ride, going over a bump, I passed out. When I came to we were in this damp and crowded prison, tired and discouraged. I had stomach cramps and a bad headache. Feeling that there was nothing to lose, I let out a yell.

"Hey, anybody there?" One of the bodies beside me stirred. It was Carol.

"What are you yelling for?"

"I want out."

"As long as we are here, we're alive."

"My stomach is in a knot. I need a can."

She giggled. "You're nuts to draw attention to yourself. Shit in your pants."

"You really think they might forget we are here? No chance. This is just to soften us up. In any case, I haven't shat in my pants since I was two. And I'm not about to undo my mother's toilet training, either."

Carol giggled again. "OK, I'll help you yell," she said. "I could use a shit myself."

We yelled in unison. Once. Twice. And again. Then there was

light. It flooded through a door, suddenly flung open. I heard Paul's voice and as my eyes accustomed themselves I saw his sturdy figure silhouetted against the strong artificial light.

"What's the matter with you people?" he asked reasonably. Without waiting for an answer he grabbed at Dean and pulled him into the light. Dean was out. Paul let him drop and turned to us again.

"So you two are awake. How come you broads are so tough these days?"

"It's the way we live," I said. "We eat good natural foods, take regular exercise, drink lots of liquid, and get to have a bowel movement at least once a day. This is the time."

Suppressed laugh from Carol. In spite of himself Paul was amused. "Comedy routines. OK. On your feet. You can use the w.c."

We staggered up, our shackled hands almost useless, our legs stiff. Paul watched dispassionately. I was first through the heavy steel-lined door of the room where we had been dumped. A long corridor ran in both directions. Rivulets of water dripped from the rough stone walls. Electric bulbs in wire cages hung down from supporting beams every twenty feet or so. We could just recognize the regular hum of a generator. It felt a long way down. In spite of myself I wondered whether this was to be the place I would die.

We moved in single file to the right, leaving Dean passed out in the storageroom. There was no one else about, no guard other than Paul. Either we weren't considered dangerous or they were low on manpower. But you don't need mere quantity with enough men of Paul's quality. He was good. Smart, efficient, well balanced. He wouldn't be conned, tricked, or caught off-guard. We moved on. I counted our steps. After 20, we turned left. The passage widened into a good-sized space about 10 by 10 metres with an elevator shaft at the far end. The elevator was old but the cables and working mechanism were new. The scope of this operation was becoming more and more evident and impressive.

Next to the shaft a part of the space had been divided off with old boards to about shoulder height. Inside was a portable toilet; essentially a plastic pail with a seat and the unmistakable smell of disinfectant all round it.

I went in first. There was paper and even reading matter. Paul and Carol waited outside.

I took my time sitting on the clammy plastic seat staring at the rough board in front of me. A small star shape scratched into the surface came into focus. I looked closer, concentrating. A mindless doodle? I scanned the surface of the wall in front of me methodically. And there it was. Another star, this time unmistakably the Star of David. And further, well out of easy reach, three letters, WOG, with a hard diagonal scratch through them. One of the Mossad boys was still alive and sanguine enough to produce what must have seemed a useless, hopeless gesture. I looked at the crossed-out initials again. Harry was dead. It had to mean that. But Sid had been alive to leave this message. Although he might be dead by now, I felt lots better. If he'd been left alive long enough to need the can, chances were they had some reason to keep him. It was good to feel less alone here in this underground prison. Maybe, just maybe there was a way out of this hole. I pulled up my pants clumsily and walked out of the toilet. Carol went in past me, her cuffed hands held in front of her. Paul still stood relaxed against the wall, gun tucked into his waistband. He motioned me to wait. I put my back against the wall and stared at the elevator. Cables hummed. Loud clanging sounds came up the shaft. Heavy counter-weights moved smoothly downward as the elevator cage rose and stopped at our level. The door opened with a strange metallic jarring noise and three men walked out. Or rather two walked out and one was dragged out. It was Sid. He'd been worked over. Instinctively I moved towards him until Paul's voice snapped me around.

"Still! Stand still." His gun now in his hand, Paul concentrated on me as his two buddies half-dragged, half-carried Sid past us and down the corridor. I stood back and watched, trying to gauge Sid's condition. His head lolled back, eyes closed, blood running from his mouth and nose. I only had time for one fast look before the three men disappeared, turning the corner in the direction from which we had come. The whole incident took no more than 40 seconds since the opening of the elevator door. Carol rejoined us almost immediately and soon we were walking back to our cell under Paul's careful direction.

Up to this point there had been no exchange between Paul and the other two security thugs but as soon as the steel door clanged behind us, we heard their raised voices. I couldn't recognize the language. I turned to Carol. In the semi-darkness I saw her busy around Dean's prone figure.

"What are they saying?" I whispered urgently. "Can you tell?"

She shook her head. It was Dean who answered. "Paul's Algerian. Good man, Paul." Then he lapsed again into semi-consciousness.

Carol lifted his left eyelid, then the right. "He's been drugged!" she exclaimed.

I chuckled. "Same stuff he gave you, by the looks of him. Serves him right."

"But why? And why not us?"

"Maybe they don't think we are dangerous, being female," I hazarded.

Carol shook her head impatiently. "Don't be silly. Maybe they only had one dose ready."

"Maybe," I answered, with no conviction.

We had our answer almost immediately. The door opened again, Paul came in, followed by the other two men. With no more than a grunt they picked up Dean, carried him out and down the corridor in the direction of the elevator. Paul stood at the door and watched them go. Then he smiled at us and said, "Interrogation. Your turn will come." Then he walked out and slammed the door behind him.

Carol lifted her head. "Listen, Helen. They are softening us up. I am not going down like a lamb. To be slaughtered. No way. We've got to get out of here. Well, what do you say?"

"I don't have any sheep blood in me, either. If I go, I go with a bang." Her teeth flashed white in the darkness. I smiled back.

"Well, what do you suggest?" she asked.

"Listen," I said and proceeded to tell her about Sid. Hurt, wounded, tortured, he was still an ally to count on. Carol found a possible alliance with an Israeli agent hard to swallow. I understood her problem — as a matter of fact, any government agent is automatically suspect in my book — but had no sympathy with squeamishness.

"This is no time to worry about political correctness. Mossad or no, we need all the help we can get. And three is better than two when it comes to a rumble."

"Three? Why not four? How about Dean?"

"That depends. For the moment Huber is treating him as an enemy, but who knows? If he is given a chance to rejoin the club, Dean will be back kissing ass and throwing his weight around. Not so?"

Carol was silent. She shrugged. "That could be true about me too, you know," she said.

"A chance I'll take." I said firmly.

"OK," Carol said with a relieved sigh.

Next we squatted down by the door jamb where a narrow stream of light entered our prison and went through our pockets methodically. Between us we had one Swiss pocketknife, two sets of keys, one packet of cigarettes, three match folders, one package of tissues, half a roll of Lifesavers, one wallet with four credit cards, $83 and a handful of change, a miniature manicure set good for picking locks as well as filing nails, one watch broken and stopped at 6:30, and Dean's map of the area which I had stuffed in my pocket what seemed like ages before.

All this took some time with handcuffs on. We split the Lifesavers between us and contemplated our remaining treasures. Carol pounced on the knife. It did look like it might be a weapon. She was surprised that they hadn't relieved me of it.

"We were taught very carefully how to disarm, search, and now they havn't bothered," she marveled.

"Happens. Paul is a professional. That means he knows really dangerous things from toys. A small folding knife like this is great for opening beer bottles and slicing cheese but as a weapon it wouldn't worry the likes of Paul. And a pick lock is only useful where there are locks. This door is barred on the outside. So much for the tools of my trade. But it's true that they've been a little careless. They should've stripped us and taken all this away. I don't expect they would exactly be scared of us but it's obvious they don't see much possibility of us escaping."

"They could be right," Carol said softly.

"Sure. We are obviously down some old mine which has been renovated and fixed up for a hideout. And underground HQ. It's miles from anywhere, no road from the outside to it, only approach is by water. That much is clear. You've never been here or heard of this place, have you?"

"Oh, I heard there was such a place. But where it is or what goes on here, no. I doubt whether Dean's ever been here either."

"That elevator didn't just rebuild itself. And arms and equipment had to be transported here. Dean must have worked on this." Then a thought struck me. I picked up Dean's map and turned it over carefully. There were faint pencil marks all over it but I couldn't make out anything in the uncertain light.

"We need to examine this under a good light. We have to get out of here." I heard the urgency in my voice.

"Let's call Paul in on some pretext and hit him over the head with a sock full of this stuff here. Money, knife, watch ... it's quite heavy." Carol was hefting our paraphernalia. I smiled.

"That might work on some dumb jail guard but not on Paul. Only thing that would stop him is a bullet."

"Well, he cannot be here all the time. Perhaps we can get at his relief."

"Too late. I hear reinforcements. Quick, let's hide this map. In your boot. Just a chance they won't search you too well." We stuffed Dean's map in Carol's elegant high boot. The rest we distributed back through our pockets. When the door opened again we were huddled together in a corner looking tired and defeated. Tired we were, all right, but defeated, no way.

"Let's go," said Paul.

We were on our way to the elevator to meet Huber.

21

I GUESS IT WASN'T UNTIL we reached the level above that I really grasped the size and importance of the operation we were bucking. Unlike the primitive arrangements below, the main level was fixed up to provide perfect living, working and training quarters for a good-sized group. There was a kitchen, a dining-room and a recreation hall with stereo, piano, table tennis and pool tables, a fully equipped gymnasium, sauna, and a shooting gallery. We glimpsed all this on our way to the interrogation rooms. And at that we only saw part of the place. There was plenty we never saw: corridors and closed doors stretched out in all directions. Storage, communication rooms, offices, I imagined.

This impressive facility was strangely empty. It seemed to await a battalion of men to make full use of it. Apart from Paul and the two men with us, we spotted only four others. They were playing pool and didn't bother to look up as we passed. The place definitely had an unlived-in feeling.

We were led to the end of one of the long passages and through a new, solid wooden door. No flimsy plywood. The inside gave me another surprise. Instead of a bare torture cell as I had half-expected, it was a well-furnished office with desk, comfortable chairs, shelves with books, one locked file cabinet and a nice portable bar. Very civilized. Only the rough ceiling, over-bright lights, and its occupants gave the room away. As we entered, a scream of pain and panic entered with us. It came from an adjoining room. The cozy little office with its civilized decor was an antechamber to hell.

I heard Carol's intake of breath and even one of our captors flinched, making a funny clucking noise deep in his throat. He too had been caught off-guard at the sound of the single scream. There was no other. Dean, for it was Dean, no question, had either passed out or had a gag slapped over his mouth.

It took me a second to realize that the scene had been carefully stage-managed for our benefit. It was clear from the smiling faces of the two men in the room. I looked them over carefully as I sat down on one of the chairs facing the desk. On my left was a short, dark man with deep-set eyes and brows meeting across his forehead. He looked young and very strong. I looked at his hands, thumbs hooked with apparent carelessness into his belt. A familiar gun butt poked out behind his left arm. It was Harry's .22 calibre killer gun. He removed one hand from his belt, revealing a bandaid on the thumb, and waved it at me. He was grinning.

"Bitch bites," he said happily. We had met previously in the VW at the Kaslo campground.

"True," I said and turned my attention to the second man, who sat behind the desk in front of me. It had to be Huber. I realized Carol had not told me anything about him except that Shoreman was scared of him.

Huber waved Paul and his two henchmen out of the room. "Now," he said in perfect, unaccented English. "Now, we can proceed. I am sorry for the unsavory sound effects. Dean is learning how to obey orders. Something you, Carol, will have to learn too. I just hope it's not too late."

The man called Huber looked to be in his forties. Large powerful body, encased in a conservative, expensive 'country' suit of brown tweed, with shining brogues on the feet and a paisley ascot at the throat. His elegantly graying, closely barbered hair fitted his well-shaped head perfectly. His face was full, smooth, with just a hint of tan. He had sharp blue eyes and a large, mobile mouth. Huber was a large, large man. He sat in a solid executive swivel chair and looked at Carol and me without a trace of emotion.

"Yes, Carol will have to be chastised, of course. We haven't got time for any extensive period of reeducation but some discipline is indicated. I am sure Dean will be glad to undertake this task, as soon as he feels a little better himself. Under Emil's instruction, naturally." He nodded at the dark man. "I hope that this unpleasant episode will be over in short order. You and Dean are valuable members of this organization but you mustn't count on my indulgence in the future. Revolutionary cadres must be perfectly disciplined. Always. Do you understand, Carol?" He fixed his eyes on her, waiting for a reply. I held my breath without looking at her.

Her whispered "yes" gave me cold shivers. Huber spoke again immediately.

"Good. That's settled then. You will go with Emil now. Tell him everything you know, everything you heard, everything you suspect, everything that's happened to you in the last 24 hours. I am especially interested in your brief sojourn with Ronald Walters. I want to know more about those three Americans. And of course anything and everything about Helen Keremos here. Clear?"

Again a soft "yes" from Carol. Huber motioned to Emil, who walked up to Carol and without any warning slapped her face. Once, then again on the other side as her head snapped round.

"Take her out."

Carol got up and left the room, closely followed by a smiling Emil.

Huber and I were alone.

"Would you care for a drink?" he said courteously.

Why didn't I throw something at him? Why didn't I fight, even against these hopeless odds? Why hadn't I defended Carol against her pain and humiliation? Why hadn't both of us died right there and then to preserve our self respect if nothing else?

Retorical questions. We had to get this creep. To do that we had to stay alive. It was no cop-out. There was no choice under the circumstances, but to play his game and beat him at it. I accepted a drink and waited.

Across the desk blue eyes contemplated me keenly. I was being evaluated. Perfectly manicured fingertips, trimmed cuticles revealing white half-moons on beautifully shined nails, played with a balloon cognac snifter.

"I suppose you are wondering why you are still alive," he said conversationally.

"I must fit into your plans somewhere, I guess," I replied in the same tone.

"Exactly. You can be very useful if you can be persuaded to cooperate."

"Persuaded?"

"Exactly. I will have to convince you that it is in your best interest to do what I say. Now, how can I do that most effectively?" He paused as if really expecting an answer.

"Fear, threats are very persuasive. Hostages are useful as a method of getting your own way. Of course, that's defining 'best interest' very narrowly."

Huber smiled at me like a schoolmaster at a bright student. "Very good," he nodded. "As long as there is direct fear of death or mutilation, 'best interest' is simply staying alive. However, that doesn't allow the controlling party very much situational flexibility." He stopped again, waiting. I mulled over the apparent direction of his words. His intent was becoming a little clearer but we were a long way from anything definite.

"The issue is options in a situation of limited choice. I must be convinced that doing what you want, even without a gun at my head, is my best, my only option. In other words, that every other possible option will produce even worse consequences."

"Very, very good. That's rational thinking. And what this situation calls for is a rational being. I see that my initial analysis was correct. You are just the person for what I have in mind."

"You mean if I appeared emotional rather than rational I would not be a possible asset?"

"Exactly. You would be only a threat, as indeed you are now, but without any possible useful function. So you would die. It's reasonable, isn't it?"

"Oh, indeed. Very reasonable."

"Good. I am very glad you understand. It makes the next steps so much easier. We are going to discuss the situation. I will tell you how I see it and invite you to point out any holes in my argument. Being a rational person you will soon see that there aren't any and then the action you must take in your own interest will be clear. You will agree to what I may suggest of your own free will."

I sipped my brandy. There was a strange feeling in the small of my back. Creepy. I didn't much like being told I had no choice.

Huber refilled our glasses, opened a fresh box of Cuban cigars, offered me one and, when I refused, lit his with deliberation.

"Now," he said, puffing carefully, "how much do you know about an organization such as ours?"

I made a non-committal sound. He smiled.

"Given your background, I am sure you know a good deal. It really would be simpler not to pretend ignorance. We have a full report on you. From an excellent source. The Mossad." He looked me right in the eye.

"Harry and Sid," I said.

"Harry? Oh yes, the unfortunate ex-member of Unit 101. Emil took a dislike to him. He's dead. But Sid has been most useful. We've kept him in storage, as it were. Every time we have a question we bring him up here and after a little persuasion he tells us what he knows. I think we have just about exhausted his usefulness. Too bad. Yes, from Sid we know about you, about Morris Beach and how the Mossad got onto us. We know you were sent here to find Carol — Sara Ann Rayamond, that is."

"That's how you knew that a message at the Jam Factory would get me." I nodded.

"Exactly. If you hadn't interfered by getting to Carol and borrowing Dean's car, we would have grabbed you safely at the Kaslo campground and all this unpleasantness could have been avoided."

"I am sorry if you were inconvenienced."

"No cheap sarcasm. Certainly I have been inconvenienced. But you cannot take all the credit for it. On the contrary, it was an internal problem." He sighed. I noted he'd used the past tense.

"Good help is hard to get nowadays," I offered.

"I have been inconvenienced by having to come here at all. You don't imagine I like sitting in a hole in the ground in the middle of nowhere when I have important work to do elsewhere?"

"What sort of work?" I asked.

"Would you like to hazard a guess? It's really off our present topic but I would be interested to know whether you have any concept ..."

"I imagine the organization you are a part of functions very much like a multinational conglomerate. My guess is that you are a fairly big head office honcho. As part of some important negotiation in Calgary, something to do with oil probably, you were sent to clear up some internal problem here. What was the trouble?"

"Exactly. Very good. It's a pleasure talking to you." He really seemed pleased. I wondered if he wasn't lonely for someone to talk to, someone who would appreciate him. It was unlikely that Emil would adequately serve this purpose. "Helen, to appreciate the situation properly you must understand that this operation is one of a network of similar facilities which we are establishing throughout the world. Locations are chosen based on various strategic considerations; a unit is sent out to reconnoiter, it produces a feasibility study and, if approved, the operation goes into effect. It sometimes takes up to two years before a base like this is established and ready for use."

"What use? From what you've just said, and from what I've seen here, these bases, as you call them, are not designed with any specific purpose in mind. Just sort of 'on spec'. Am I right?"

"Exactly. The directive calls for 'undercover bases, i.e. safe houses, training and supply facilities to be established throughout the world in strategically important and tactically vulnerable locations.' That's a quotation."

"Go on," I urged, fascinated. "What else does the directive say?"

"Two other instructions are pertinent. There must be adequate local support. It is clearly impossible for us to operate even on a small scale without involvement of local people. Reconnaissance must establish the existence of indigenous support, either current or latent. There has to be a secure above ground component. The other instruction is also common sense. No offensive action of any kind can be undertaken anywhere in the vicinity of the base until it is formally activated by headquarters in line with an overall plan. Until then function of the local unit is strictly preparatory; construction, conservation of equipment and other housekeeping chores. They are not empowered to organize as an offensive unit. So you see the problem." He stopped.

"So you really have no immediate need for these bases. There are no specific plans for their use. What you have is a lot of people who need to be kept busy. The whole thing is a make-work project, and the problem is that the poor slobs involved don't know it. They believe they are part of some gigantic scheme to destroy capitalism, free the workers, and establish a new society." I couldn't keep the awe out of my voice.

"Oh, that is certainly our overall aim. The issue is discipline. All this private initiative is the trouble. Sometimes our own people, like Al Shoreman, are not content to wait quietly for orders in a backwater like this. They have to get mixed up with local talent like Dean and start making independent plans! Empire builders, jumped-up little nobodies endangering the whole enterprise, disobeying orders!"

"Branch plant insubordination, eh. That's the way it is these days. Everyone looking after Number One, with nary a thought for the corporate good."

"There is no question that the caliber of personnel one has to work with nowadays is diverse, to say the least. There was a time we could count on idealistic young people ready to lay down their lives for the cause, disciplined and dedicated. Now what do we get! Gun-struck kids, adventurers, megalomaniacs, fanatics."

"So Shoreman and Dean planned to conquer the U.S.A., not to mention Canada, all on their own. How were they going to do that?"

"Oh, it never got that far. It became clear to local leadership that Dean was having delusions of grandeur. Dreams of some sort of private organization with himself as leader. Nothing is further from his mind that any real revolution."

"And Shoreman?" I asked.

"Very skilled and, with the right direction, useful operator. Needs a strong hand. It wasn't provided. Instead, he got bored, spent too much time with Dean, fantasizing what smart guys they were and how they could run the operation, conduct action, make a name for themselves. To cut a long story short, we were notified by local leadership of what was going on and I was delegated to make a short detour here to sort things out. A month later I am still here." He grimaced. "It's been pretty routine. But it takes time. Security cell had to be reactivated; they'd been badly demoralized through lack of leadership. Now it's just a tidying-up operation. Everything is under control."

"So what do you need me for?" I said, adding "There are some loose ends, aren't there?"

Slowly Huber turned his half-smoked cigar so it would burn evenly.

"Just so. Walters' appearance on the scene is an inconvenience. I don't deny it."

"Walters is here because of the disappearance of Harry and Sid." I stated the obvious again.

Huber waved an impatient hand." We are quite familiar with Walters. I've seen his dossier. He's a professional."

I remained silent. Matters were coming to a head. Huber put down the stub of his cigar, took a sip of cognac, moved his chair closer to the desk, put his forearms on it, pointed at me, and said, "You are going to talk to Walters for me."

"Ah," I said.

"I think the situation is now sufficiently clear for a deal to be made. Listen. You will be dropped off on the main road. I leave it to you to get to Walters." I nodded. "You will tell him that I have a proposition for him and that he'd better listen. One, he's to persuade local law enforcement to accept Harry and Sid as Soteroff's murderers and close the case. We will supply more evidence if required. Two, he's to deal with Beach, tell him to keep his people out of here, and quit making waves. I am sure there is some *quid pro quo* he can offer. Three, he's to cool any unauthorised interest in Carol."

I nodded.

"Now here's what I offer in return," Huber continued. "We will pack up this unit. Close up. Shoreman, Dean and Carol will leave the area for some good, legitimate, above-ground reason. Paul, Emil and the rest will be removed underground the way they came. ARC will be deactivated. I need a month or two of no harassment, no trouble from him, from the Mossad, the RCMP or the CIA. Understand?"

"Why should he go along?"

"Because if he doesn't accept my deal, we will make the Iranian Embassy drama appear like a minor episode by comparison. Potentially, we have all of western U.S. as our hostage. If he sits on all this and lets us pack up quietly he will avoid a major, and I mean major, international fracas not to mention a confrontation between Canada and the U.S."

"What can you actually do from an old hole in the ground, miles from anywhere, with twenty men and a boy? Now who is having delusions of grandeur?"

"We have a lot more than that. Not just here, but across the line. Walters will understand."

"What have you got 'across the line'?"

"We have the ability to trigger a potent media campaign focussing attention on developments here. I mean that, unless it's in our interest, Walters won't be able to keep quiet what happens here. If he tries to mop us up surreptitiously we announce in the States that we have plans to destroy the Columbia water system. Then we just step back and let Walters and Canada take the flack. Now, that's clear, isn't it?"

"Why don't you do it anyway? What would stop you?"

"Let's just say that we would prefer to withdraw from this area quietly. But if we have no choice we will use the opportunity to create an international incident. You and I both know that the Canadians have no option but to let us go, to forget about Ben, Sid and Harry, and to muzzle the Israelis. You will be go-between. Let's get on with it."

"You've made your point. What exactly do you want from me?"

"Here is a schedule of what we want Walters to do and by when." He passed on a single sheet of paper. I read it carefully. He continued. "All you have to do is tell Walters how matters stand, and get his answer. Yes or no. That's all."

"How do I pass on his answer to you?"

"Don't you worry about that. We'll be in touch."

"I was afraid of that."

He laughed. "That's the way it is. Take it or leave it."

I took it. I wanted to live.

Huber glanced at his watch, pushed a button on the intercom, asked whomever answered whether they were ready, hung up and turned to me.

"Before you go I want you to see something. You're quite bright. Much better material than average. You might consider joining us at some point. I realize that right now you are under strain and probably hate my guts, but it won't last. Eventually you will see that we are working for the future. That's all that matters. Individuals don't."

I remained silent.

"You will go next door. Our treatment room. Just like regular mental hospitals. Injection, electric shock. Fuzzes up the nervous system beautifully. You see, we are very up-to-date. There will be hardly be a mark on her, yet after a course of treatment she will be as docile as a lamb. No initiative at all. We need her like that, of course. Senator Raymond's daughter. She will be great on TV, if it comes to that," he added.

"Lovely," I said. "And what about Dean?"

"Him we hurt. Oh yes. He will remember the pain. That's the stick. He will be Carol's control. You understand? That's the carrot. He will act under our orders and through him so will she. There is no need to keep them locked up." Huber leaned back in his chair, smiling happily. "On the contrary, they won't be here very long. And if you plan any rescue operation while they are still here, we will kill them. "

"When do I leave?"

"Oh, no great hurry. Have a good breakfast. See Carol again, and Dean if you like. I would rather you didn't take my word for any of this." He lifted the phone. "Paul? Come get Helen. Feed her and let her talk to Carol and Dean. Then take her out. Usual precautions." He stood up. "It's been a pleasure. Give my regards to Walters."

I too stood up and without another look at him I left the room. Paul was right outside.

The room from which Dean's scream had come was right next door to Huber's office. Large, bright with fluorescent light and fitted out as a cross between an operating theatre and a torture chamber. There were two tables-cum-beds with straps to hold down their occupants. An impressive stainless steel machine, like an electric stove on wheels, with a wired headset plus other attachments on tidily coiled cords. A closed cabinet, presumably holding other instruments without which no up-to-date operation of this kind would be complete. Emil and another man stood at a small table putting things away. In front of them, laid out on a towel, were assorted boxes of hospital quality sponges, ampoules and swabs, and a neat row of scalpels, probes and surgical pliers. They both wore white lab coats and looked rather like your friendly neighbourhood pharmacists. Dean sat on one of the operating tables, his body held stiffly as if avoiding any motion. He was dressed in a shirt and pants — no shoes or socks. I looked for Carol but saw only some of her clothes, including boots, in a heap on the floor. Paul motioned at another door.

"Carol's in there. Go see her. She's dressing."

I nodded without speaking, picked up Carol's clothes, and walked into the closet-sized bathroom. There was a basin with running water, a shower and a chemical toilet with Carol sitting on it. Her eyes focused on me and a small frown of concentration appeared on her face. I held her clothes in front of her.

"Here're your duds. Pants, jacket and boots." All she had on was a shirt. Her underwear lay on the floor. "Thanks for looking after the map for me," I said softly. I took it out of her boot and shoved it behind the waistband at the back of my pants. She smiled weakly, still trying to concentrate.

"I forgot. I guess I forgot about it," she said.

"That's OK. Nobody knew you had it. Now I have it. It's OK." Without consciously intending to, I spoke as if to a child. "D'you need any help?" I asked.

"No. Yes, please. I'm not feeling so good."

I was helping her dress when Dean opened the door and walked in uncertainly, heading towards the toilet to relieve himself. He groaned and almost doubled over at the pain. There was blood in his urine. Very thorough, those gentlemen of the security cell, I thought. Very well trained and efficient. No wasted motion, no silly sadism. Just good, clean, means to an end.

I walked back into the torture room, looked for Paul, and said, "I am ready."

He led me back up the corridor towards the communal kitchen and diningroom. Again we passed the recreation hall. Only two men were at the pool table.

"Now let's have some eats," said Paul. For some reason I had no appetite.

22

Outside it was a beautiful day. I felt it even with the blind-fold which Paul didn't remove throughout the bumpy truck ride, not until we were on the boat well out on the lake. I sat in the cabin below, watching the sun on the foamy water without trying to follow the boat's twists and turns. It wasn't possible anyway. I couldn't see any landmarks, I had no watch to time our changes in direction. All I could feel was the sun. Our general direction was south but that wasn't any help. They dropped me off at a spot on the map called Kaskonook, near Creston at the southern end of Kootenay Lake. Paul waved as they left with a flash of bright water. The place was nowhere. It took me four hours to get to Nelson and another to contact Walters.

Sitting at the Jam Factory restaurant and waiting for the car Walters was to send for me, I tried to imagine what else I could do besides go along with Huber's orders. There was no phone at Women's Acres so I couldn't get in touch with them. I had no idea how to reach Win. So I called Jessica at home in Vancouver. No answer. Then Alice. No answer. Finally I left a message on their office tape. One of them would pick it up next day. That made me feel better until I realized it was Saturday. No one would be in the office tomorrow.

Feeling mightily alone I sipped my third coffee. I felt a man beside me. He touched my arm. It was Walters' agent. I rose and left. Outside I got into Walters' very average totally incon-spicuous car and let myself be driven to his trailer headquarters. There was nothing else I could think to do.

Ronald Walters presided over his phalanx of machines — com-puter, copier, teletype, shredder, radio, telephone, typewriters, electric pencil sharpener, coffee maker, tape recorders and doubtless an assortment of weapons — wearing a sporty blue-green checked shirt, beige pants of fashionable cut and cowboy boots with modified heels. 'Weekend in the country' attire. All new and already looking tacky. There was something about

Walters which made elegance impossible.

I watched him pour out two cups of coffee. He put one of them down in front of me without a glance in my direction. There was no sign of that ebullience of the day before.

"Treasury Board cut the agency's appropriations?" I hazarded.

He allowed himself a weak grin.

"What spoiled your day?" I continued.

Walters sighed and ran his hand over his bald spot. I speculated on the amount of time that I spent in this case talking to powerful men hidden behind desks. Walters and Huber were different yet had much in common. They were both managers and executives making decisions in small rooms surrounded by bureaucratic paraphernalia. How much did they actually know first-hand? How much did they have to rely on subordinates and outside documentation? My wondering mind was brought up short by a copy of *Newsweek* being thrust in front of my face.

"Look at that." Walters smacked the magazine onto the desk. Prominent on the cover was the serious senatorial face of Republican candidate for President of United States Raymond of Arizona. Under it ran the legend 'Republican Front-Runner on the Trail of the Nomination'. "According to this rag he's a shoo-in for the nomination in July. That's a month away. With a good chance in November," Walters continued.

I thought about the timing. I nodded and said, "So? Why this sudden interest in American civics?"

"So my information is that Carol Latimer, whom you talked me into letting you take away from here, is this bum's daughter. Where is she, Helen?"

To gain time I picked up the magazine and glanced through the pages. Words, photos danced in front of my eyes.

"It's a long story, Ron."

"It had better be good. Oh, boy. President's daughter! And I let you walk out of here with her and lose her!" I didn't much like the look in his eye.

"When do we expect the Marines? Did her fingerprints trace her?" I concentrated on the magazine.

Reluctantly Walters quit glaring at me, sat down and picked

up a pencil.

"No. Soon as I heard who she might be I cancelled the trace. It never reached Washington. But ..."

"Good. Then there is a chance." I closed the magazine and threw it down. "Let me tell you my story." And proceeded to do so without omitting very much. Walters listened attentively. Finally he grunted.

"That checks out with my information ..."

"Information from who?" I asked.

"Now, Helen, you know that's out of the question."

"Let me guess. Echo. He's got to be your agent here."

"Yes. But no way is Huber getting that."

I waved an arm at him. "Cool it. He won't. But I had to know. By the way, how did you recruit him?"

Walters was glad to oblige. "It's the usual story. We picked him up on the coast just as he was about to get 2-less-a-day for punching out some Macmillan-Bloedel employee. There was talk of damage to a company truck, too. It seemed a bunch of hippies squatted on company land, piece of coast on Galiano Island. Locals got pissed off with their goings-on and got Mac 'nd Blow to burn and bulldoze the whole bunch of weirdos right into the sea. There was a bit of a fracas. We moved in and handpicked Echo in the melee. Echo was quite a hero, a real hot-shot activist. It's always useful to have someone inside." Walters grinned.

"That must have been long ago," I said.

"Oh, sure. Seventies. He did four months then trained in the U.S. and then moved here to keep an eye on things for us. And people. The radical Doukhobors, American draft dodgers. Other subversives. Nothing much happened until last year. Then bingo. It all paid off." He looked at me, willing me to make a dumb comment, to disapprove.

"Congratulations. How does he get his information?"

"Informants. Gossip. The usual." Walters wasn't so uncomfortable any more.

"And what has he been feeding you? Anything you can confirm independently? Anything that couldn't be common knowledge?"

Walters shook his head. "He had some very specific information about sabotage on the Columbia. That's what brought me here. It occurred to me that he could've been had, but it's unlikely."

"If you say so. It was just a random thought." I lied. "What do you make of it all, Ron? You gonna go along with Huber?"

He looked at me fixedly for a minute. "Go along? Sure I will, as far as it goes. I can leave, write off the Israelis, close the Soteroff case. Nothing to that. But Huber doesn't expect me to believe him, does he? And I wouldn't believe me if I were him either," he added as an afterthought.

"All he really wants from you is time, that's clear."

"Time." Walters nodded. "Hell, who's he think he's kidding anyway? This Carol is his trump card. Supposing Raymond gets elected Pres of the U.S. And terrorists have his daughter. What a gift!"

"Yeah. That's why he's so ready to evacuate here. But wouldn't want to use her until after her papa's been elected. So he's bluffing. Think of the opportunity he could lose if it got out before the election that a nominee's daughter was a hostage. Especially a willing hostage. Remember Patty Hearst."

"I remember," he said and fell silent. Wheels were turning. "It's not bluff if I don't dare call it. Oh well. We'll see. You can tell Huber I'll play it his way. At least until after the Republican Convention. If Raymond doesn't get nominated things will be a little easier. Of course, I'm not responsible for what you or your private army care to do in the interim."

"My private army?" I asked, taken aback.

"Yes. Three of your friends from Vancouver just happened to drop in. They are in a hotel in Kaslo. Our old pal Frank Hanusek, a fancy lawyer-lady Jessica Tsukada, and a sharp-lipped youngster called Alice Caplan. They say they are here for the weekend."

"Ah," I managed to say. But I was grinning too.

I wanted to be gone. To see Jessica, Alice and Frank. To take a look at the map at my back. To figure out some of the odd angles in this case. So I asked for and got a lift to Kaslo. As I left, for the first time in my life I felt sorry for Ronald Walters and his kind. Not very sorry, but a little.

23

WALTERS' SILENT AGENT dropped me off on Kaslo's main street. I walked to the nearest hotel. On the way I picked up a copy of the same *Newsweek* that Ron Walters had waved at me, and a *Time* magazine for good measure. I wanted confirmation of a crazy idea cruising through my head.

I got as far as the hotel lobby when a tall, skinny guy with a silvery crewcut, a pipe and a nice smile rose up from one of the battered old armchairs.

"Frank," I said, delighted.

"No other," he said, grabbed my arm with both hands and shook it. "You're OK."

"Yes. But only just. Where's Jessica and Alice? We can't talk here."

"Upstairs, Room 31. We've been taking turns scouting for you."

"Great. Let's order some sandwiches and beer. I've got lots to tell you."

A few minutes later we were tapping gently in rhythm on the door of Room 31. It opened on the chain and Alice's eye peered out for a second. Then the door sprang open and we were welcomed in.

It's difficult to describe the pleasure I felt on seeing Jessica and Alice. We exchanged frantic hugs and glad cries. I am considered pretty tough; it helps in my kind of business. But my kind of tough doesn't mean unfeeling! An outsider might have concluded that the three of us hadn't seen each other for months, if not years. But it was only an indication of the bonds between us magnified by our common awareness of isolation and danger.

Throughout it all Frank stood by grinning sheepishly. Without directly sharing in our relationship, he was a staunch friend, honest and supportive. He, too, was happy to be there, glad to see me safe, and keen to help. If he thought that Alice, Jessica and I were over-dramatic in our greetings, or took too long to get down to business and generally didn't behave like proper naval persons, he didn't say so. Ability to react spontaneously as we did had long been destroyed in him, leaving only a little simple embarrassment and a lot of deep-seated longing. He wished he could but he couldn't. This lack discomfited him and he accepted it as a weakness on his part, not as a strength.

"I've got so much to tell you." I started to pull myself together and finally begin. I felt an urgency, a need to be up and doing just when I had to sit down to talk and plan. The presence of these three people — my private army, as Walters had called them — stimulated my appetite for action together with my imagination. I again felt able to affect events rather than merely endure them. I was tired of being an object, a chess piece in other people's games. Sure, I could just leave Huber and Walters to fake each other out. They were masters at it, manoevring to win points, to preserve their special empires. Damn them. It was too personal now.

I looked around the shabby hotel room. After the initial emotional outburst everyone was busy settling down. Alice flipped the caps off four beer bottles and shared out the sandwiches. I pulled out the map from behind my back and set it squarely in front of me together with the two magazines. Jessica leaned over with interest.

"What's this?" she said, picking up the map.

"With any luck it will pinpoint for us exactly where I spent the last 24 hours," I couldn't resist saying. Frank reached for the map.

Jessica held out her hand and stopped him. "Helen, quit grandstanding. What's been happening, eh? Come on, Helen. I know you will play to the gallery given an opportunity. I didn't come all this way, missing a good sailing weekend, to participate in guessing games."

Alice and Frank looked a little taken aback at what appeared to be an unwarranted attack. But I knew that while they might be enjoying themselves, seeing the whole thing as an adventure, Jessica, fully aware of the reality of danger, hated the whole process. She wanted solid facts, detailed plans and fast resolution. She didn't get off on the romance of action. It was only a means to an end to be attained as quickly and simply as possible.

So she could go back to the satisfying, controllable life of law practice and sailboat.

I took a bite at my sandwich, swallowed and smiled at Jessica, letting Alice and Frank know everything was OK.

"Right. Quite right. Let me fill you in."

Very carefully I explained everything that had happened since my trip to Vancouver, with some special detours for the benefit of Frank who wasn't as up-to-date as the two women. I went over Ben's death and my ideas about it. Frank wanted to know how Ben had died.

"Good question," I answered. "Nobody's talking about that very much. Official version at the moment is that he was killed by a 9 mm. at close range. He'd been shot all right but whether that's how he died, I've my doubts."

"You're suggesting he was killed elsewhere and transported, by boat, to the park road. Right?"

"Yeah. So suspicion could be thrown on the two strangers in the station wagon. Quite a nifty plan but it's coming unstuck. Now I'd better tell you about Carol Latimer, Women's Acres, and L'il Abner Dean." And I went on, with frequent interruption from one or the other of my attentive audience. They were all fascinated with the women at Women's Acres. Alice thought she'd heard of Nancy but couldn't be sure. Anyway, we discussed the practical implication of their political position vis à vis Carol and 'the ARC gang', as Frank had started to call them.

"How can they be so naive? I know lesbian feminists who hold separatist sentiments, but this is absurd, surely!" said Alice.

"Their politics aren't really separatist, not considering that they offer unconditional shelter and support to a straight woman like Carol whose political activism is hardly on a feminist model. To me they seem highly principled if somewhat unrealistic," was Jessica's comment.

"Their politics work as long as the outside world is kept out. Once it stops working as it has now, it does become a trifle absurd. But there is internal consistency in Rita's position, you know. She isn't interested in being 'realistic', she isn't a fair-weather feminist with principles to fit the circumstances. Nancy is just as principled but different. She suspects that it's virtually impossible to live as a lesbian separatist and be a feminist activist at the same time," I commented.

"The fact is that their space was invaded by men with guns and people were removed against their will. So much for sanctuaries from the male world." Alice was a lesbian and a fledgling feminist with no patience for anyone who choose to withdraw from the fray for any reason. Wisely, Frank didn't comment.

"Yes. Will they ignore the whole episode, pretend it never happened, pretend it doesn't concern them? Just burrow deeper. Or will they do something to defend the integrity of their life and their chosen position?" Jessica went on.

"Personally, if someone just walked into my place and snatched people, I would be angry as hell. Not to mention concerned at what happened to those people. That's what I am counting on; enough anger and concern on the part of the Acres women to get them acting along with us," I said. "But I am getting ahead of myself. Let me go on." Quickly, I described the underground base, Dean's disposal, and my glimpse of Sid. Then I plunged into the scene with Huber, sparing them no detail. Smiling Emil; Carol's reaction; the torture room and Huber. Huber and his offer to Ronald Walters. All three listened attentively. Fear, horror and anger chased each other across Alice's mobile face. Frank held the bowl of his long-cold pipe with both hands and bit the stem. Jessica sat totally still, her eyes big. Somewhere in my narrative I turned to Frank.

"Somehow, I don't think calling this operation 'the ARC gang' is very appropriate, Frank. That suggests just a bunch of hoods. They cannot be dealt with on that basis."

Jessica had been listening silently. As usual she had picked up more than the others.

"Helen. That's not all there is, I can tell," she said. "You've got something up your sleeve, haven't you? For God's sake, let's have it and get on with it," she said. There was no sharpness in her voice. Just quiet confidence and determination. Jessica's authority was so innate, it was hard to resent. Besides, she was so bright!

I picked up the copy of *Newsweek* and started to flip through it. "I've told you exactly what happened so you can draw your own conclusions. But here is a kicker." I laid the magazine open on the little coffee table, got out my wallet and took Carol Latimer's picture out of it. I put it down on page 5 of *Newsweek*, next to a photograph of a family group. The caption under it read: "Senator Raymond and (left to right) wife Ruth, sons John and Lee, daughter Sara Ann, celebrating the Fourth of July, 1967 at their Arizona ranch. The last time together." A snapshot of the all-American family. Three heads bent over the table to examine the two pictures. Jessica first looked up at me, then down again. Frank said nothing, sucking at his pipe. Alice was first to burst out.

"But that's not Carol! I mean that's not Sara Ann!"

"Right. The 1967 photograph I was given by my clients in San Francisco, remember them? is not of Sara Ann Raymond in 1967. That's for sure. But it is a photograph of a woman we now know as Carol Latimer. So Carol isn't Sara Ann Raymond. There is a resemblance and it's possible to confuse present-day Carol with this old picture of Sara Ann in the family group. But the two pictures taken in the same year are of different people. Carol Latimer is not the long-lost daughter of Senator Raymond, Presidential candidate. Now, what does that do to our case?"

24

IT IS LIKE SHAKING a kaleidoscope. The coloured pieces shift position. They remain the same but the picture changes.

It was clear that my clients were phonies and that the purpose of my being hired was to connect Carol Latimer with Sara Ann Raymond and draw attention to her.

The Hardy boys, who had to be John and Lee Raymond, were sicked onto me to confirm Sara Ann's presence in the West Kootenays. Of course I could not be allowed to find Carol and certainly neither could they. Just traces of her. Presumably all this was designed to lend credibility to any blackmail demands on old man Raymond. Having a fugitive for a daughter is not good for Presidential chances; having one who is a hostage of terrorists is deadly. And whose grand scheme was this? Not Huber's. He'd only appeared on the scene a month ago. It took much longer than that to set up the plan. Clearly this was the private enterprise of the trio of Dean, Shoreman and Carol. For she had to be in it. The key figure. This thought really shook me for a while as the four of us mulled over all the possible permutations and possibilities revealed by the shadowy photographic images. It certainly changed my feelings about Carol.

Jessica sighed, snapped open her briefcase impatiently, took out a pad of paper, a pen, and said, "All right. Let's get some order into this chaos. How many different participant groups can we identify and what do we know about each. Helen? You start."

"Huber and the security cell. Whatever Dean and Shoreman worked up previously, it's Huber who's in charge now."

"I knew you would start with Huber," said Jessica, shaking her head. "Never mind. Let's go back in chronological order so we can follow the process."

"Huber is on my mind. And for good reason. But OK. Here goes." I lifted a finger. "First comes the Raymond Conspiracy group — let's call it that for convenience. Includes my clients Pat and Bob in San Francisco, who passed Carol's photo for

Sara Ann's, presumably Dean, Shoreman and positively Carol Latimer." I stopped. No one spoke. I continued. "I have no idea where Carol stands at the moment. Or what their moves might be in any given situation. Damn!"

I continued quickly. "Next, Israeli Intelligence — Beach in Vancouver and Harry and Sid here. The last two are dead."

"You don't know for sure Sid's dead," corrected Frank.

"That's the probability," I replied and went on. "Then there are the women at the commune. Plus probably quite an extensive network both locally and on the coast. Rita and Nancy are the key people. They are another question mark." I sighed. "Who's next? Oh yes. Echo and Win. We know Echo works for Ron Walters but I rather think he's playing some little game of his own. And Win ... I have a theory about Win." I hesitated. "We should count Win as one of the 'local leadership'. I am not 100 per cent sure but I'll bet he's one of this nebulous unidentified group who sent for Huber. Or, more correctly, complained to Headquarters about Dean, Shoreman and Carol's shenanigans. Huber is what they got and I suspect it was a lot more than they bargained for."

"Whoa, there!" said Alice. "I've nothing against wild guesses but how did you get this sordid idea? I thought Win was an OK guy from your description, and now you are saying he's a mad dog of a terrorist."

I was about to reply when Frank broke in. He was standing now, waving his hands and his inseparable pipe.

"Yes, yes. We sit here talking about this and that; terrorists, security cells, plots. Who are these people? Who is Huber? What do they want! Doesn't this organization have a name, a location, a leader? I've heard of the Baader-Meinhof gang and the Red Brigades. Is that where Huber and Shoreman come from? I want to get a handle on all this."

"Yeah, don't tell me Win goes around kneecapping people," broke in Alice. "I still don't see where he fits in."

"Terrorism comes in many shapes, sizes and flavours. Various national liberation groups start out using it as a tactic. Like the Basques in Spain and Uruguayan Tupamaros. And the PLO and the IRA. Then there are the right-wing execution squads. Remember Argentina, Mao Blanco, El Salvador? Violence attracts. And the people it attracts aren't necessarily in it for the highest motives. It becomes common banditry and takes on a life of its own. Look, terrorism is a growth industry these days. It spins off, it adapts, it multiplies like an amoeba. For various reasons there are countries which support it, train personnel, supply money. Naturally there are connections between groups, there are factions, a lot of personal enterprise, attempts at control. It proliferates. This day and age provides an excellent environment for proliferation of violence. As with any other growth area, it throws up big and small units; successful and less so amateurs and professionals both get into the act. You keep thinking in terms of established institutions. But the name of this lot doesn't matter. It isn't registered in any bureaucracy. Anyone can use any name, any time. Leaders, operators change names, locations, faces. All we know about this outfit is that it has long-range plans. That's unusual. And that Huber ties in with oil. That's not unusual. And that it issues directives and seems to have a surplus of personnel. That's dangerous. Perhaps someone is building an underground empire, using long-time professional operators like Shoreman and Huber and amateurs like Win and Dean. Local people like Win and Dean would be told whatever would sell them. Naivety is very dangerous. For Dean it is a return to his activist days. Promise of power and excitement. A great recruiting tool. Ask the Armed Forces advertising agency."

"And Carol?"

"We know nothing about Carol. But I bet her background is pretty close to that of the real Sara Ann. Probably arrived in Canada with some American draft resister, like Dean. Maybe it was Dean. They knew about Sara Ann Raymond, perhaps knew her personally. Figured out a scheme to impersonate her. It wasn't part of any overall plan of the organization but private initiative. Just taking advantage of an opportunity. It's meant trouble all round. Perhaps that's what the squabble was about between the ARC cell people — Dean, Shoreman, Carol — and the leadership cell people — like Win and ..." I stopped. Who else? Echo? Could he have been turned? It was possible. Especially given his background and the circumstances of his recruitment by Ronald Walters' boys. Who else? Who would I recruit if I were setting up a base in this area? Doukhobors? For sure someone in the Doukhobor community. It stood to reason. Ben. What if Ben had been in local leadership! I was getting lost in what ifs and perhapses.

"OK. OK. We get the picture. What we are interested in now is getting out there and doing something about it all. Here and now," Alice interrupted my momentary silence.

Jessica nodded and put away her notepad with the list partly completed. "I don't think we really have enough data to go at this systematically. I can make lists but so what? It won't help. So I agree with Alice. We need to get going."

Jessica was famous for stepping out of character like that and surprising everybody.

"But, but," Frank sputtered. "What do we do?"

"We follow Helen's nose. Right, Jessica?" Alice said smiling.

"I think so. Helen, you work on hunches, don't you? Just off the top of your head, what's the next step?"

"Well, I don't usually have this number of people to have hunches for. Just me."

"What would you do if you were alone, then?" Jessica continued to deal with me as if I was a backward child. Without a second thought I reached for the map. Dean's map with all its markings.

"I would try to get back to that underground base. With reinforcements. And damn Ron Walters."

"Didn't Huber tell you that Dean and Carol wouldn't be there? Perhaps no one would be. Anyway, how can you believe this map? It could be a trick. You cannot trust Carol now."

"Why not? Because she isn't Sara Ann Raymond? You know what just struck me? That Huber doesn't realize she's a fake! That he's taken over the impersonation plot not knowing it's an impersonation! He's threatening Walters with putting Carol on TV. He wouldn't dare do that unless he thought she was

Sara Ann. Nobody told him different."

"If Huber is proceeding out of this mistaken idea then he's likely to keep on with the blackmail because he thinks he has all the cards. Once that certainty is shaken he could do anything. Kill Carol, for sure. Maybe blow the dams. Damn!"

"We cannot call his bluff because he doesn't realize it's a bluff. So where does that get us?"

"Back to square one," I said. "Let's go find Win. He's been looking for me, I've been told. Let him find me."

"What about us?" Alice was impatient for action.

"Sit tight." Before anyone could object I left the room. All this rapping to and fro wasn't getting us anywhere. If you want action, go out and rattle somebody or something. It's always worked for me in the past. It had better work now.

25

I WALKED DOWN THE STAIRS. In the lobby the first person I saw was Win. He stood in shadow against an outside wall, next to the window, waiting. Although it was Saturday he had his work clothes on; boots, workpants, check shirt, combat jacket and a baseball hat. He looked tired and uncertain. Very unlike the bright, determined man of the day before. Suddenly he turned towards the outside door. I saw Rita's dark head and high, tense shoulders among a group of tourists barging in through the swing doors. Simultaneously she saw me and so did Win. For a split second all of us stood quite still. Then Win and I started off towards Rita who immediately turned and ducked out the door again. Seconds later the three of us found ourselves together on the sidewalk outside the hotel. Rita stopped, turned to me, and smiled.

"You OK." It was half statement, half question.

I nodded, childishly pleased at her smile and her concern.

I looked up and down the comfortable, busy, Saturday-afternoon-in-a-small-town street. A car was stopped in mid-street, blocking an intersection while the grizzled driver conferred with a woman with a baby buggy. Three youths with incipient Burt Reynolds moustaches and flashy vests shouldered their way into the liquor store. Kitty-corner from where we stood, two friends had just met and stopped in front of the post office on their way to pick up their mail. A daily ritual neither would miss for the world. They conferred earnestly. It was busiest around the IGA grocery store. The consistent traffic was generally unhurried and good-humoured except for an occasional worried looking Mama and Papa weighed down with grocery bags and small children. A RCMP constable walked out smiling from the corner gas station, followed by a gesticulating owner. He said a few soothing words, nodded briefly at a passer-by, and got back into his cruiser. I heard the crackle of his radio. He spoke a few words into the mike, smoothly and efficiently executed an illegal U-turn and drove out of sight. Without being aware of it, all three of us relaxed. Rita's greeting to me was followed by an awkward moment of uncertainty and indecision.

Rita broke the momentary stalemate. "Let's go to the car. We'll fill you in," she said and moved off to the right without waiting for us. "The less visible Win can be, the better," she added. At least now I knew she and Win were allies. But why was Win in danger in the street? I didn't ask but followed her obediently.

We turned a corner and there was my jeep! It was almost nostalgic to see its businesslike lines, piggy snout and big black all-weather tires. The door swung open and Nancy's face appeared. She gave a brief grin of welcome. Without a word Rita and Win scrambled into the back. I got behind the familiar wheel.

"Get this crate out of here. We'll talk as you drive," Nancy said.

I started the engine and moved out gently into the stream of traffic. It was obvious that Rita and Nancy had things under control. This was my day for picking up friends and allies.

"Where to?" I asked.

"Thrums. The Soteroff place."

I glanced back at Win. He looked depressed, if not despairing.

"Win," I said tentatively.

"Yeah, Helen. It's all over. I've been a fool. I guess you know that."

"Never mind. We'll get it all sorted out."

In the rear-view mirror Win's face showed pale as if all the warmth and colour had drained out.

"I hope so. I sure hope so," he said, but there was little conviction in his voice. "I think they are after me."

An impatient movement from Rita and the need to cope with traffic leaving town brought me up short and reminded me of my three other allies still cooped up in Room 31.

"I left some friends of mine in that hotel. We should bring them along or at least tell them where I'm going."

"Helen, we discussed it and decided not to involve any outsiders. Like your friends. You can call them later."

"Oh, I'll call them all right. But don't you think we'll need all the help we can get? I am not clued in on the situation here and you seem to have changed your mind about becoming involved in male politics. Would Win have something to do with it?" I don't know whether it sounded snarky or not.

"Oh, come off it, you two," Nancy said impatiently. "Yes, it has to do with Win but only indirectly. After you and Carol and Dean were snatched, consensus was to take action. As a start we contacted Win. We knew you were meeting with him so we reckoned he would give us a lead. Well, he did."

"I told them of my part in all this. Everything was falling apart anyway. They'd killed Ben. I had to do something. So I got a boat and this afternoon we went over to Terra-One base. Where you had been held."

As he spoke my excitement mounted. Terra! Now we had at least one name. Frank would be pleased. Win continued with difficulty. "It was empty. Quite empty. They had completed evacuation. When we got back we got word that you were out and about. So I looked for you in Kaslo. Rita and Nancy came to pick me up and here we are. No further ahead. Sorry." He lapsed into silence.

"Oh, I wouldn't quite say that," Rita commented quietly. "We've found Shoreman. And we have him cornered."

Win woke up. "You have Shoreman cornered! I don't believe it! Where? How?" he shouted.

"Well, you know we went to Ursula's place. Guess what happened. Albert Shoreman. He came in, very scared, waving a gun. So we took it away from him but he had another and he's holed up in the root cellar." What Nancy's description lacked in colour and detail it sure made up in impact. Instinctively my foot grew heavier on the gas pedal. The jeep jumped forward in a hurry to get to Thrums.

"You took away his gun," Win repeated unbelievingly. "And have him holed up in the root cellar. Who's keeping him there?"

"Artemis. She has his gun. She's to keep him pegged down until we get there."

I thought of Artemis in connection with guns. I remembered tools scattered about the Women's Acres yard and Laura's scathing comments. Then I thought of Shoreman, the weapons expert. And shook my head.

"I just hope she's all right," I said.

"Don't worry, she is," Nancy said with conviction.

"Where's Ursula? Was she there when you left? Was anyone?" Win asked urgently.

"No." The single monosyllable hung in the air. Win sighed, I think with relief.

We were speeding along the lake road, south. Soon we would reach Nelson and the road down to Thrums. Suddenly I felt very afraid for Artemis. I stepped on the brake and pulled over to a squealing stop at a roadside telephone booth.

"Anyone got a quarter?" I asked. Nobody asked me why I'd stopped or who I intended to call. I expect Rita and Nancy were having some second thoughts about the spot in which they had left Artemis. The heat of accomplishment was cooling off. Win looked dully in front of him doubtless regretting more than just this day's events. I got Room 31 and gave Alice my message. Back in the car we took up our breakneck speed. The whole thing had only taken three minutes. But you can go five miles in three minutes. My jeep's four-cylinder engine whined at corners, tires spitting gravel. I prayed we weren't stopped by any officious Mounties like Carol's American captors had been.

We reached Nelson. I had to concentrate on driving through the bustling little town just winding down from Saturday afternoon and winding up for Saturday night. We were lucky. No cops.

26

I ALMOST OVERSHOT the side road leading to the Soteroff place. The wide rutted road ran between small fields. A checkerboard of fruit trees, vegetable patches, corn and pasture studded with cows and horses. There were no houses immediately on this road, and only a few at the far end facing the next side road. I realized how isolated this place was as I pulled the jeep through the wide, easy turn-circle just inside the gate. The little farm was tucked in under the mountain. It looked peaceful, bucolic. The front yard with fruit trees under which I had sat with Win, Echo and Ben (not to mention the dog), and the sturdy farmhouse came in sight first. The farmyard and outbuildings were hidden behind, showing only a bit of shining barn roof reflecting the evening light. I came to a halt and looked about. There was no movement from the house.

"So where's the root cellar? We've got to find Artemis. If she's still here, alive and well," I said without much hope. "Win, you know this place. So play scout and reconnoiter. We have to know the situation before we go in en masse."

"I know this place too, and I know where we left Artemis. She might shoot Win by mistake if he just shows up."

I could understand that. Rita didn't like my taking charge but that was no reason to let her do anything stupid.

"Rita, it must be three, four hours since you left Artemis here holding an unfamiliar gun on a guy who's an expert with them. What are the chances the situation has remained the same?"

"I bet she's still got him. Artemis is a good woman. Everyone sells her short because she's a bit spacy but I know what she can do," Rita said stubbornly.

"OK, OK. Both of you go. But one at least must come back here and report immediately."

Win and Rita ducked out of the jeep and after some waving of arms and whispered discussion set off towards the buildings, one following the right-hand fence and the other dodging from fruit tree to tree. Nancy and I sat like spectators in the front seat of the jeep, watching.

"Should we let them go in like that, alone?" she whispered.

"No. I sure would rather not. But all we have is one rifle. It would be dumb to act like U.S. cavalry. Let's see what happens. It's sound strategy not to commit all your forces at once. Follow?"

"You're probably right. It's the smart thing to do. But I cannot let Artemis and Rita deal with this alone. I've got to go too." She opened her door and stepped out.

"Oh, all right. Let's all go," I said. "I'm getting pretty itchy sitting here myself. You follow Rita, I'll take the other side. OK?"

"OK," she said, and completely ignoring my suggestion started directly down the path past the house at a dead run.

"Shit!" I said, tucked my Remington .30.30 under my arm and followed her. What else could I do?

Shots rang out when we were barely halfway to the farm buildings. Not at us. Just shots on the other side of the house. Handgun, it sounded like.

"That's where the root cellar is," panted Nancy over her shoulder and speeded up. It was doubtful that she could really tell where the shots came from, but the cellar was as good a place as any to start. We passed the house and turned the corner into the barnyard. Instinctively I threw myself against the barn wall behind a pile of manure and took a good look around. For a change Nancy followed my example. At first glance there was nothing to be seen. Then Nancy pointed at the open door of the root cellar. It faced us on the left in a direct line between the house and the barn. The chicken coop and implement shed were on the right side of the yard. Two large gravel trucks, conspicuously marked 'ARC', sat across the yard from us. So far, so good.

"Psst, psst." Someone was trying to get our attention through the barn wall. The barn was made of single boards, with no fancy dovetailing.

"It's me, Artemis. Nancy, is that you?" Artemis's forlorn voice sounded in my ear. She was barely inches away, on the other side of the thin weather-beaten board.

"It's me, it's me. And Helen. Are you all right?" Nancy answered back.

"I am fine. But where is Rita? I hope she's OK. They are all in there, you know. Across the yard. In the root cellar. They've been shooting at me sporadically just so I keep my head down ...."

"Who's there? Who are you talking about, Artemis?" I broke in urgently.

"Dean and a bunch of the other guys. One of them, called Paul, is the guy who came to get you at Women's Acres. I don't know the others."

"In the root cellar?"

"Yes. They arrived in those two trucks and started unloading stuff. Then they realized something was up. You see, I took a shot at Paul. That's how they found out I was hiding here."

"You shot at Paul! Why on earth did you give yourself away like that?"

"He was carrying a machinegun. Sort of little but I didn't like it so I shot him so he couldn't use it."

"You mean you hit him! With a handgun!"

"Oh, yes. It's not far. He shouldn't have invaded our space like he did. Men are a menace." Artemis seemed quite serious and unconcerned.

I tried to get my mind around her information. "What 'stuff' were they unloading? And where did they disappear to?"

"Just stuff. In crates. Very heavy. And they went down the cellar. Where Shoreman disappeared. I haven't seen anyone since. They just send a couple of bullets in this direction." Artemis was uninterested in my questions. "They were just like Alice's white rabbit, going down that hole. Never appeared again."

"What about Shoreman? Has he shown?"

"Haven't seen him since Rita and Nancy left me on guard here."

"Is there another entrance to that cellar?" I asked the obvious question. I knew by now that there had to be. But neither Nancy nor Artemis knew anything about any other entrance.

"Where's Rita, for God's sake?" said Nancy.

"Yeah, and Win."

"He went in the direction of the house," I said, trying to

remember where Rita was when I saw her last. "And if that cellar has another entrance it might well be in the house."

Instinctively both Nancy and I peered at the entrance to the cellar. Both sides of the solid wood double door had been flung open against the earthen sides of the burrow, which looked for all the world like a back-garden bomb shelter. Except the doors were too big for that. They looked wide enough for a pickup although not for any five-ton gravel truck. Some root cellar! I thought. No farm had any business with anything like this. The house was a good 200 metres away but a tunnel wasn't inconceivable under the circumstances. I began to have my suspicions about dear old Ben of sainted memory, and perhaps the hard-to-find Ursula. The kaleidoscope moved. The outlines of the case shifted again. 'Local leadership' — wouldn't Huber's minions sent to research this area have instructions to recruit representatives from each main group? Wouldn't their bosses insist on having a Doukhobor on board? I would, in their place. Douks, Indians, American 'new people' ...

Another thought occurred. Who was in on the Sara Ann impersonation? I recalled the ARC foreman. He gave me Carol Latimer with no problem. Obliging and garrulous. Very convenient. People in the coop, woman in an apron, then Dean. Had I been passed along from hand to hand, so to speak? At each step the identity of Carol as Sara Ann Raymond confirmed, solidified. But she couldn't be found or shown on TV as Huber had threatened.

The ultimate purpose of the original conspirators was clear. Prevent the election of a right-wing Republican. Any plot involving a real Sara Ann had to be different from one involving a fake Sara Ann. Huber for one wasn't aware it was an impersonation. He got here late and didn't read the situation accurately. Nobody had dared to tell him Carol wasn't Raymond's daughter for real. Had Carol been Sara Ann it would make more sense to let Raymond get elected and then put on the pressure! That would be the big pay-off.

Nancy nudged me. Suddenly all my detection seemed like an academic exercise. "I am going back to the house. Coming?

Artemis will stay and watch this door. We have to find Rita."

"Right," I said and moved along the barn wall back the way we had come.

We didn't find Rita, although we covered the side orchard very carefully, even turning over mounds of straw and hay spread between the trees to keep down weeds. In case she'd been knocked down and left unconscious. That idea had been my contribution.

"Win?" asked Nancy.

"Win."

"Why?"

"Win is up to his neck in this. He could have knocked her out to give himself a clear field. To deal with whatever is in the house. He'd asked whether Ursula was here."

"I just remembered. I think Ursula and Win are married. To each other. I heard Dean make some racist crack about that last year. Does that mean anything, d'you think?" she asked naively.

I sighed. It was one thing to reject patriarchal customs like marriage and quite another to ignore them and their implications.

"I wouldn't be surprised."

"So what do we do?"

"Check out the house. And I do not mean rush in like a herd of stampeding buffalo."

Nancy nodded and grinned.

The house showed no sign of life. Windows loomed black and empty. The side door, through which Win and presumably Rita had entered, was closed.

"What do we do?" Nancy asked again. We were lying down in a hollow between two trees, well hidden from immediate sight.

"Let's start something. They've been keeping Artemis' attention on the cellar by sending shots her way once in a while. If we pump one or two into that door, they might show up to investigate. I'll fire, then we run like hell, take cover over there." I motioned to the back of the chicken coop. "OK? Keep your head down."

Wrapping myself around the little Remington, a present from my father I had gotten years ago, I deliberately fired three shots into the side door and the window next to it. We ran back to the chicken run.

It took them only a minute to respond. With a breaking of glass in an upstairs window came the sharp, staccato rattle of a semi. The chicken coop vibrated, splinters flew.

"They know where we are," whispered Nancy, much subdued now that she'd actually been shot at. Canadians, no matter how radical, are not familiar with the sound and effects of machineguns. We lead sheltered lives.

"I think we can retire with honour now and join Artemis. We know they are in there and they know we are out here."

"I'd rather wait until it stops."

"Suit yourself. But we are in more danger of splinters in here than bullets out there," I said as a bit of flying debris hit my shoulder.

We crawled back towards the barn. Shooting stopped before we reached our cosy spot between the ramp up to the barn's upper level and the manure pile. Artemis, shut up in the warm darkness, was anxious about us.

"So what happened? All that racket. Did you find Rita?"

We told her that we suspected Win had grabbed Rita and she was being held in the house. Immediately Artemis was insisting on a rescue operation.

"We cannot leave her in there," Artemis said and proceeded to action. She decided to join us on the outside, her chore of guarding the cellar door quite forgotten.

It turned out that she had been locked in the ground floor of the barn by the ARC group before they did their white rabbit act down the cellar. Her plan was to climb up the bales of hay and come down the outside chute from the upper level.

"Wouldn't it be easier and faster if I just went around the front of the barn and let you out? The doors are barred from the outside."

"Would you! But isn't it dangerous? They could shoot you from the cellar entrance."

"They could but I suspect they don't want too much shooting in the farmyard. My guess is that those trucks are full of arms and ammo. A hit on a fuel tank and it's goodbye. That's why they haven't rushed you yet and got you out of the way. Just kept you penned up for later disposal.''

"And I thought I was keeping them penned up," Artemis chortled. She was neither concerned nor upset at this turn of events. It just struck her as amusing. I began to understand why Nancy and Rita had such faith in her ability to survive.

Keeping low, just on the chance I was wrong, I opened the barn door. Artemis followed me out to our smelly hiding place. Before I could talk them out of it, she and Nancy were off to find Rita. They hadn't reached the chicken coop when a machinegun opened up again. Someone had seen them. I looked up to see a gun barrel and a man's arms poking over the corner of the roof. I wondered why they didn't just come and get us. After all, we were just three women with a hunting rifle and a handgun, even if it was Shoreman's 9 mm Browning. What's that, compared to machineguns? Paul's having been shot by one of these women would have been some discouragement, but it was only a matter of time. I realized that, like me, the men inside the house and cellar were waiting for reinforcements. Whose would arrive first? With luck, my private army from Room 31 could be only half an hour to an hour behind us. They had a car, rented in Castlegar, and my instructions were pretty explicit. Was Walters having them watched? At this point I didn't care. Just as long as someone on our side got here before more ARC personnel arrived.

I tried to imagine who was here and why. It was obvious that, having evacuated Terra One, Huber's boys were stashing some of the arms at this quiet farm with its specially built 'root-cellar'. So much for Huber's promise given to Walters via me that he would leave the area. There was nothing surprising in that. Huber's position wasn't hard to figure. He knew now that Carol wasn't Sara Ann. The local situation had turned sour. He and his men of the security cell didn't really amount to much without a sound local base of support. And that seemed to have disintegrated. Was it likely that he meant to sit it out here for a while, until the situation clarified? It was possible. Perhaps Ursula was in there with them to supply 'above ground' cover. And Win, too, for that matter.

Speculation was all very well. Waiting for our reinforcements was all very well. I had two very impatient amateurs on my hands who were likely to do something foolhardy at any moment. Better all three of us do something useful, if dangerous, than get killed on some hair-brained scheme. So I came up with my own foolhardy scheme — going down the root cellar. After all, I hadn't been shot at when I opened the barn door. If there was a passage through to the house, as there must be, then most likely the wounded Paul, Dean and their henchmen had passed through it. Leaving perhaps one guard to send a shot in Artemis's direction once in a while.

Nancy and Artemis, all out of breath from their short foray, loved my idea. But I had trouble getting them to agree to my actual plan, such as it was. As usual they seemed all for a 'mass' assault.

"No way," I said. "And this time do what I say, Nancy. Or we are all dead ducks." For some reason this homely threat worked. I was allowed to proceed. It was my intention to creep up on the root cellar door and surprise the lone shooter, trusting he was indeed alone, as he came up near the entrance to let loose his salvo. It turned out not to be a bad plan. It worked.

Long shadows of the impending night helped. The evening sun slipped behind the mountain at our back. For a while the eastern slopes burned with a distracting ruddy glow, foreshortening distance. Then it turned dark quite suddenly. I slipped across the yard, past the ominous bulks of arms-laden trucks, and hunkered down on one side of the double doors to the cellar. A few minutes of waiting and a cigarette butt sailed out of the dark cellar. It fell not three feet in front of me. There was a low grunt, a sigh and the barrel of a rifle poked out, aimed in the general direction of the barn.

What happened next is hard to describe but was relatively easy to accomplish. I took a deep breath and smacked down with the butt of my old faithful Remington at the menacing rifle barrel. Caught unawares, the man dropped his rifle. Not that it mattered. My next swing with the butt hit him square on the left ear. He staggered, fell and lay still. For a few seconds all I could hear was my own heavy breathing. There was no sound from the dark, dungeon-like interior of the tunnel. I waved at Nancy and Artemis. They came running, agitated and uneasy.

"He's dead!" I said nothing, but handed Nancy the man's rifle and two clips of ammunition I had found in his pockets. There was also a gun in his belt. "Let's go." I didn't stop to check whether he was indeed dead or not. In the middle of action like this the probability of death does not penetrate. That comes later. For now there was only the next moment, the pressure to action, the drive to survive.

Using the man's flashlight we plunged into the blackness of the 'cellar'. The cone of light illuminated numerous large, heavy crates. Some were stacked in tidy rows along both walls, others left carelessly about. We were still in the bomb-shelter-like structure. It was about four cars wide and at least 10 metres long. Near the entrance stood a small forklift obviously used for unloading and stacking the boxes of arms, ammo and other equipment.

I checked some of the crates. SA-7 shoulder-fired missiles, disassembled; an open crate of Uzis in their original packing; carefully stacked steel crates with stencilled codes I couldn't decipher. I would have liked to explore further but it obviously wasn't the time.

"The thing to do is to walk quietly through this storeroom and down this tunnel to the house — I assume that's where it leads — and sneak up on them. So a diversion would be nice. How about the two of you going back to the yard and taking pot shots at the house from a safe distance? We now have two rifles." I looked longingly at the armoury around us but it was useless. Take too long to assemble, clean off the preserving grease, find the right ammo.

"Yeah, let's." They were glad to be out of there. But felt concerned about me. "What about you? Going to try a sneak job or barging right in?"

I hefted the Makarov police pistol I had taken off the still body of the guard. It was loaded and there was plenty of spare ammo. I was as ready as I was going to get.

"I think I'll sneak up on them, if I can. Look after that little rifle of mine. It's a family heirloom." They each gave me a hug, sprinted away across the yard. I watched Artemis's bright red, hand-embroidered blouse and Nancy's hand-me-down Jak shirt disappear around the corner of the barn.

Moving deeper into the storage chamber, I passed more crates of weapons lying silently in their place, like legendary knights waiting to be awakened to deal death. What were they designed to be used for in this peaceful valley?

27

THE TUNNEL DID INDEED LEAD to the house but the whole system was more extensive than I thought. About 100 metres in, a narrower passage joined the main track from the right. I figured it led to an extra escape hatch; it was too tight for more than one body at a time to squeeze through. Although also underground, this maze of passages had quite a different feeling from the military monumentality of the Terra-One base where I had been captive. Once through the main storage mound, which although covered with earth wasn't below ground level, these tunnels seemed like something out of Stalag 17 — low, tight, with no more work in them than absolutely necessary. I looked at the sturdy poles and the solid two-by-six boards supporting the uneven ceiling. Good lumber, sparingly used. Thin coating of gravel underfoot on the seldom-used pathway. This wasn't a hideout for any army of guerrillas. Just normal precautionary measures for the 'local leadership' cell, built by locals with gopher blood in their veins.

Slowly I followed my cone of light along the main passage, listening for approaching sounds. A final bend and I was brought up short by the house foundation, a wall of cement and concrete blocks. A hole had been cut and a door installed. Horizontally above the solid door ran a new steel rail, replacing the destroyed foundation support at this point.

Very nice, I thought, putting my ear to the door. Beyond it must be the actual basement of the house. Voices. But not immediately behind the door. The door wasn't locked, just latched by a simple farmer's latch, such as one finds in stables and barns. I pressed and pushed, my heart hammering. The door swung open on newly-oiled hinges. I was in the furnace room. Homely clutter. Orienting myself to the plan of the house I noted two doors. One was a regular house door to the main part of the basement. The voices came from there. I heard steps going up the cellar stairs to the main floor. And shots. Nice to know Nancy and Artemis were out there making a racket. The other door, small and old, caught my attention. It was padlocked. Why? I put my ear to it. Small sounds like that of mice or other small rodents. It didn't take long to break off the flimsy hardware on the door jamb. Inside, surrounded by shelves of pickles and jams, lay Rita, semi-conscious and bound with her own belt and laundry cord. Next to her was Sid. He lay on his back, his hands held awkwardly in front of him on his belly. He stared at me with eyes like little grey lumps of stone against his pasty face. I could see him concentrating on me. His lips moved, revealing bloody gums.

"What ...." he managed to spill out from them.

"Helen. Helen Keremos, Sid. Remember me? It's OK. Will get you out of here. Just sit tight."

There was nothing I could do for him right there. I bent down to untie Rita. She moaned and started to come to. With what must have been tremendous effort Sid grabbed my arm and pulled himself to a sitting position.

"A gun, gimme a gun," he babbled through his mangled mouth.

"I only have the one. But if you can get yourself out of here and along that tunnel, there's a roomful of all the weapons you can possibly want waiting for you. Including Uzis."

"Uzi," he repeated.

"Yeah. Can you walk?"

A minute later he was standing up holding onto the wall. His breath bubbled out of his lungs and out between his lips. Red saliva dribbled down his chin. I don't know how long he would have stayed vertical. By now Rita was awake, sitting holding her head and groaning.

"Come on, Rita," I said. "There is no time. You've been knocked out. But you're OK. This is Sid. Israeli agent. He's far from OK. You must get out of here and help him. Hey, look at him. And you think you've been hurt!" It might have been cruel but compared to Sid, Rita was in fact not hurt. I couldn't take the time to commiserate with her. She staggered onto her feet, wobbled for a while, then nodded and said, "All right. Here, Sid, hold on to me. Helen, point us in the right direction."

"Out that door. Down the tunnel. It will be hard but follow it all the way. You will come to the armoury. Then out across the yard towards the barn. There is a place between the barn wall and the side of the ramp which is relatively safe. Nancy and Artemis should join you there very soon. Got that?"

Sid made a sound.

"Hush. Quiet. There are baddies on the other side of that door. Go!"

I helped them out of the cellar, through the big door into the dark tunnel. Reluctantly I relinquished my flashlight. Guess I would leave through the upstairs door. If I left alive.

Closing the door behind them, I concentrated on sounds from next door and upstairs. There was some coming and going, some shots, but it was clear that Artemis and Nancy had not completely succeeded in drawing everyone out of the basement. There were people, a number of them, still in there, talking.

I got an empty jar, carefully knocked out the bottom, put it against the door and my ear against the other end. Now the muffled conversation came through loud and clear. I didn't recognize the woman's voice.

"We don't need Huber. We don't want him and his bunch of hoodlums. Why don't we take the game away from him now?"

"What game?" This seemed to be Dean. "Game's over. We'll be lucky to survive." Dean's voice took on a petulant tinge. "Anyway, Ursula, it's your fault. If you hadn't bleated on us, we wouldn't have Huber to deal with. And we would be sitting pretty."

"If you hadn't been such idiots we wouldn't have complained." Ursula's tone indicated that this had been said a number of times before. The next voice, also unknown to me, confirmed it. It sounded amused and confident.

"Oh, shut up, children. What's done is done. No point blaming each other now. Huber's got the bit between his teeth and is likely to do for all of us. He'll fix us and deal with Carol and whoever else gets in his way. He's got his orders, his job to do. We're small fry but we've been disobedient and stupid. At least we shouldn't have lied about Carol. We will pay, believe it. Remember that nobody gets away with spoiling the organization's long-range plans and endangering one of its best. Nobody." In spite of the speaker's obviously precarious position he sounded proud. Loyal. I figured it would be Shoreman.

"I want to know about these long range plans. We weren't told anything about this when we agreed to cooperate. I won't be manipulated by any bunch of foreign white men." This was Win. The words were strong but the voice seemed uncertain.

"Oh, my, the natives are restless. Our red brother wants to know our plans. Well, well. You've sure been a lot of help. What have you done except feed Echo his lines? Damn all. And those 'foreigners' aren't all white. You'd better be careful or you'll say something terribly politically incorrect." Shoreman's icy voice carried both contempt and fear.

"For Christ's sake! Let's decide what to do!" Dean again.

There was a step on the stairs.

"Shut up! Paul's coming back."

I couldn't understand the next bit as everyone seemed to speak at once. It took me a moment to isolate Paul's quiet, decisive, French-accented voice.

"There are just a couple of broads out there. With two rifles. Nothing serious."

"One of those broads sure winged you good. If it was me I'd have her guts by now without waiting for reinforcements. What's the matter, Paul, losing your nerve?" Shoreman didn't exactly go in for making friends. I suspect that meant he was plenty nervous. Lots of people are like that — when they are scared they get obnoxious. Paul must have read him that way too, for all he replied was, "Quiet yourself, Albert. We are not asked for heroics. They will be taken care of without endangering any of our people. If you want to go out there and get shot at like a fool, be my guest. The trucks will be here soon enough. Don't worry, we will be out of here tonight, leaving everything good and tidy."

Now that Paul was back the conversation became routine. They were bored and nervous. The really important subjects — what to do about the Sara Ann impersonation and what had been planned for their unit and for the Terra-One base — obviously couldn't be discussed in front of Paul. I moved carefully away from the wall and squatted down for a moment to consider what I had heard. First of all, where was Huber? It wasn't him they were waiting for but more trucks, presumably carrying arms. They must have moved all this stuff out of Terra-One during the period when Dean and I were having our confrontation in Kaslo. The evacuation must have been almost complete when I was held there. Most of the equipment would be sacrificed but not the weapons. This farm was the alternate arms dump. With ARC trucks it wouldn't take long and with Echo on their side feeding Walters whatever they wanted him to know, it would be pretty safe for a while. All that was clear. What next? It seemed to me that we were in a pretty good position to take this whole bunch out of circulation before their reinforcements arrived. Especially as my reinforcements — Jessica, Alice and Frank — could be here any moment. I hoped Rita and Sid had had time to get out of the tunnel and hide as I had suggested. If not, too bad. I checked my gun, stood up, returned to my listening post and cursed. They had turned on the TV, making their own conversation inaudible. All I could hear was a solemn American male voice, intoning. I was at the point of giving up when something rivetted my attention. The man making the speech was an American Presidential candidate. He was talking about oil and — what else — water! Over the static and the room voices I heard a few phrases — "continental resource strategy", "our northern neighbours", "pipelines", "Alaska oil", "Columbia water system". Then the segment was over and an announcer with perfect diction came on.

"You have just heard excerpts from a speech by Republican Presidential hopeful Senator Raymond, given last night at a Chamber of Commerce meeting in Milwaukee. Senator Raymond stressed his commitment to a continental strategy and promised that as President he would work with Canada and Mexico towards pooling continental resources in all fields, thus making North America independent and invincible. And now news in sports. The Montreal Expos ..." Someone turned the set off. There was a moment of silence, then Win's voice clear and strong.

"Bastard! 'Continental resource strategy' is just another American grab! He mustn't get elected! If making it public that guerrillas hold his daughter will blow his chances, why doesn't Huber do it right now? Or why don't we? What is this deal with Walters? The whole thing stinks!"

"Calm down, Win." Paul was at it again, keeping this nervous company cooled down. "We have plans for Raymond. Huber knows what he's doing."

"Yes, what makes you an expert in international politics, eh? God, you are stupid. Huber wants Raymond elected, you fool! Has been working like a little beaver to make it happen."

"Shut up, Shoreman! You talk too much." Paul's voice cut through Shoreman's nastiness. "Get out and check on the two prisoners next door. Now! Dean, you go upstairs and relieve Emil in keeping an eye on those two women. Ursula, we want something to eat. Win can help you. Go!"

Nobody dared protest. There was a scraping of chairs. I heard Shoreman's reluctant steps in the direction of the door behind which I was standing. On the off chance that I could get away with it, I slipped behind the furnace, gun in hand, and stood still. Shoreman walked in and without a glance in my direction stared at the little door with the broken padlock hasp. He made a sound in his throat, flung open the door, took one look at the empty closet and shouted "They're gone!" and disappeared through the door in the foundation and into the tunnel.

"OK, everybody upstairs," I heard Paul order. "Time to take out the two broads out there. And I want those prisoners found and everyone accounted for before the trucks get here." He was calm but the others weren't. Dean and Ursula kept asking questions. I noticed Win didn't. Hadn't he told them I was around, that he'd arrived with three of us, not just two? That would've given Paul a clue, he wouldn't have been quite so sanguine about the situation.

Dean, Ursula and Win went upstairs with Paul bringing up the rear. I followed them. First into the basement room where they had sat. It was fixed up as a family room, with easy chairs, coffee table, TV and even a pool table. Then up the stairs behind them, very slowly and carefully. About halfway up the sound of a fusillade got me running. I was up and in the large farm kitchen in three strides. Outside it seemed like a young war was going on. I moved over to one of the kitchen windows which looked out on the side of the house. Suddenly there came the clatter of fast-moving feet on the stairs from the second floor and Emil appeared behind me. He carried a rifle, his face was red and tired.

"I need more ammo," he said then recognized me. In a flash the empty rifle hit the floor as he reached for the gun in his belt. Harry's gun. I shot him just about where the gun would be. He dropped backwards and lay still.

The sound of the Makarov going off had reverberated in the small house like thunder. There was no mistaking a shot inside the kitchen for the noise outside. I had to get out of there before Paul and the others came to investigate. They were on the other side of the house, the side which faced the chicken coop and the barn. That's where Nancy and Artemis were, possibly Rita and Sid by now. That's where I had to get. It would be unbelievably stupid to get caught inside a house full of people with guns.

I sprang through the side door, raced over the uneven straw-strewn orchard, dodging between trees as best I could. Once I tripped just in time as the patter of machinegun bullets rustled in the dead grasses around me.

"You're short, you turd," I whispered to myself. "Missed me!" A flash of red. Artemis. It was now pretty dark but whatever gleam of light there was made her bright blouse stand out. I looked at myself and was grateful for my blue knitted top, dirty as it was. I realized I hadn't been out of it for 36 — or was it 48 — hours. Never mind. Time for bed, sleep, bath, food soon. Maybe.

I reached the spot where Artemis had been seconds before. No Artemis. I lay quietly a second, breathing hard. Shooting had stopped for the moment. I looked up at the house. Nothing. I never knew what made me look behind me, back towards the way I had come from the side of the house. What I saw was the shadowy outline of a man holding a gun. Pointed at me.

I had been stalked! Lying on my belly in the grass I could neither run nor get my gun on him. It was Dean.

"Hello Helen Keremos," he said. "Goodbye Helen Keremos." He lifted his gun. The round barrel stared at me. I threw myself as far as I could to the right. As I did it I knew it was not far enough. His gun jumped in his hand. In fact his whole body jumped. Machinegun bullets passed over me and cut into him. Dean fell all in one piece. Instantly. Standing not five metres on my other side was Sid, an Uzi still pointed my way.

"Christ!" I said as Sid disappeared again behind the ruins of the chicken coop.

The house exploded in machinegun fire. I hugged the earth and wondered whether Paul had found Emil yet. I wondered what he would do next. He's lost at least three men, he himself was wounded although not badly. Soon it would be too dark to see to shoot, and the sound of our encounter must eventually bring in the outside world. My guess was he would try to skedaddle in the two ARC trucks.

On my belly, knees and elbows I snaked my way in the direction where Sid had vanished.

"Sid, hey Sid! Rita? It's me, Helen."

"We're here." Hands grabbed me and pulled me into a dusty hollow made by chickens for their dust baths. As I fell I got a powerful hit of the ammonia-laden smell of disturbed chicken shit. I lay on my back staring up at Rita and Sid crouching above me. They had an Uzi apiece.

"Nice place you've got here. Could use an air freshener, though."

Sid grinned without understanding. He didn't look well at all. In fact he didn't look like he would last long. There is something about the eyes. They tell it all. I've seen it too often in the past to make a mistake. Sid was dying. There was nothing to be done about it.

"Who did for old Ben, Sid? Do you know?"

He stared at me, remembering, then shook his head. His speech was fuzzy, disjointed. "He was already dead. I don't know how.

Then they fired a shot into his belly and took his body away somewhere. Shoreman was in charge." Sid stopped, reliving those moments in the park. "Harry was dead by then too. Emil shot him. I couldn't help. They ambushed us." His face contorted. He stopped. Disconnected sentences did make a kind of sense. It was all I wanted to know right then. Quickly I changed the subject, just a little.

"Well, I got Emil. In the house right now. He'd been the sniper on the roof. They are losing men. Paul must do something. I reckon he'll try for those trucks. Where's Artemis and Nancy at, Rita? I thought I saw Artemis back there a while ago."

"They've gone to the car. Your jeep. I wonder if they've made it. Shouldn't your Vancouver friends be here? And how about the neighbours? They must have heard this racket."

"Yeah. The question is when? When will anyone arrive and who will get here first? They are expecting more trucks with arms. I bet Paul won't wait. He cannot afford to. What do you think?" I asked, looking at the two white smudges of their faces in the gathering dusk.

"We blow the trucks," Sid said finally. Rita nodded. We'd all come to the same conclusion.

"OK. How about you stay here and keep them busy and Rita and I will go do in the trucks?" I wasn't sure he could make it.

"I think it's too late. Look!" Rita grabbed my arm and the three of us looked at the house. It was dark and silent. I picked up a chicken water-dish and waved it above my head. It glinted in the remaining rays of the sun. No reaction.

"They've gone down the tunnel to try to get to the trucks. Shoreman's already there. Let's go!" We rose and ran back towards the barn and the farmyard where the two ARC trucks sat like waiting monsters. As we turned the corner by the barn, the same corner Artemis and I had navigated safely a couple of times, a spatter of shots rang out. I felt rather than saw Rita fall. Sid kept going. He almost threw himself between the two trucks and disappeared. I squatted by Rita feverishly trying to gauge where and how seriously she'd been hit. There was black, sticky stuff on her neck, on my hands. Blood pumped steadily out.

She was certainly alive but with such a blood loss wouldn't stay that way for long. I ripped her shirt and wound it around her head. I wasn't sure whether she wouldn't be better sitting up so I grabbed her by the shoulders and dragged her into the shadow of the barn, propping her up there. Then turned my attention back to the goings-on in the yard.

Sid was either dead or lying doggo. I glimpsed figures running out of the root cellar door in the direction of the trucks. Paul was evacuating, as I'd predicted. Engine in the second truck was running now. It was only a question of seconds before both would be on their way. I took careful aim at the front tire of the nearest truck. Before I could squeeze the trigger the world exploded in front of me. I was flung down like a rag, and it rained dirt, stones and bits of scrap metal for what seemed like hours. Some of this debris must have hit me. I passed out.

28

When I came to, I thought I was blind. Darkness rose above me. Raising my head brought on nausea like a wave. I closed my eyes again and lay still, consciously working on getting myself together. Heavy metallic taste persisted in my mouth. Then my fingertips touched the edge of a stretcher. Reality returned. I reopened my eyes and focused. It was dark because the stars had been extinguished by the light of flames pouring up out of the ruin of the farmhouse. I felt more than saw the urgent hustle of people around me. Strangely my nausea subsided. I tried to turn onto my side to see better. I was on a stretcher lying in the cool grass on the edge of the front yard. All around me police, firefighters, trucks, ambulances came and went. Uniformed men waved their hands, shouting orders over the roar of the fire and the engines. Nearby two sweating men were loading an ambulance with still, blanket-shrouded bodies on stretchers. The dead. Several more lay with military precision in a row, awaiting their turn. I gagged. A hand found and touched my forehead and a plastic cup of water appeared in front of me. I sipped carefully, Jessica's watchful eyes following my every move. Squatting beside her was Alice. I was in good hands.

"Is everybody else dead?" I croaked finally.

"No, no," Alice hastened to assure me, probably afraid I was in shock. "One woman, I think it was Rita, was wounded." I nodded, wincing. "She's been taken to hospital. The other two women are OK. They took your jeep." Alice still wasn't sure whether I was in good enough shape to be told all this.

"Yes. And two of the men survived," Jessica carried on, presumably having decided I could take it. "I believe one was Shoreman. The other looked bad but was still alive. They went to hospital under guard. So far they've recovered eight bodies. One a woman," Jessica reported.

"Ursula," I whispered. My mind kept counting — Ursula, Dean, Paul, Emil, Win, Shoreman, and of course Sid, a number of nameless men — I got muddled and stopped.

"Don't think about it," Alice instructed me. "How do you feel?"

"Lousy but OK. If you see what I mean." I was sitting up by now and fighting down vomit which rose into my throat. Painfully I scrambled to my feet and was promptly very sick. Almost immediately I felt better. Leaning against an Emergency Squad vehicle I sipped water and took deep breaths. My body was bruised and scratched, my clothes filthy and torn, but I was intact. Alice and Jessica looked at me anxiously.

"Really. I am OK," I assured them. "Tell me." I waved my arm at the organized chaos around. Nobody was taking any notice of us.

"It was quite a party. We were late getting here because we had trouble with our rented car. Then we got held up on the road by a couple of very slow ARC trucks. Heavily loaded and coming this way. We figured something was wrong. When we got off the highway we heard all the shooting. So did the men in the trucks. They speeded up. So did we. Suddenly, just up this road, they stopped and tried to take us out."

Jessica told the story calmly and chronologically with Alice immediately ready to take over if she took more than a breath's pause.

"Take you out," I said stupidly. That gave Alice a chance to break in.

"Yeah, yeah. It was really exciting. Then the cops arrived. Frank was mad because that spoiled the fun but I must say I was never more glad to see Mountie cars in my life. Anyway we milled around for a minute, sort of sorting out who was who and how much of a fight the guys in the trucks were going to put up. Then pow! One hell of an explosion! Like Canada Day at the PNE! Fireworks! A real blast. The cops called up reinforcements and the fire department and started to pick up the pieces." We were silent together.

"Where's Frank?" I asked.

"In the melee somewhere. You don't think he would miss an operation like this! Borrowed a helmet from the fire department and went right into the debris before the dust settled. Of course, they wouldn't let us in. Females, you know."

The fire was dying but more from lack of burnable material than from the efforts of the men. The barn had disappeared, leaving behind a crushed mass of timbers scattered over the whole area as far as could be seen. Remnants smouldered here and there. The backyard was a crater; there was no sign of the 'root cellar'. Giant clods of earth and piles of loose soil rose in unexpected places.

"There's a man waving at you over there," Jessica broke into our contemplation of the scene around us. A familiar nondescript car sat out of the way of the jumble of official vehicles.

"That's Ronald Walters. Figures he'd be here," I said. "I'd better go talk to him."

"You sure you're well enough?"

"Sure." Painfully I moved away under my own steam, having refused Alice's offer of an arm. I walked slowly up the farm lane, past the mess of trucks and police cars all with flashing lights and engines running. The sights and sounds of a disaster.

Before I reached Walters, his agent rose from the shadows and checked me over. Walters waited patiently, sitting in the passenger seat with a clipboard full of papers on his lap. I leaned against the door and looked at him through the window.

"Well, I see you survived," he said, and seemed pleased about it. No thanks to you! I thought ungratefully.

"Many didn't," I said. We watched a private mortuary wagon pull up — they'd run out of ambulances — and the last two blanket-shrouded bodies were put on board.

"It was quite a rumble. Three in hospital. The woman with a bullet wound, Albert Shoreman with suspected concussion. They will be OK. Can be interrogated tomorrow, I hope. But young Wingard is bad. May not live." Walters looked at the lists in his lap. In spite of myself I was impressed. The smoke hadn't cleared and he had lists, names, reports. Great staff work.

Walters looked at me, and what he saw made him move over, making room for me on the bench seat. I slid in and slammed the door.

"Huber wasn't here. Neither was Carol. One of these uniden-tified males must be Sid Bazerman, one of your friend Morris

Beach's Mossad agents. So now they are both dead. Well, that should take care of Ben's murder. At least as far as the RCMP are concerned," I told him.

"Hell, that's the least of our troubles. What do we do with this mess? Anyway, don't change the subject on me. I want to know about that blast and what happened here. We captured two trucks of assorted weapons on their way here. Well?"

"I think we can thank Sid for the blast and for most of the dead. He sent two other trucks full of arms and ammo up just as Ursula, Paul, Win and at least one other guy got aboard. He must have died with them. There was an arms dump back there, underground. It went up in the blast. There's a crater back there you could lose a house in."

Walters nodded. "Now, fill me in," he said.

So I did. This time I told him everything. About Win's involvement, about Echo's part and especially about Carol's impersonation. He bit his pencil, made notes on his lap, and stared ahead through the windshield as I spoke into his ear. Every so often he would glance up at me, then look down at his notes.

"A mess. I'll have to talk to that Win. Let's hope he survives. You telling me that he and Ursula were the entire local leadership? Two kids like that? No way. Never mind about that. Locals we can deal with. Huber. It's Huber that concerns me. What's your guess about his plans? What's he up to?"

Up to this point we were talking like old pals, no conflict. I guess circumstances of death, fire and general destruction do affect the most hard-headed of us. It had been reasonable to assume that even Walters in all his professionalism unbent a little. But there was something phony in his inquiry about Huber. Just a chatty, idle question, but it wasn't a chatty, idle moment. I skirted it.

"Some of it isn't hard to figure. They were moving some of their arms stash here so that mine shaft (they called it Terra-One base, can you believe it?) could be cleaned up as per Huber's so-called deal with you. But the evacuation had started earlier. At least a day earlier. Their plan was already in place."

"What plan? They weren't really up for blowing Columbia.

Silly bluff. Four truck-loads of assorted hardware is to play cowboys with and scare innocent bystanders, that's all. Short of a nuclear blast, it would take tons of explosives to do major damage. We checked ARC storage, warehouses, garage. Nothing to indicate more than what we see here. And I have a team going over that old mine headquarters. Terra-One! Comic book stuff." Now that he believed it was all over Walters could pretend it was very amusing.

"I wouldn't have put it that way," I said, rather severely perhaps, "under the circumstances." He acknowledged my rebuke.

"Yes, of course. I didn't mean it that way. But that base they built. Impressive but not functional." He paused then. "After we clean up this mess, I'd better take care of Huber." Again that rising inflection, like an unspoken question. Deliberately ignoring the obvious inconsistencies of the situation, even his own doubts about the identity of some of the local participants, Walters was probing me about Huber.

"Should I worry about him?" he continued, when I didn't react. He badly wanted to know what I knew or suspected.

"That depends on what he represents. Outside of this unit here which has ceased to exist. You let him go, didn't you? Huber. And Carol. Right?"

Walters struggled too elaborately. "That was part of the deal you helped make between us. Remember?"

"Nuts. That deal was a phony. You and he made a real deal under cover of that one. Anyway, he's gone, isn't he? Safe and sound."

Walters didn't answer for a while. When he did it was with reference to another statement of mine. "I don't know exactly what and who Huber represents. But I know he's got friends." He sighed and stabbed the roof of the car with his index finger, meaning 'upstairs'.

"Aha. Yes. It's not easy being a faithful servant of the powers-that-be. When the interests of all the powers-that-be do not coincide."

"You're too smart for your own good, Helen. I am a servant, as you put it, of Canada. When the interests of the United States coincide with ours that's one thing. But otherwise I don't care

— 187 —

what the President of the United States says or wants." He purposely misunderstood me.

"Beautifully said. Who defines the interests of Canada for you? What price the Canadian federal system, these days? Huber has friends in high places. You let him go. That speaks for itself."

"I had no choice." Walters said tonelessly.

"You've answered your own question. Worry about him." I opened the car door and started to leave.

"We will need a statement from you. I am going to try to keep this down. Call it just local trouble getting out of hand. Doukhobors, you know. Religious fanatics. Can be blamed for anything, especially when it involves fire. They are famous firebugs. So that's all right. Give me a statement which won't contradict that."

"You draft it. I'll see whether I'll sign it." I slid out of the car. "And keep the Horsemen out of my hair."

Jessica, Alice and a very dirty and excited Frank were walking towards me.

"Let's get out of here. I need about 12 hours' sleep."

29

18 HOURS LATER I stood in a private hospital room watching Win come to life. A young, suspicious Mountie in garish mufti watched me in turn. Two doctors hovered expectantly while a nurse did something technical to the tangle of tubes and wires which connected Win to his life-support system.

As we watched, Win opened his eyes and tried to focus. Immediately the doctors got into the act, ignoring the rest of us. It took a while but by the time Ronald Walters arrived, out of breath and with his faithful shadow, Win was conscious and able to talk. At a sign from Walters the Mountie escorted all three hospital functionaries out of the room. He would have thrown me out bodily too had Walters not indicated that I was privileged to stay in spite of lack of official status. While the Mountie stood at the door and sulked, Walters' good, grey agent stared out of the window. Walters and I tried to get all we could out of Win. This was easy as he badly wanted to talk.

His first concern was Ursula. He spoke directly to me, largely ignoring Walters.

"Helen. About Ursula. She's dead, isn't she?"

I indicated that she was.

"We were in this together. Did you know she was my wife? We believed that things had to be changed. Can you imagine what it was like? An Indian and a Douk. We had no chance. A couple of strangers came to us; Dean brought them. They talked, they promised. We would be part of an international organization, they said. Resources, facilities, leadership. It all made sense. They knew all the words. The Indian Act, Wounded Knee, land claims. Settlement." He stopped for a while, breathing noisily. I moved to call a nurse but he shook his head and continued. "I'm OK. Just let me rest once in a while. Yes, yes. We had to do something. Had to act. Before they took everything away from us. So we agreed. We joined. It took some time. Maybe four, six months. It was Ursula they were after, really. They had trouble recruiting Douks. You see, they had to have represen-tatives from each major group in the area. The Douks, the Indians, the Americans. Otherwise their bosses wouldn't let them set up a base here. Ben wouldn't even talk to them but Ursula and her mother went along. Douk women can be dynamite. They got me as a bonus."

"What was your job?"

"Initially to recruit more brothers. Everyone thought it would be easy. But in fact very few would play. The young men wouldn't join with white men. And the older guys were real uncomfortable about working with women. Especially Douk women."

"Saved by their biases," I said. It was somewhat amusing.

"Yeah. More recently my job was keeping track of Echo. You know about Echo?"

"Sure. A stoolie for the feds. This here is Echo's boss, Ronald Waters." I indicated the silent man beside me.

"Well, maybe. Echo cooperated with us, you know. I mean about Terra-One. I fed him information he'd pass on to his boss. I never quite understood why we attracted attention to ourselves even if it was misleading. I was told we needed someone senior on the job to deal with."

In a conversational tone Walters amplified. "Sure. It's standard practice. An organization like theirs needs well-established contacts at a high level. What they are up to is too sophisticated to be left to local authorities. It's preferable to have someone knowledgeable and well-researched to deal with."

"What a lovely symbiotic arrangement! Never mind now. Go on, Win," I said. "Tell us what was happening at that farmhouse last night. What was the plan?"

"As far as I knew we were just storing some arms for future use. Huber ordered Terra-One evacuated the same night they tried to snatch you at Kaslo and didn't make it. I was there. Disillusioned and angry, I guess you could say. I figured Shoreman had killed Ben. Such a dirty business. I had no idea to start with. All very romantic. Anyway, I wanted to find out what you knew and whether you would go on looking for the real killer. I reckoned you would ..."

"You reckoned you could let me find Terra-One once it was empty. Not really betraying Terra but making sure the hunt for Ben's killer went on. Right?"

"Right. I guess I was confused."

"You could say that." Walters stepped in, for the first time, impatience in his voice. "What's Huber up to? D'you know?"

"No." Win looked away and let himself drift off.

"Boy, you are some interrogator," I said to Walters as we left the room. "I had him talking and you had to get heavy."

"Nah! He doesn't know much more. He wasn't exactly one of the chiefs." And he went away chuckling to himself. Let's be charitable and call it nerves.

"Damn, I wanted to ask Win about his private life with the Soteroff family." I said to Alice, who had been waiting outside in the hospital lobby. "I wonder whether he and Ursula had a child. Now that idiot Walters has blown it."

Frank and Jessica had gone back to Vancouver to tend their respective businesses. No amount of pressure or threats by Jessica had persuaded Alice to leave the case now that she was in it. She had insisted on tagging along.

"A child? Why would a child be of any interest?"

"Oh, I don't know. Kids are kind of cute."

"Damn it, Helen! What's gotten into you? What are you up to?"

"It's just my ghastly sense of humour. Let's go eat. I am starved."

We decided to walk down from the hospital to the Jam Factory through Nelson's busy Monday traffic. It took a while and we got there hot and hungry. Alice went on ahead; I hung back and from force of habit checked the message board. It was there. A short cryptic note signed 'Beach'. Frank had passed on my query to Morris Beach and he was ready to talk to me. Alone.

Over an enormous salad, homemade bread and two beers I said to Alice. "I think I will take a walk and then a nap. Still need a lot of rest after the last few days. See you at the hotel tonight."

Alice looked at me skeptically but I guess I looked like I needed rest so she let it go. Before she could change her mind, I finished my meal, left the restaurant and made my way downstairs into the pottery studio. I was admiring a finely made jug when a man touched my arm.

"Beach," he said, and without a further glance at me walked out. I followed across the railroad tracks, past another old warehouse building to a stack of lumber awaiting shipment on the lakeside. He nodded casually in the direction of the neat piles of squared logs and kept going. A middle-aged man in an expensive business suit sat on one of the logs, well-hidden from passers-by. A good place to meet. I sat down beside him and we looked each other over. I don't know what he saw other than one tired, brown-faced woman with graying hair dressed in old but clean outdoorsy clothes. What I saw was a man with too much on his mind, too much stress in his life, who coped by taking one too many martinis whenever possible. No amount of squash in expensive clubs quite compensates for the combination of stress, rich food and booze. Beach was clearly losing the battle. All the disasters of male mid-life were upon him; thinning hair, soft paunch, loose jowls, shaking hands, gray face. Only his eyes, under groomed eyebrows, still held something of consequence.

"I'm sorry about Harry and Sid. They had no business here you know," I said.

"We have legitimate interests ..."

"No, you don't. Anyway that's not what I meant. They should never have been sent here like that. No support, no local knowledge, no nothing. That's why they died."

"I didn't send them here. No one can blame me. I gave them all the help I could."

"Sure you did. Never mind, now. I need some information. Information that they had."

"What information? Why?"

"I want to know more about that deposit Huber made in Calgary. Remember? $100,000 in gold certificates."

"Why?" Beach repeated, looking at me suspiciously. "You won't be able to get at it anyway."

"It's a lead to Huber."

He stared at me some more. Then shrugged and said, "What do you want to know?"

"Which branch, when, in what name? Like that."

He told me. When I had all I needed and all he knew, he pulled out an old, familiar map rather the worse for wear, and handed it to me.

"From Frank Hanusek. He told me that he took it back to Vancouver by mistake. In case you need it." I had conveniently forgotten about that damn map. Probably because it reminded me of Carol. I put it away.

"Thanks. What are your plans?"

"Nothing. Walters notified me about what happened. I am here to sort out this business, that's all. Harry and Sid ..."

"Yes. I am sorry," I said again. "Shalom."

"Shalom. Good luck."

I went back to the hotel, undressed, lay down on the soft mattress and examined Dean's map. It was dirty, stained and had been folded often enough to wear out on the folds. Looking closely it was just possible to make out barely decipherable markings. Presumably made by Dean in his meticulous tiny hand-writing with a very fine marking pen. One of these marks approximated the location of the Soteroff farm. Another was probably the Terra-One base but I couldn't be sure. I debated whether to dress and get a magnifying glass or dress and give the map to Walters. I compromised and did neither. Instead I phoned for flight information to Calgary. I was interested in Huber.

30

TRIP TO CALGARY was uneventful. Nobody stopped me and there didn't seem to be a shadow. I hoped that Walters had forgotten me but I wasn't counting on it. I changed taxis three times just to be sure.

It was half an hour to closing time on Tuesday when I walked into the branch of the Canadian Imperial Bank of Commerce where Huber had deposited his petty cash. I couldn't recognize my reflection in the solid plate glass doors. Instead of scruffy investigator, I looked the picture of a respectable female lawyer of the new breed. Pleated pants with a lovely drape, trendy silk shirt, spiffy blazer and an expensive briefcase. Only my shoes were a bit off but there is no way I can cope with high heels even for a good cause.

The assistant manager was young and keen. He wanted to seem well-versed in international machinations. Perhaps he was. Anyway keen, young and anxious-to-impress types are easy to con since they cannot admit to ignorance and hate to consult anyone else. I presented myself as Jessica Tsukada, who had come all the way from my Vancouver law office to do business with a Mr. B. Misurali (a.k.a. Huber), a foreign gentleman of great wealth who had given this bank as one reference in a very hush-hush deal. I was the go-between, checking up on Misurali on behalf of my client, who had to remain nameless.

"An arm's-length deal, you see, Mr. Bridgeman," I said mysteriously. "Our agents are checking into matters overseas and I have to do so here. When I am satisfied, I have the authority to conclude the transaction. It's a great responsibility as I am sure you are aware from your own experience. One has to be very, very sure that everything is in order. That's why I've come to you."

Bridgeman nodded eagerly, opening his eyes very wide as if to take in as much as he could of this exciting emissary from the glamorous world of international finance.

"Of course, Ms. Tsukada, of course," he enunciated carefully. "I am at your service. Mr. Misurali is a valued client of ours. He has done considerable business through us in Alberta. Import and export I understand. Very impressive list of clients he deals with, very impressive. Major oil companies, the provincial government. Really, I assure you your client will be in excellent company."

I remained unconvinced. "Yes, yes. But I need chapter and verse. Who, what, when and how much. And of course that $100,000 in gold certificates which Mr. Misurali deposited with you for us as a guarantee of his good faith. That's all been arranged so I do not expect any problems. I am sure you are a busy man so let's proceed as expeditiously as possible."

Bridgeman looked uncomfortable, as well he might. The Misurali file lay in front of him and he kept flipping it open and closing it again. He knew the contents by heart and therefore knew that it didn't contain any authority to hand over information or money to any third party. Bridgeman was in a spot.

"I am afraid we haven't yet received the appropriate instructions from Mr. Misurali. So ..."

"Not received them yet! What do you mean, not 'yet'! You got them over a month ago! Come now, Mr. Bridgeman, I appreciate that you have to safeguard your client, but you cannot take it upon yourself to ignore his instructions."

"I haven't got any such instructions, I assure you, Ms. Tsukada. I am very sorry." And indeed he looked devastated.

"It's your problem, Mr. Bridgeman, if they are not in that file. The bank received instructions. If the bank mislaid them that is your inefficiency and the bank is liable for any cost or loss incurred thereby." I sounded very impressive, even to myself.

Ten minutes later I had him on the run. He tried unsuccessfully to get Misurali on the phone at his Calgary location. Then he let me look at the list of companies and individuals with whom Misurali had done business through the bank. It seemed very one-sided: i.e. all out-go and very little return. Except for ARC and a trucking company ART. I concluded that they did real business, as well as fronts. What all those other payments were was anybody's guess but the sums were considerable.

"Now about that $100,000 I have to accept that you cannot transfer it to us but I insist that it be transferred to another closed account until further notice. Otherwise I can't conclude the deal between Misurali and my client. You see my problem? My instructions were clear on that point. That money must no longer be accessible to Mr. Misurali unilaterally, otherwise it doesn't represent any commitment on his part. Perhaps a trust account requiring both our signatures?"

"I am afraid I cannot do that either without authority from Mr. Misurali. As soon as that is available ..."

"You mean as soon as you find it where your inefficiency has lost it. Very well. I am at the Calgary Inn. Call me immediately. I will have to inform my office of this delay. It may be costly. I suggest you find that authority as soon as possible. Good day."

I rose and departed with as much impressive indignation as I could muster.

Misurali (Canada) Export/Import Sales had a tiny office in the top floor of a six storey building. By sheer coincidence no doubt, ART was located in the same building. The Misurali office was locked and empty; no wonder Bridgeman's call went unanswered. I let myself in with no trouble. It contained a desk, a file cabinet, two chairs, a telephone and a lot of undisturbed dust. Obviously unused and not designed to be used. Merely a front, in case anyone came round to see. I went down, found the ART dispatcher at the garage area ramp, and putting on my best bureaucratic manner asked for Mr. Misurali. I was an inspector from the Provincial Taxation Department whose letters hadn't been answered for months.

"Just routine, you understand. Paperwork. Must be done." I was bored, apologetic, and impressed by his mustache. It turned out that Mr. Misurali hadn't been seen for a month and my informant knew nothing about him. What's more, he doubted that anyone at ART Trucking could help me.

"But he's down as part-owner of this business," I said. "It is our understanding ART is a Misurali enterprise."

Lively mustache wriggled unhappily. "I just work here. All I know is he's not one of the bosses who give me orders. Saw him, oh, maybe month, six weeks ago. He came by, said hello, and went upstairs to his office. That's the last I saw of him."

"He didn't talk to anyone in your office?" I put lots of skepticism in my voice.

"Now I think of it, he did have a word with Jerry Lipman. He's the office manager. But I don't think it was more than a hello."

"OK. Thanks for your time. I'll go see Mr. Lipman."

"Jeez. I am sorry. Jerry hasn't been to work since last week. Death in the family. His mother died in Edmonton, I think."

"Sorry to hear it. Well, I'll be along."

I got a cab and went back to a modest motel near the airport. My rented car sat in front. So far I had struck out. Huber/Misurali apparently hadn't gone back to Calgary. Yet I was sure he would be back. If only to close his account. $100,000 is a lot of small change.

On an impulse I looked up Gerald Lipman in the phone book. Stopping only once for a quick sandwich I drove to the address. It was a newish 'Adults Only' apartment building boasting a canopy and a uniformed doorman. Seemed a bit upscale for a trucking company office manager. There was no answer to my ring. The doorman was new and didn't remember Mr. Lipman and never heard of Misurali. I was about to give up when a man quickly entered the lobby, let himself in with a key and made straight for the elevators. He was only in sight for thirty seconds but there was something familiar about him.

"Isn't that Mr. Lipman?" I asked the doorman.

"Oh, no, Miss. That's a new tenant, Mr. Peter Matakoff. He's subletting Apartment 1210."

Peter Matakoff, ARC general foreman!

"Is there a Mrs. Matakoff?" I asked, remembering the episode with Carol and Albert Shoreman. People tend to follow patterns. And there is nobody as anonymous as a 'Mrs.'.

"No, Miss. There is no lady with Mr. Matakoff. But he did tell me a gentleman friend was joining him tomorrow."

I wondered how long this obliging doorman would keep his new job. Lack of curiosity and a closed mouth are the preferred characteristics of door-keepers. This one was tall, dark and handsome which would help and East Indian which wouldn't. I debated whether or not to warn him against being friendly and open with people like myself but decided he might not take it in the spirit in which it was meant. Cultural and gender differences make communication tricky. I thanked him politely for his courtesy. Then it struck me that he would be just as indiscriminate about talking to tenants. Chances were good that Matakoff (and Lipman when he got back) would very shortly be aware of my interest. As a further blow, I couldn't now stake out the building without being spotted. That put a decided crimp in my plans which at this point were based on the assumption that the 'gentleman friend' was Huber. It couldn't be coincidence that Lipman of ART Trucking and Matakoff of ARC Construction had apartments in the same building. Huber had to be around. Since the apartment house seemed a dead loss for now, I went back to my original plan of getting to Huber through the bank. I couldn't believe that he would leave that $100,000 untouched. If Bridgeman ran true to form he would call the Calgary Inn immediately Huber surfaced. All I could do was go back to my motel, keep in touch with my contact at the Calgary Inn and hope Lipman and Matakoff didn't warn off Huber.

It worked. There was a message from Bridgeman asking me to present myself at the bank at 9 a.m. the next morning, before opening time. I called him back immediately and managed to get some interesting information out of him. He'd gotten a wire from Misurali from the road urgently demanding a meeting next day as early as possible. Hence the 9 a.m. appointment. The other news was that a 'considerable sum of money' had been transferred into Misurali's account that afternoon from a stateside bank. $500,000 to be exact. Being a bright boy, Bridgeman had connected those two events with my arrival and was convinced that some very fancy international business was about to be conducted before his very eyes. I asked him whether Misurali had been notified that I was in town. Bridgeman tried to explain very apologetically that Mr. Misurali was in transit and therefore unreachable, but we would all meet as soon as feasible so it didn't matter. I allowed myself to be mollified.

31

THEN I MADE MY PLANS for next day. They involved many phone calls and some leg work. I got both my Calgary contacts at first try.

Willy was a compulsive gambler and a pretty fair informant and go-fer. Just back from the track, he was about to leave for a charity casino — an Albertan specialty — when I caught him. I described Huber and for a price he promised to have the Lipman/Matakoff building staked out — front and back — until 9 a.m. next day and let me know right away if and when Huber showed.

Lester was an American ex-G.I. who split after Cambodia, moved to Calgary, married a local woman and now drove an airport limo and still dreamed of homesteading in the Peace River. He'd been training as a jockey when the draft got him. Now he concentrated on being the best wheelman, with the fastest vehicle and the best knowledge of streets and roads in and around Calgary. He was happy to make his skills available to me next day.

All complications aside, I counted this a lucky day. By 10 p.m. that night I had done all I could to be reasonably sure that next day I would get my hands on both Huber and the money.

I left my motel at 8 a.m. next morning. Earlier Willy had reported no action on the Lipman/Matakoff front either coming or going. Presumably Huber would only arrive that morning, or else was sacking out somewhere else. Of course he could have phoned them; I had no way of having their phones tapped on such short notice. It was a chance I took.

Scene in front of the downtown bank was the usual morning rush-hour bustle. I found a coffee-shop with a view of the front door and was lucky to grab a stool from under an indignant Calgarian. Over a stale coffee and fresh danish, I watched the crowds and the traffic. At 8:40 a blue stretched limo with a small uniformed chauffeur drew up and parked illegally across the street from the bank. The driver was alone. He pulled out a paper and absorbed himself in it. At 8:55 I walked past him, crossed over to the bank and went up the steps to the door. For a few seconds I stood there with a clutch of employees until let in by a young man with an obvious hangover. He tried to keep me out but my old friend Mr. Bridgeman was on the case and rescued me most gallantly. We repaired to his office to await Mr. Misurali. I was offered coffee and kind inquiries about business in Vancouver. Then we got onto the weather. Bridgeman was tense and worried. I hoped it was nothing other than the natural nerves of a man out of his depth.

At 9.06 the phone rang. Mr. Misurali's party waited outside. Party? Instinctively I patted my new expensive briefcase. Bridgeman bustled forward as the door opened. First person into the room was Carol, followed by Huber.

"Mrs. Misurali?" Bridgeman said uncertainly.

Carol just smiled and said nothing. As the door closed Huber glanced around the office. Nothing registered on his face when he saw me. He was going to play this one right through. There was $600,000 and his safety riding on it. To get his hands on the money he had to prevent Bridgeman from smelling a rat. Meaning that Huber couldn't just blow the whistle on me. In fact nothing crude or suspicious could happen as long as the money wasn't in his possession. After messing up the Kootenay operation, for which he would have to take responsibility regardless, he couldn't afford to make any more errors or incur any other losses.

We looked at each other with total understanding. Both of us had made our preparations before coming into the bank. Doubtless he had Matakoff stashed somewhere awaiting developments. I had Lester and his limo. The joker was Carol. Even though he knew by now that she wasn't Sara Ann she had managed to work her way somewhere into his plans. And so stay alive and healthy. Amazing, the survival capacity of this woman.

By now Bridgeman was behind his desk again fiddling with the file. Carol had sat down in the prime customer chair on the other side of the desk which left Huber and me to perch side by side on two little straight chairs near the door. It wasn't a big office. Our elbows touched.

"I'm Jessica Tsukada, Mr. Misurali. It's a real pleasure to meet you at last." I said, giving him his cue. "Did you have a good trip from the states? I understand that after this primary Senator Raymond has the Republican nomination all sewn up. That should be good for business." Huber's face went even more rigid, if that was possible. I was getting under his skin, and we had barely begun. I glanced at Carol. The smile was still stuck on but her eyes were bright and knowing. She gave the impression of tightly restrained energy just waiting to be released. Now Huber and Bridgeman were talking to each other, apparently ignoring us. Bridgeman apologizing for mislaying his instructions to deal with me and Huber patiently humouring him.

"That's quite all right, quite all right. These things happen in the best regulated organization. As a matter of fact this delay permits me to meet the delightful Miss Tsukada." Huber just oozed patriarchal charm in my direction. Then he cut it. "Now that we are all here our business can be concluded all the more speedily. Gold certificates for $600,000, I believe that's correct?" Without waiting for Bridgeman's affirmative answer, Huber proceeded. "I will require them right away. Let's get all the necessary paperwork out of the way at once. Must catch the next Air Canada flight to Edmonton. Urgent business, you see. Which is why I put you to the inconvenience of meeting us at such an early hour." Huber was talking too much. Realizing that, he stopped. Bridgeman was on his feet, more than eager to follow any instruction which took him out of the tense atmosphere of his tiny office.

"That's $100,000 for us, remember, Mr. Bridgeman." I said. Again before the banker could answer Huber chimed in.

"Yes, yes. Of course. Mr. Bridgeman knows that." Huber wanted to expedite the transaction and get out of there. Was he really going to let me walk out with 100 big ones? No way! Something nasty was waiting for me the minute we were out of here. Then he would have his money back.

"I think I would rather have a cashier's cheque, 'For deposit only' to our office account in Vancouver, J. Tsukada, Barrister and Solicitor. Those gold certificates are transferable. It's not safe to travel with them." There was no reason to make it easy on Huber. He was about to lose $100,000.

Not able to think of any reasonable excuse to prevent the money being transferred in this form, Huber grimaced and nodded as Bridgeman disappeared behind the door. There was a stifled sound from Carol. She was laughing! Huber ignored her and turned to me. I had a bet with myself about what his first words would be. "It's a great mistake to get in my way, Helen. A mistake you will regret." I gave myself no marks for being right.

"You're a pompous ass, among other things, Huber. Take it easy. You're about to take off with $500,000 anyway. Unless you make waves, that is. And you wouldn't want to screw-up anything else after the Kootenay fiasco."

"My dear Helen, this is all small change. And that Kootenay operation including the Terra-One base, was just a minor issue. You should've known that by now. My real job has been here and in the states. And that's gone very well. We have a deal which makes us silent partner of the President of the United States. Even without all that stupid business with Carol." Huber apparently couldn't resist boasting.

Carol looked at me fixedly, a small smile still on her face. I shook my head.

"Not yet, Huber, not President yet. Either you are conning me or you've been conned. But just to humour you, I'll ask the big question. What did you promise to deliver to this 'leader of the free world'?"

"Raymond wants 'self-sufficiency'in vital natural resources. He promised it to the American people. For a start that means a reliable oil supply from Canada and Mexico. We will deliver that."

"Raymond is an exemplary politician. He fulfills his campaign promises. Then I take it that there is a similar operation going on in Mexico."

"Right. Much remains to be done there. But here we are well underway. Continental resource policy makes a lot of sense. Even Ottawa now understands that, witness the free trade agreement. But so far it's just words on paper. We will make it real."

"I see. The free trade deal has been a mixed blessing for you guys. It sent up too many warning flags in Canada. Direct political pressure could backfire on the Americans. Raymond needs you people to do the dirty work for him. And you will be happy to do it. Have him in your pocket for ever."

"Exactly. And everyone benefits really. It's a good deal all round."

"So you're a success?"

"Exactly. And it's in the bag, as they say. It took three years. But, eventually everyone who matters saw things our way."

"I'll bet. Congratulations. And your payoff from Raymond is a piece of the action."

"Just a piece of the action, yes." Huber smiled at me benevolently.

"And water is next ..."

Just then Bridgeman came back in, followed by a curious underling carrying another file. She put it down on the desk, gave us an interested glance and reluctantly left. Then Bridgeman proved capable of opening the file all by himself, removing what looked like a regular withdrawal slip and handing it to Huber. Huber signed quickly. Bridgeman in turn took out a cheque and handed it to me. I stood up.

"Perfect. Thank you. Well, Mr. Misurali, it's been a pleasure. Our client will be in touch very soon. Count on it. Thanks again. I'll leave you gentlemen to complete your business. Goodbye." I moved to the door. Suddenly Carol was on her feet.

"I need some air. It's so stuffy here and you know how I hate your silly business meetings. I'll wait for you outside." Huber didn't bother to reply, concentrating on the gold certificates which were due to pop out of the magical file. Curiouser and curiouser, I thought. He doesn't care whether Carol or I leave before him. As I walked out the front door with Carol close beside me, I understood. A sharp poke in the ribs. A gun in Carol's hand. And parked two doors down the block, a Mercedes with Peter Matakoff at the wheel. I stopped and faced her.

"You aren't going to shoot me. Not right here on the sidewalk in front of the bank with Huber still inside. In fact I don't think you are going to shoot me at all, anywhere. Why would you want to?"

"I don't. But I want to live even more. As long as I am useful, I live."

"Not much of a life. Why don't you split?"

"I haven't a dime, no passport, not even a credit card. How far would I get?"

"Fair enough. So let's take Huber's piggy-bank away from him. $500,000 is good travelling money."

"I don't think I have the nerve. Not after ... all that happened. And Peter is watching us, you know. It's too dangerous."

"What's your choice? Huber will get rid of you any day now."

"I'm getting a posting to Mexico. I can be useful there."

"A posting, eh. Like the diplomatic service. Well, if you believe in the tooth fairy you can buy that. Why don't we just stroll over to Peter and see if we can't persuade him to cooperate. Then when Huber arrives we will take away his marbles," I said and began walking towards the blue Mercedes through the mid-morning crowds, swinging my briefcase. Across the road Lester put down his paper, yawned and started the big limo.

Action at the Mercedes was soon over. At the time, of course, it always seems to be in slow motion, but in fact it's too fast for unsuspecting passers-by to grasp. As I approached, followed by Carol, Peter leaned over from the wheel seat to open the passenger door for me. I was in like a flash, the long clumsy barrel of my gun pointing at him. At the same time Lester double-parked alongside, was out of the limo and at the Mercedes driver's door. Some quick work with a leather cosh and seconds later we were helping a stunned gentleman into his private limousine. The pint-sized chauffeur was already behind the wheel ready for a quick exit. The whole episode didn't take 40 seconds.

It was all ridiculously easy and fast. Only worked because of Matakoff's touching faith that Carol had a gun on me and would use it. An experienced operator — like Paul had been — would not have let himself get trapped that way but then Matakoff was in fact a construction foreman, not a street-smart urban guerrilla. Lipman, if he was around, was also unlikely to be a skilled gun. Huber might fancy himself a mover and a shaker on an international scale, but the quality of his current support staff left much to be desired.

Lester's limo with its unconscious passenger was out of sight, heading for a predetermined rendezvous point, when Huber appeared out of the bank. By this time Carol and I were both in the back seat trying to look like captor and captive. Huber frowned at Matakoff's absence but without thinking slid into the front passenger seat.

"Where's Peter? I told him to stay with the car no matter how long it took." His angry, commanding voice boded ill for Peter.

"He's been unavoidably called away," I said. "Move over behind the wheel and drive." I leaned against the back of the front seat, just by his head, and briefly showed him my gun.

Have to hand it to Huber. He took it like a pro. Without a word he slid into the driver's seat and started the engine. Simultaneously I rushed out of the back and into the just vacated front passenger seat. Again, nobody seemed to notice the gun in my hand. The only way to go in situations like that is open and fast. Being clandestine on a busy street takes precious moments. Unless a shot is actually fired, nobody is likely to notice even totally outrageous things if they happen fast enough.

With my gun pointing at his vital parts and a silent but wary Carol at his back, Huber pulled away from the curb. Following my instructions we were going west in the direction of Banff. It was a bright cool morning. The road is one of the most scenic you can imagine. Perhaps overcome by the beauty of nature, Huber slowed down a little and attempted to engage Carol in conversation, ignoring me completely.

"I am really sorry, Carol, that you are signing your own death warrant like this. But it's not too late to reconsider. You have a gun. Use it on Helen. Shoot. I will take my chances with her gun."

For a moment I didn't think she would reply, but she did.

"No, I'll take my chances with Helen. You've already signed my death warrant. I sure owe you nothing."

During this dialogue I moved swiftly under Huber's suit jacket and relieved him of the gun in his shoulder holster. He probably had some other hardware stashed on his body but I didn't want to take the unnecessary risk that he would grab or hit me as I was frisking him more thoroughly. Shoulder holsters are the most accessible.

Huber had nothing to say to Carol's statement. He had no card. Nothing he could offer her. Which meant that he would have to make a move himself, sooner or later. He didn't know that we were meeting Lester very soon in a rest area just off the Banff highway. He didn't know Lester existed. I imagine he intended to wait until we stopped and he could get at me somehow. On impulse I checked the glove compartment. A nasty little .32. One-handed I threw it into the back of the car. "Unload it," I asked Carol. She did. Next I moved the gun into my left hand and keeping my eyes on Huber, leaned over and felt under the car seat. A Coke can, a cigarette pack, an oily rag, a torn piece of paper. Lousy upkeep. I couldn't reach any further.

"Carol," I said, "know of any other hardware in this car?"

"We didn't arrive with Peter. I never saw this car before."

"You better check under the seats from your side. I can't reach." Obediently she disappeared behind the seat. My gun was in my right hand again, steady and pointed at Huber. He'd increased speed again.

"Slow down, slow down." Obediently he eased on the gas.

"I can't see very well this way." Carol was down on the floor of the car at the back.

That's when Huber made his move. In one urgent turn of the wheel he swerved sharp left into the empty passing lane. This threw me towards him; instinctively I steadied myself with my gun hand. Immediately he spun the wheel right with his left hand at the same time grabbing for my gun with his right. I pulled the trigger.

It almost worked. Two inches out and the bullet would have missed his thigh and gone harmlessly into the seat. By then he might have gotten the gun away from me. But I didn't miss. There was a muffled thump, the gun jumped and my hand was covered with blood, and bits of brown wool from Huber's suit. He cried out incoherently and his foot fell useless off the gas pedal. I grabbed the wheel and we coasted off the pavement onto the shoulder. Again, it seemed at the time to take hours. In fact it took seconds; less time than it takes to describe.

Once the car stopped, I set the hand-brake, and put her in park. Huber was barely conscious from shock and was losing blood. Carol and I pulled him out and laid him down, sheltered from the highway by the car.

"Get a tourniquet on that leg, Carol. He'll be all right, you know. Don't feel sorry for him. He'd have killed both of us without a qualm." I should have known better. Carol worked like a demon to stop the blood flow but wasn't wasting any sympathy on her erstwhile boss and torturer. Meanwhile I searched him, found the package of gold certificates, a gun strapped to his calf, a knife in his sleeve, two passports and $630 American.

"Let's get him into the back and this car on the road again before some curious Good Samaritan shows up. Or a Mountie stops to investigate."

The tourniquet was a piece of Huber's shirt twisted with the .32. Good use for a deadly weapon. We stretched Huber on the back seat, and Carol got in beside him.

I remembered to kick dirt on the bloodstain on the ground but the mess on the car seat would have to wait. Spreading Huber's jacket over it, I sat down and got us on the road again.

We drove for the next few kilometres in silence while our pulse rates moderated. What had been started had to be finished soon. I glanced at Carol in the rear-view mirror and spoke very calmly and softly.

"We will be meeting up with Lester, that's the limo driver, soon. A decision has to be made about Peter Matakoff. What's to be done with him?"

"Done with him?" Carol repeated. She hadn't been thinking of Matakoff. "Let him go home, of course."

"He's part of the Terra operation. He was here with Huber. He has some responsibility for what happened."

"He's a victim who chose this way to strike back at his oppressors. You cannot hold him responsible. It's not fair!"

"It's quite fair. Anyway what's fair got to do with it?"

"Are you holding me responsible then? As you do Peter? For

Terra and Huber? Are you going to turn me in to Ronald Walters again? So all that talk about travelling money was just a con."

"No con. Take the money and run. Your situation is a bit different from Matakoff's. You've got nowhere to go back to. A lot of people will be looking for you. Huber's people, Walters. And those stateside hoods who picked you up once before."

"You mean the young Raymond brothers and their heavy-weight back-up. The way I see it, Raymond's sons really believed that Huber was out to scuttle their father's chances of election by using their sister Ray. So they tried to find her by following you. First by themselves; when that didn't work by hiring some hangers-on of their father to come here and snatch Sara Ann — that is me — away from Huber. They aren't serious or dangerous." Carol was thinking aloud

"Yeah, real pathetic young lads. Fully justified in waving guns, kidnapping and threatening people. Just helping out dear old dad. Don't you just feel for them."

"Oh, stop it, Helen. They aren't worth it. They know by now that I am not Sara Ann. Forget it."

"OK. I will. Anyway, here's Lester. We've arrived."

32

LESTER'S BLUE MONSTER OF A LIMO sat serenely across the entrance
to the rest area. I pulled in beside it. Lester and Peter Matakoff
sat smoking and talking in the front seat, Peter towering head
and shoulders above the ex-jockey.

I drew Lester aside while Carol went to speak to Peter.

"Well? You two seem very friendly. What's with him?"

"He's OK. A religious nut, sort of. Fighting against Satan and
all that. He figures governments are the devil. Was helping to
destroy them. He's just a harmless nut."

"Nobody is harmless. Nuts can pull triggers and push buttons."

"He's just a confused local yokel. Don't make a federal case
out of it."

"All right, all right. I've been outvoted. Tell him we will give
him a lift to the nearest bus. He's to go home and keep mum.
Real low profile. Maybe Walters won't look for him too hard.
Oh, yeah. Give him this." I handed over Huber's $630. "600
beans will get him home first class. But tell him to stay low. OK?"

"Done. Anything else?"

"Just sit tight. Peter is the least of our problems. We've got
a badly shot-up man back there. And the whole damn world
will be looking for him and us anytime now."

Lester looked at me soberly. I plunged into my pocket and
took out a gold certificate.

"Be worth it to you. First we must move him to your limo.
It's OK, he's not bleeding anymore. Then we will get rid of Carol."

"Rid of her?" said Lester distractedly, examining the $10,000
certificate I had given him. "Is this any good? I've never seen
anything like it."

"It's good. You'll have no trouble cashing it. Or you can save
it for that Peace River spread you were planning to get."

Lester grinned up at me. "No, this will send Alma to college."

"Good. The rest of this lot goes with Carol. That's how we
will get rid of her. She has to disappear. Come on, we can talk

about it with her."

Soon Huber lay in the limousine, while Lester conferred with Peter giving him the money and explaining our arrangements. Both of them glanced at me once in a while but otherwise all seemed to be going well.

Carol came up to me. "Well, I guess this is where I'd better leave. How much are you going to give me of that money?"

"All but the $10,000 I gave Lester. That should be plenty. Take the Mercedes. It will get you out of this area. I doubt that there are any calls out on it. I looked in the glove compartment. It's registered to a Mr. G. Lipman, who passes as office manager of Arrow Road Trucking. Sound familiar?"

Carol shivered, tucking the money quickly into her bag. "I'd better ditch it soon then. Thanks. Just as a matter of interest, what are your plans for Matakoff and Huber?"

"Matakoff goes home. Lester agreed with you about that. I just hope he knows enough to keep his mouth shut. And Huber needs medical attention. Walters will want to talk to him eventually."

"I see. Fair enough. He will survive, you know. Men like him always do. It's the Deans, Peters and Ursulas who die."

"Nuts. Peter didn't die. And either did you. But Emil and Paul did. Not to mention a number of other nasties. Nobody's immortal. Let's not glamorize Huber and his kind. He bleeds just like anyone else."

"I'll remember you, Helen. More than anyone else in this awful business. Goodbye."

"Goodbye." We hugged briefly.

She waved at Lester and Peter and without another glance in the direction of Huber, got into the Mercedes, backed it carefully and was gone.

I wondered if I was right to let her go. I wondered whether I would even see her again.

An hour later we dropped Peter Matakoff at a truckstop where he intended to get a hitch back home. While Lester was gassing up at a self-service pump I went into the snack bar and made some phone calls. Walters was first.

"Ron. I have Huber. He has to be hospitalized. I don't intend to be around to do any explaining. Where do I take him?"

"What's that? Where the hell are you, Helen?"

"Never mind. You heard my question. Do you want him dumped in Alberta, B.C., or no preference?"

"Wait a minute." Walters might have liked to trace my call. Maybe he tried. But he was back on the line very soon. "If you can get him to Golden before he croaks I will take it from there. And be obliged."

"OK. Hospital in Golden, right?"

"Right. I'll set it up."

"Don't set it up to prevent me leaving, Ron. I won't talk to any local cop. I'll see you pretty soon anyway. Talk to you then. By the way, if you're not too busy check Misurali Export/Import in Calgary."

"Good enough." He hung up.

Next I tried to get Alice Caplan at the hotel. I figured she would be mad at me for taking off for Calgary without her. Still, I expected she would stick around and wait for me. However, the hotel told me she'd checked out. I debated whether to call Jessica in Vancouver about her wayward colleague and decided it was more urgent to get out of there and get rid of Huber.

"We're going to Golden," I told Lester. "Huber's to be taken to the hospital there."

"Not any too soon, I tell you. He's not good. I bet he'll lose that leg." Lester had dressed Huber's leg as best he could. We fed him codeine pills crushed into a milkshake. He drank it and passed out.

It was one of the most beautiful drives I remember. Through Banff, Yoho National Parks and into the little town of Golden, British Columbia. You sweep over a curve high on the side of a mountain and suddenly look down into it. A river, a valley and mountains all around.

We found the local hospital with no trouble. Two obliging young people helped Lester half-drag, half-carry Huber into Emergency while I remained in the limo. A moment later Lester was out again and we pulled away. No one tried to stop us but I noticed an idle-looking man with a short haircut making a note of the licence number.

"Lester, sooner or later you are going to have official visitors. This fancy set of wheels is hardly inconspicuous."

"Who me? I know from nothing. I've been at the track all day, hanging out with my pals. So somebody took this tub for a joyride. OK?"

"It will do. As long as they don't stop you in these mountains somewhere on your way home."

"Will they?" A simple question but there was no mistaking the anxiety in his voice.

"They won't. That man will merely report back. A piece of data. Security people are compulsive about information. Any and all. It will go into a file. Perhaps someone will have to check into it sometime. So you will have callers. No sweat."

"OK. I've got my papers, my wife and daughter are Canadians. What can they do to me? What now?"

"Drop me in town and go home. That's it."

"Right."

"It's been a pleasure doing business with you."

"Likewise. Sure beats ferrying drunken businessmen to the airport. But I wouldn't want it as a steady job."

"It's not a steady job," I laughed.

33

DRIVING BACK SOUTH-WEST to the Kootenays in a rented car the next day I was overwhelmed by a sense of anti-climax. Sort of like a post partum depression. Huber's minions dead or dispersed, the core of the conspiracy in the Kootenays had been destroyed. A lot of bits and pieces remained, of course. Loose ends to be tidied up. Most of them were best left to Walters. I had enough faith in Walters' professionalism to expect that this time, he would be able to keep Huber out of circulation. As for the deal, assuming it really existed, between Raymond and Huber's organization, there was nothing any of us could do about it.

There were some personal matters I had to take care of. Like getting my jeep back. Saying goodby to the women at the Acres. Finding Alice, if she wasn't already back in Vancouver. Picking up my borrowed trailer at Castlegar airport. Part of me wished I could be satisfied to leave well enough alone and just go home. Part of me wanted answers to questions which no longer seemed terribly relevant. For instance, who really killed Ben? How had he died? Considering how many others had died during the course of the last week or so, it did seem strange to be bothered with one old man. But unfinished business goes on nagging me. I missed that sense of completion which comes when no substantive questions remain. I didn't expect any surprises but I had to know for sure.

Resigned to mere routine and momentarily depressed at the end of excitement, I pulled into Castlegar's airport parking lot. And was pleasantly surprised to find my trailer gone. Perhaps there was a little life left in this case after all. A helpful attendant informed me that a 'lady in a jeep' had arrived two days earlier, paid all parking charges, hitched the trailer up to the jeep and took off. After I identified myself he handed me a letter from Alice.

"Would serve you right if I just vanished with your jeep and you never heard of either of us again. However, I decided to be merciful and let you find us. Love, Alice."

Driving back up the lake road to Kaslo and points north I decided to stop off at Walters' local headquarters. Behind the barn a well-informed flunky told me that Win was out of danger, Shoreman was in custody pending a hearing on his status, Rita had been released from hospital and Ron Walters was 'elsewhere'. When I asked if 'elsewhere' might not be Golden he gave me a knowing look but kept his mouth shut.

I signed a careful statement on the Soteroff farm 'fire', told the agent to give my regards to Ron and was on my way again. It was clear that Ben's murder was closed and that the whole episode would be swept under the rug in a classically Canadian manner. The three monkeys have nothing on us.

34

WOMEN'S ACRES was a very different place from what it had been when I'd seen it last. The first thing I saw was the little trailer parked right smack in the middle of the yard, with Rita on a makeshift bed the centre of a lively group. On one side were Alice and Nancy deep in private conversation. Sitting around Rita were Artemis with a book in her lap, Laura rolling a joint and Chris playing with a dog. Sun poured down on them. I wondered what my arrival would do to this serene picture. In fact there was very little immediate reaction. I went up to Rita and inquired about her wound. She was formal but, for Rita, friendly. She was better, thank you. It had been quite an adventure. She hated violence but it had been exciting. We agreed that indeed it had been that. Now it was over. Thank goodness. We agreed again. I thought it significant that she didn't ask me about Carol.

Artemis pretended to read, Laura busily removed seeds out of the homegrown grass, Chris went off somewhere. All the conventional things having been said, conversation flagged. I guess Alice was waiting for that moment for she got up suddenly, came up to me, and hugged me. Everyone relaxed. Alice's affirmation of me was like a sign. I realized that in two days she had been accepted by those women as I would never be. Part of it was the age difference, part my job, part just me. There was a hard edge of experience which I brought with me which they mistrusted. Alice was different. She, like the other women there, was still becoming. Trying out life, lovers, jobs, experiences, personalities, political positions. From part-time student to part-time actress, to part-time legal secretary, perhaps to part-time communard. Whatever the future, now Alice was at home, happy and excited with her new friends, new surroundings. And, yes, even at seeing me there.

"So you got my message, eh. I over-tipped that parking lot attendant to make sure. Isn't it great here?"

"You could've left me a note at the hotel. Wouldn't have cost anything."

"I never thought of it until I got to the Castlegar airport. Then it occurred to me to leave word. Want a beer?"

"Typical," I laughed. "Yeah, I'll have a beer."

We sat down by Rita's cot and talked. Alice filled me in on events since my sudden departure for Calgary, which she wouldn't forgive me for. Nancy asked about Carol. Very tentatively I said that she was safely out of the country. They knew that Carol had lied to them, had used them. The realization that willing or not they had been part of the political game they despised did not come easy. Carol had manipulated them, conned them. Loyally, they had closed ranks to protect her even against their better judgement. All in the name of a solidarity which she obviously did not share. It was a hard lesson to learn, and they were learning it reluctantly. I hoped they wouldn't over-react and turn back on their principles. I needn't have worried, as I was soon to find out.

Apart from Carol, I kept pretty quiet about Huber and developments in Calgary. There didn't seem any point. Actually, nobody seemed much interested. There appeared to be an unnatural lack of curiosity about Terra-One and the Soteroffs. Just to test my impression, I said, "Well, it looks like the powers-that-be will write the whole thing off. Shoreman will go down in the books as Ben's killer whether he's convicted or not. They will deport him quietly if they have a chance. I wonder about Win, though."

There was a moment of awkwardness and Nancy said in a tone of finality, "Win will be OK. It's all over, that's great. I guess you'll be going back home soon." This was about the third time a similar sentiment had been expressed.

"What's the matter? Bad breath? Everyone wants to get rid of me," I ventured. There were fervent cries of denial. It wasn't that I wasn't welcome but merely that everyone wanted the case closed, finished, forgotten and my presence made that difficult. Laura articulated it quite unambiguously.

"Well, as long as you are here I guess we have trouble believing that you aren't working. Like, digging into things some more. Not letting things alone. That's all."

"Oh. Is there more?"

"Of course not," Rita was firm. "It's just that we connect you with all that trouble and death. I guess you must be used to that."

"Used to trouble and death or used to people connecting me with them? Neither, I assure you. Look, Rita, I didn't bring this on. It wasn't me who let terror into your lives. Don't blame the messenger."

"Hey, hey. Enough already, you two. Everyone relax. What is all this bullshit anyway? Helen's OK." That was Alice trying to defuse the situation.

Having established to my satisfaction that they were indeed trying to hide something I had to decide whether it was worth uncovering. I had a pretty good idea what it was, of course, and wasn't at all keen to deal with it. Unfortunately, my fatal flaw is that I cannot leave well enough alone. A quality which is an asset for an investigator but a nuisance otherwise. I have gotten fatalistic about it. Just go on doing whatever comes naturally and cope with the fallout when it happens.

Without consciously planning it I turned to Alice and inquired about the map which I had left in the trailer along with my other stuff on leaving for Calgary.

"Map? What map?" she replied lamely. And I knew that I had again stepped over the line. There was nothing for it but to press on.

"Dean's map. The one Carol had. Now, come on, Alice, don't play dumb. What other map could it be?"

"Oh, that map. Well, I don't know where it is. I don't think I've seen it in the trailer. Where did you leave it?"

"In the middle of the bed together with all the rest of the things I had in the hotel. You couldn't miss it. I'll go look."

There was a growing silence as I went off. The map wasn't in the trailer. Could these good, innocent women really believe I wouldn't miss it? Could they have destroyed it? I came back slowly, thinking and looking at them all huddled together watching me carefully.

"All right. What happened to the map. And why?"

"Oh, why don't you forget it? What use would it be to you now? What good would it do?" Alice was uncomfortable with the issue. She kept glancing at Nancy, Rita and the rest. Artemis stepped in to help her out.

"We burned that map. Dean had pinpointed everyone involved in this Terra thing on it. Little dots all over. Would have made trouble for a lot of innocent people. God, he was compulsive. What was his sign? Anyone know?" Pause. "Anyway it's better destroyed. That's all."

I started to laugh.

"You really are an amazing lot. OK, OK so you destroyed the map. Good riddance. Why did you assume I would make trouble for 'innocent' people? Why not let me in on this protective operation?"

My old friend Alice did have the grace to look embarrassed but Rita, for one, only looked stubborn.

"We did the right thing. Once it's gone, it's gone. No more can be done about it. Let's forget it."

"Yes, and let sleeping dogs lie," I said, amused. I should have stopped there but they was still something else and I wasn't about to let them get away with it any more. "And speaking of dogs. Wasn't that Ben's little mutt Chris was playing with when I arrived? And then she disappeared with it?"

Laura slapped her knee, leaned over and hugged me. The others grinned. Alice said triumphantly, "See, I told you. She's a detective, you know. I told you she would spot the whole thing. Oh, come on. Let's show her."

Reluctantly Nancy and Artemis helped Rita to her feet and soon the lot of us were making our way past the familiar outhouse into the bush behind the house. The path was fresh, slashed haphazardly through the scant undergrowth. The earth and some of the bigger trees were scarred by the passage of vehicles, trucks and front-end loaders. We walked for maybe 10 minutes, taking turns helping Rita. Now it was a game. We laughed and teased each other. No one would tell me what they were hiding. I kept being told to wait and see. Finally Artemis, who was in the lead, stopped and everyone crowded behind her. We had reached a tiny clearing, where a creek and a rockfall down the side of a small cliff created a natural open space. A cabin roughly made of cedar poles, mill-ends and junk lumber stood against the raw rock wall. On one side was an enclosure for goats. A middle-aged woman with blue eyes and strong hands looked up at us from weeding a small garden patch. Beside her on the ground lay a baby, dressed in a diaper.

"That's Ursula's baby," someone half-whispered behind me.

"Yes, and that's Ursula's mother," I said. I didn't add that she had been active in 'local leadership'. The women at Acres didn't give a damn about that. They would protect her and her grandchild to their last breath. Judgmental busybodies like me could lump it.

"Hullo, Maria." Artemis pronounced the name as in *West Side Story*. She moved tentatively towards the silent older woman, who had meantime seen and recognized me. I felt her eyeing me speculatively. There was something about her. I wondered how I had missed it before. Then I realized that, like everyone else, I had discounted her. She was invisible, just Ben's hardworking, stupid woman. That's why Ronald Walters wouldn't even bother looking for her. She didn't count. Middle-aged women who work on the land and in the kitchen don't really register as people. How could a grandmother who bakes bread also blow up dams, blackmail Presidents, hide arms, or kill people?

"When is Win coming to join you?" I couldn't resist asking.

"Who needs him? Men are lazy bums. We do better without him," Maria answered. Laura giggled and looked at me sideways.

"Just because Ben was like that doesn't mean Win would be. It's his baby, isn't it?"

"Big deal. Don't need him. Good riddance."

"I am sorry you feel that way. Personally I thought Win rather a nice guy. But it's your business. None of mine."

"Yes, none of yours." Maria bent down to her weeding.

"She'll be OK, won't she, Helen? The goverment won't bother her here, will they?" inquired Laura with sudden urgency. I stayed silent, looking at Nancy, Rita and Artemis whose idea this utopian hideout had to be. Alice stayed away, clearly not feeling comfortable with the situation.

"Probably not. Not the security people. But she cannot just disappear. She is next-of-kin. There are legal matters. Someone will have to look after what's left of the farm, and Ben and Ursula's belongings. It would be very noticeable if she doesn't show up to deal with all that."

"Alice suggested that Maria hire Jessica to represent her. All that can be dealt with at third-hand. People will assume she left the area, went back to her people or something. Taking the baby. That way no one will try to find them." Nancy drew a long breath, looked me right in the eye and added, "We think it's a good idea."

I considered. "Yeah. It will probably work. Why not? The authorities won't give her a second thought. Does she have many friends who might miss her?"

"She says not. Been too busy to make friends. That's what she says."

"Her ex-comrades might wonder, though. Still, that lot isn't likely to do anything. Would have been useful to have that map pinpointing them all, you know."

"Well, I am glad we don't. She can stay here all summer. In winter, we'll see. There isn't very much room in the main house."

"She could come with me to Victoria," Laura suggested casually.

"Oh, all that's months away. Meanwhile she and the baby are safe here."

The present is all in this kind of hand-to-mouth living.

As we talked around and over her head, Maria finished weeding, picked up the baby and went into the little shack. I followed her inside, alone.

First gesture was hers. Maria picked up a pot from the propane stove and without a word poured us mugs of strong black Indian tea. She put two spoons of honey into hers, sat down on an old kitchen chair and sipped. The baby beside her moved in its sleep.

"What's you want from me?" she said. We eyed each other warily.

"Why are you here?" I asked. "You don't belong with these women."

"Oh, nice kids. They want to look after us. I let them. What you want?" Obviously I didn't qualify as a nice kid who wanted to look after her.

"About Ben. How did he die?"

"Why do you care? Many died. Many more will die. What does it matter?"

"Idle curiosity, let's just say. Albert Shoreman didn't kill him, did he?"

"Who then you think killed him?"

"You."

There was a pause while she rolled a cigarette from a fresh pouch of Export tobacco. I watched her hardened fingers meticulously tuck in the ends, then set a match to the tip.

"If I tell you, will you go away and leave us alone?"

"Yes." I didn't hesitate.

"OK. I killed him. Stabbed him with a goat hoof knife. Like this." Her arm moved suddenly and there in her hand was a strange, wicked-looking object. A knife with a thick, short, curved blade. She put it down on the table between us.

"Why?" I asked, trying to keep my cool as best I could.

"He'd set it up to talk to these agents. Going to meet them. Our boys grabbed them just in time. But sooner or later he'd have given us away. He was an idle, useless old man. Full of self-importance. Liked to know things, make trouble, do nothing himself."

"Did you kill him for Terra, then? Or for personal reasons?"

"Who knows? It's all one, isn't it? Now you know, leave me be. Go away and leave us alone."

"Who knows about you? About the murder. They don't, do they?" I gestured towards the group of women outside. Through the open door we saw them clustered around Rita, talking, smoking, having a good time. Alice and Nancy holding hands. I saw that Chris had joined them.

"No. You going to tell them?"

"They don't want to know," I stated.

"No."

I stood up. As I did, a small collie arrived panting at the door. Dotchka. She gave me a friendly sniff then threw herself at Maria in a paroxysm of joy, love and abandon.

So much for canine instincts, I thought, as I left to join the group under the trees. Looking at them, I knew that it would soon be time for me to leave this magic place.

MAJOR NEW CRIME TITLES FROM VIRAGO

THE DOG COLLAR MURDERS

Barbara Wilson

**'Someone screamed, very loudly,
"You've *all* killed her!" '**

Loie Marsh, prominent anti-pornography activist, is found
strangled by a dog collar at a Seattle conference on sexuality.
The clues point to any number of suspects and it's up to Pam
Nilsen, the printer-sleuth of Barbara Wilson's earlier
mysteries, *Murder in the Collective* and *Sisters of the Road,* to find
the killer. Was it someone who wanted to prevent Loie from
speaking on her panel? The local lesbian sadomasochists?
Feminist activists opposed to censorship, or Loie's ex-lover
and former research collaborator? Or someone from Loie's
distant past? In investigating Loie's death, Pam begins to come
to terms with some of her own fears and desires. Meanwhile
the murderer is still at large and strikes again . . .

MAJOR NEW CRIME TITLES FROM VIRAGO

MURDER BEHIND LOCKED DOORS

Ellen Godfrey

A gripping murder mystery set in the cutthroat world of computers, technology, mergers and takeovers

Jane Tregar works at a large headhunting firm, finding top executives to fill high-powered jobs. Competent and successful, she nonetheless finds working in this overridingly male world as taxing as the 'constant speaking of a foreign language'. When the vice-president of a large software company is found dead in a locked computer room, Jane is asked to find a replacement. But suspicion surrounds his death and, worse still, the only suspects are the other five on the management team. When Jane's own life is threatened as she unravels the mystery, she is forced to recognise that values like loyalty have little currency where corporate manipulation and personal ambition are involved.